THE
TREES

Published by Influx Press
The Greenhouse
49 Green Lanes, London, N16 9BU
www.influxpress.com / @InfluxPress

This edition 2022.

Printed and bound in the UK by Clays Ltd, Elcograf S.p.A.
First published in the USA in 2021 by Graywolf Press.
Paperback ISBN: 9781914391170
Ebook ISBN: 9781914391187
Cover design: Jamie Keenan
Interior design: Vince Haig

THE
TREES

A Novel

PERCIVAL
EVERETT

For Steve, Katie, Marisa, Caroline, Anitra, and Fiona

The art of war is simple enough. Find out where your enemy is. Get at him as soon as you can. Strike at him as hard as you can and as often as you can, and keep moving on.

—U. S. Grant

RISE

1

Money, Mississippi, looks exactly like it sounds. Named in that persistent Southern tradition of irony and with the attendant tradition of nescience, the name becomes slightly sad, a marker of self-conscious ignorance that might as well be embraced because, let's face it, it isn't going away.

Just outside Money, there was what might have loosely been considered a suburb, perhaps even called a neighborhood, a not-so small collection of vinyl-sided, split-level ranch and shotgun houses called, unofficially, Small Change. In one of the dying grass backyards, around the fraying edges of an empty above ground pool, one adorned with faded mermaids, a small family gathering was happening. The gathering was neither festive nor special, but usual. It was the home of Wheat Bryant and his wife, Charlene. Wheat was between jobs, was constantly, ever, always between jobs. Charlene was always quick to point out that the word *between* usually suggested something at either end, two somethings, or destinations, and that Wheat had held only one job in his whole life, so he wasn't between anything. Charlene worked as a receptionist at the Money Tractor Exchange J. Edgar Price Proprietor (the official business name, no commas), for both sales and service, though the business had not exchanged many tractors of late, or even repaired many. Times were hard in and around the town of Money. Charlene always wore a yellow halter top the same color as her dyed and poofed hair, and she did this because it made Wheat angry. Wheat chain-drank cans of Falstaff beer and chain-smoked Virginia Slims cigarettes, claiming to be one of those feminists because he did, telling his children that the drinks were necessary to keep his big belly properly inflated, and the smokes were important to his bowel regularity.

When outside, Wheat's mother—Granny Carolyn, or Granny C—wheeled herself around in one of those wide-tired electric buggies from Sam's Club. It was not simply like the buggies from Sam's Club; it was, in fact, permanently borrowed from the Sam's Club down in Greenwood. It was red and had white letters that spelled *am's Clu*. The hardworking electric motor emitted a constant, loud whir that made conversation with the old woman more than a bit of a challenge.

Granny C always looked a little sad. And why not? Wheat was her son. Charlene hated the woman nearly as much as she hated Wheat, but never showed it; she was an old woman, and in the South you respect your elders. Her four grandchildren, three years to ten, looked nothing like each other, but couldn't possibly have belonged anywhere else or to anyone else. They called their father by his first name, and they called their mother Hot Mama Yeller, the CB handle she used when she chatted with truckers late at night after the family was asleep, and occasionally while she cooked.

That CB chatter made Wheat angry, partly because it reminded him of the one job he'd had: driving a semitrailer truck full of fruits and vegetables for the Piggly Wiggly chain of grocery markets. He lost that job when he fell asleep and drove his truck off the Tallahatchie Bridge. Not completely off, as the cab dangled over the Little Tallahatchie River for many hours before he was rescued. He was saved by climbing into the bucket of an excavator brought over from Leflore. He might actually have held on to his job had the truck not held on, had simply and quickly plunged immediately and anticlimactically off the bridge and into the muddy river below. But as it happened, there was ample time for the story to blow up and show up on CNN and Fox and YouTube, repeated every twelve minutes and going viral. The killing image was the clip of some forty empty cans of Falstaff beer spilling from the cab and raining into the current below. Even that might not have been so bad had he not been clutching a can in his fat fist as he climbed through the teeth off the excavator bucket.

Also at the gathering was Granny C's brother's youngest boy, Junior Junior. His father, J. W. Milam, was called Junior, and so his son was Junior Junior, never J. Junior, never Junior J., never J. J., but Junior Junior. The older, called Just Junior after the birth of his son, had died of "the cancer" as Granny C called it some ten years earlier. He passed away within a month of Roy, her husband and Wheat's daddy. She considered it somehow important that they died of the same thing.

"Granny C, ain't you hot in that ridiculous hat?" Charlene shouted at the old woman over the whir of her buggy.

"What say?"

"I mean, that hat ain't even straw. It's like a vinyl tarp or something. And it ain't got no breathing holes in it."

"What?"

"She cain't hear you, Hot Mama Yeller," her ten-year-old said. "She cain't hear nothing. She's deaf as a post."

"Hell, Lulabelle, I know that. But you cain't say I didn't tell her about that hat when she up and keels over from heatstroke." She looked down at Granny C again. "And that contraption she rolls around in gets all hot too. That makes you even hotter!" she yelled at the woman. "How does she keep living? That's what I want to know."

"Leave my mama alone," Wheat said, half-laughing. He might have been half-laughing. Who could tell? His mouth was twisted in a permanent lopsided sneer. Many believed he'd suffered a mild stroke while eating ribs months before.

"She's wearing that ridiculous hot hat again," Charlene said. "Gonna make herself sick."

"So? She don't mind. The hell you care, anyway?" Wheat said.

Junior Junior screwed the cap back onto his paper bag–wrapped bottle and said, "Why the fuck y'all ain't got no water in this pool?"

"Damn thing leaks," Wheat said. "Got a crack in the wall from where Mavis Dill fell into the side of it with her fat ass. She weren't even tryin' to go swimming, just walkin' by and fell on it."

"How did she manage to fall?"

"She's just fat, Junior Junior," Charlene said. "The load gets leanin' one way and that's the way it's gotta go. Gravity. Wheat can tell you all about that. Ain't that right, Wheat? You know all about gravity."

"Fuck you," Wheat said.

"I won't have that kind of talk around my grands," Granny C said. "And how the hell did she hear that?" Charlene said. "She cain't hear screaming, but she can hear that."

"I hear plenty," the old woman said. "Don't I hear plenty, Lulabelle?"

"Y'all sure do," the girl said. She had climbed onto her grandmother's lap. "You can hear just about anything. Cain't you, Granny C? Y'all is damn near dead, but y'all can hear just fine. Right, Granny C?"

"Sho 'nuff, baby doll."

"So, what you gonna do with this pool?" Junior Junior asked. "Why?" Wheat asked. "You want to buy it? I'll sell it to you in a heartbeat. Make me an offer."

"I can put me some pigs in this thing. Just carve out the bottom and stick them pigs in there."

"Take it away," Wheat said.

"I could just bring them pigs here. That would be easier, don't you think?"

Wheat shook his head. "But then we'd be smelling your hogs. I don't want to be smelling your hogs."

"But you got it all set up and staked out so nice-like. Gonna be a lot of work to move it." Junior Junior lit a skinny green cigar. "You can keep one of them hogs for yourself. How about that?"

"I don't need no fucking hog," Wheat said.

"Language!" Granny C shouted.

"If I want bacon, I go to the store," Wheat said.

"And buy it with my money," Charlene said. "Bring them pigs on over, Junior Junior, but I want to keep two of 'em, big ones, and you butcher 'em."

"Deal."

Wheat didn't say anything. He walked across the yard and helped the four-year-old climb into her pink plastic car.

Granny C stared off into space. Charlene studied her for

a minute. "Granny C, you okay?"

The old woman didn't reply. "Granny C?"

"What's wrong with her?" Junior Junior asked, leaning in. "She havin' a stroke or something?"

Granny C startled them. "No, you rednecked talking turnip, I ain't havin' no stroke. I swear, a person cain't reflect on her life around here without some fool accusing her of havin' a stroke. Are *you* havin' a stroke? You the one show symptoms."

"How come you jumpin' on me?" Junior Junior asked. "Charlene was staring at you first."

"Never mind him," Charlene said. "What was you thinking on, Granny C?"

Granny C stared off again. "About something I wished I hadn't done. About the lie I told all them years back on that nigger boy."

"Oh Lawd," Charlene said. "We on that again."

"I wronged that little pickaninny. Like it say in the good book, what goes around comes around."

"What good book is that?" Charlene asked. "*Guns and Ammo*?"

"No, the Bible, you heathen."

The yard became quiet. The old woman went on. "I didn't say he said something to me, but Bob and J. W., they insisted he did, and so I went along with it. I wish to Jesus I hadn't. J. W. hated him some niggers."

"Well, it's all done and past history now, Granny C. So you just relax. Ain't nothing can change what happened. You cain't bring the boy back."

2

Deputy Sheriff Delroy Digby was driving his twelve-year-old Crown Victoria squad car across the Tallahatchie Bridge when he received a call to go to Small Change. He pulled into the front yard of Junior Junior Milam and saw the man's wife, Daisy, pacing and crying, gesticulating wildly. Delroy had dated Daisy briefly in high school, and it had stopped when she actually bit his tongue. Then he went into the army and became a clerk in the quartermaster's corp. He returned home to Mississippi to find Daisy married to Junior Junior and pregnant with her fourth child. That child was on her hip as she paced now, and the other three were sitting like zombies on the first step of the porch.

"What's goin' on, Daisy?" Delroy asked.

Daisy stopped waving her arms and stared at him. Her face was crunched from crying, her eyes red and sunken.

"What is it? What happened, Daisy?" he asked.

"The room all the way in the back," she said. "It's Junior Junior. Oh Lawd, I think he's dead," she whispered so the children couldn't hear. "He got to be dead. We all just got back from the big swap meet in the Sam's Club parking lot. The babies ain't seen nothing. Lawd, it's just awful."

"Okay, Daisy. You stay here."

"There's something else back there too," she said. Delroy

put his hand on his pistol. "What?"

"Somebody. He's dead too. Must be dead. Oh, he's dead. Gotta be dead. You'll see."

Delroy was confused and now more than a little scared. All he ever did in the service was count rolls of toilet paper. He went back to his patrol car and grabbed the radio. "Hattie, this here is Delroy. I'm out at Junior Junior Milam's place and I think I'm gonna need me some backup."

"Brady's not far from there. I'll send him over."

"Thank you, Hattie, ma'am. Tell him I'll be in the back of the house." Delroy put down the handset and returned to Daisy. "I'm gonna take me a little look-see. You send Brady back there when he arrives."

"The room is just off the kitchen," she said. "Delroy." She put her hand gently on his arm. "You know, I always liked you when we was in high school. I didn't mean to bite your tongue, and I'm awfully sorry about that. Fast Phyllis Tucker told me all the boys liked that and so I did it. You didn't like it. I guess I did it too hard."

"Okay, Daisy." He started away and then turned back to the woman. "Daisy, you didn't kill him, did you?"

"Delroy, I'm the one who called the police." Delroy stared at her.

"No, I did not kill him. Either one of them."

Delroy didn't draw his weapon as he entered the house, but he kept his hand heavy on it. He walked slowly through the front room. It was dark because the windows were so remarkably small. There was a line of small bowling trophies on the mantel. The fireplace was filled with stacks of brightly colored plastic bowls, plates, and cups. The house was so still and quiet he got more frightened and pulled his pistol. What if the killer was still there? Should he go back outside and wait for Brady? If he did that, Daisy might think he was a coward. Brady would certainly laugh at him and call him a yellow chicken. So, he kept moving forward. He gave each bedroom a cursory look, then stood in the kitchen for a long while before pushing on into the back room. His boots made a lot of noise on the buckled linoleum.

He stopped in his tracks once inside the room. He couldn't move. He had never seen two people so dead in his entire life. And he'd been in a goddamn war. Who or what he took to be Junior Junior had a bloody, bashed-in skull. He could see part of his brain. A long length of rusty barbed wire was wrapped several times around his neck. One of his eyes had been either gouged out or carved out and lay next to his thigh, looking up at him. There was blood everywhere. One of his arms was twisted at an impossible angle behind his back. His pants were undone and pulled down to below his knees. His groin was covered with matted blood, and it looked like his scrotum was missing. Some ten feet from Junior Junior was the body of a small Black man. His face was horribly beaten, his head swollen, his neck scarred and seemingly stitched together. He was not bleeding, it seemed, but there was no doubt that he was dead. The Black man wore a dark blue suit. Delroy looked again at Junior Junior. The man's exposed legs looked strangely alive.

Delroy jumped a little when Brady appeared behind him. "Good Lord Almighty!" Brady said. "Goddamn! Is that Junior Junior?"

"I think so," Delroy said. "Any idea who the nigger is?"

"None."

"What a mess," Brady said. "Lord, Lordy, Lord, Lord, Jesus.

Looky at that. His balls ain't on him!"

"I see that."

"I think they're in the nigger's hand," Brady said. "You're right." Delroy leaned in for a closer look.

"Don't touch nothing. Don't touch a gawddamn thing. We got ourselves some kind of crime here. Lordy."

3

"Goddamnit, I hate murder more than just about anything," said Sheriff Red Jetty. "It can just ruin a day."

"Because it's such a waste of life?" the coroner, Reverend Cad Fondle, asked. He had just pronounced Junior Junior and the unidentified Black man dead without so much as touching them.

"No, it's because it's a mess."

"It is a lot of blood," Fondle said.

"I don't give a shit about the blood. It's the goddamn paperwork." Jetty pointed at the floor. "What you gonna do about Milam's balls there?"

"Tell your boys to bag 'em. Can't see there's much point in sewin' them back on him. But the mortician can decide that with the family."

Sheriff Jetty squatted, being careful not to land on a knee, and studied the Black corpse, tilted his head.

"What you seein', Red?" Fondle asked. "Don't he look familiar?"

"I can't tell what he looks like. That's a lot of damage. Besides, they all look alike to me."

"You think Junior Junior did that to him?" Fondle shook his head. "None of it looks fresh."

"Well, let's get 'em in the wagon and take them to the morgue." Jetty looked back into the kitchen. "Delroy! Get the bags."

"You want we should dust for prints?" Delroy asked. "We ain't touched nothing. In this room, anyway."

"Why bother? Oh sure, why the hell not. You and Brady do that. Then help clean up all this blood."

"That ain't in my job description," Brady said. "You want to keep a job to describe?" Jetty asked.

"Clean up the blood," Brady repeated. "Come on, Delroy."

4

Sheriff Jetty parked his private car, a well-maintained Buick 225 that had belonged to his mother but had since been repainted, in a diagonal space in front of the coroner's brick office building at the edge of town. It was dinnertime and his big belly was growling loud enough for others to hear. He walked in and then straight past the man at the desk whose name he could never remember.

Doctor Reverend Fondle was sitting on a metal table in the autopsy room. The big light was on but turned away from him.

"What's up, Cad? Why am I here in this fucking icebox instead of at dinner with my homely family?"

"We got us a problem," Fondle said. "What kind of problem?"

Fondle walked over to one of the four cadaver drawers set into the far wall. "This here is where I put that dead nigger."

"Yeah? And?"

Fondle pulled opened the door and pulled out an empty platform. Jetty stepped closer and looked at the gleaming metal surface.

"There ain't nobody there."

"So you see it too," Fondle said. "Well the Black sumbitch was in here forty-five minutes ago."

"What are tellin' me? Are you saying that the body is missin'?"

"I'm sayin' I don't know where it is."

"Damnit to hell, Fondle. Dead people just don't get up and walk away," Jetty said. "Do they?"

"Only one that I know of," Fondle said. "And who was that?"

Fondle frowned. "Our Lawd Jesus Christ Almighty, you heathen. You need to drag your ass to church now and again."

Jetty shook his head. "You didn't misplace him?"

"Apparently I have. I even checked the other three drawers. Milam's in that one. I looked in the closet. I looked in the wagon. I tell you, somebody done stole that nigger's body."

"This is fucked up," the sheriff said. "Pardon my French, Pastor."

"Who would have done this?"

"We don't even know who the hell he was. Maybe something will come back on his prints." Jetty looked at the door he had come through and at the windows. "When were you out of the office?"

"Around two I went to pick up some manure for my wife. Gone twenty minutes tops. Dill was at his desk, though."

"Goddamnit." Jetty pulled out his cell phone and looked at it. "Brady, where the hell are you?"

"Cleaning up the blood, per your instructions," Brady said. "Don't give me attitude, you peckerwood. You and Delroy get your asses to the coroner's office pronto."

"What about the blood?" Brady asked.

"Forget the goddamn blood and get your asses over here." He ended the call with the tip of his fat finger. "Do you remember how good it used to feel to slam down the receiver on somebody? I hate these little sissy phones. Get Dill in here."

Fondle pressed the wall intercom. "Dill, come in here, please."

"Dill a good man?" Jetty asked.

"Yeah. I'm sure he ain't got no use for a dead nigger."

Dill entered the room. "Yes, Doctor Reverend, sir?"

"You remember the body of that Black man we brought in this morning?" Fondle asked.

"Remember? What do you mean 'remember'?"

"The body's gone," Sheriff Jetty said. "Were you at your desk all day?"

"Yep. Even ate my lunch there. Egg salad."

"Didn't get up to take a shit?"

"I do that at seven every night like clockwork? Then I watch a *Maverick* rerun before making myself a bowl of Cream of Wheat."

"Step out of the office for any reason?"

"Nope."

"You're tellin' me that there was no time that somebody could have gotten by you and into this room?"

"That's what I'm sayin'."

"Back door?"

"Been stuck closed for two years," Fondle said.

"A damn fire hazard," Dill said.

"Where do you live, Dill?" the sheriff asked.

"I live with my mama, on the edge of Change."

"Oh, you're Mavis Dill's boy," Jetty said.

Dill nodded.

"How is she?" he asked.

"Fat. Happy. Fat. Are you tellin' me that a body disappeared from in here?"

"Looks like it," Fondle said.

"Any ideas?" Jetty asked Dill.

"I didn't take him."

"Y'all say that back door is locked," Jetty said.

"Stuck," said Dill.

"Let's go look at it anyway." Jetty followed Dill and Fondle through a dirty, equipment-cluttered hallway.

"That switch is over here on this wall someplace," Fondle said. He reached behind a tall metal cabinet and found the switch, turned on the light. The fluorescent bulbs hummed and flickered.

The back door was open, the lock clearly broken, one of the rusted-over hinges showing the threads of screws.

"Would you look the hell at that?" Dill said. "That there door ain't been open in ten years."

Jetty examined the lock. No key had been inserted into that rusted and dirt-covered hole. "Who could have pulled this open?"

"I mean this thing was stuck solid," Dill said.

"That's a fact," Fondle said. "I'll tell you who is at work here."

"The devil?" Dill asked.

Fondle nodded. "The devil hisself. Jesus save us."

Jetty looked at the little concrete landing outside the heavy door. "Dill, go sit at your desk and wait there. Don't touch anything. And I mean anything."

"What about me?" Fondle said.

"You don't touch anything either." He used his phone again. "Hattie, tell Jethro to get over here with his fingerprint kit." He put the phone back in his pocket and shook his head. "Lord."

5

Junior Junior's new widow, Daisy, pulled into the yard of Wheat and Charlene Bryant. She was crying when Charlene came out to greet her.

"Where is Junior Junior with them pigs?" Charlene asked. Then she saw the tears. "What's wrong with you? Did that lowlife, cocksuckin', ball o' shit bastard hit you again? I swear I'm gonna kick that boy's lily-white ass."

Daisy shooed the children around to the back of the house. "It ain't that, Charlene. He's dead," she said.

"Who's dead?" Charlene asked.

Granny C rolled onto the porch in her inside-the-house wheelchair. Wheat was behind her.

"Hey, Granny C. Hey, Wheat," Daisy said.

"Who's dead, Daisy?" Charlene asked again.

"Junior Junior. Junior Junior is dead, kilt by a nigger in our own home. Junior Junior done passed on."

"Have mercy," Wheat said.

"What happened, chile?" Granny C asked.

"Oh, Granny C, it was awful, just awful." Daisy ran onto the porch and put her head in the old woman's lap. "I was with the kids at the swap meet in the Sam's Club parking lot. You know the one. I went early because they was having a sale on them halter tops like Charlene wears, and I wanted me a lime-green one, but all they had was blue, powder blue. The lines was like superlong inside the Sam's Club, and Triple J had a dumbass fit because I wouldn't buy him no sour Skittles. People was lookin' at us like they never seen a baby cry before."

"People are just awful," Granny C said.

"Get on with the goddamn story, Daisy," Wheat said.

"Hush up, boy," Granny C said. "Go on, chile."

"So, we come home. You know, they didn't have no lime-green ones. I said that. I put the children down in the yard and went on inside the house. I just knew somethin' was wrong soon I got in there. I could smell somethin', feel it. I walked through the kitchen and into the back room and there he was. It was awful."

"You said that," Wheat said. "What was awful?"

Granny C cut Wheat a hard look.

Daisy raked at the tears on her face and wiped her nose with the back of her hand. Her mascara made bars down her face. "It was Junior Junior. He was lyin' all twistylike on the floor, like one of the Gumby toys, the bendy ones. There was blood everywhere. His head was all clobbered in. I mean all caved in like a cantaloupe what you done drove over with a tractor."

"Jesus," Charlene said. "Oh, Daisy."

Daisy's five-year-old boy came running around to the front of the house. "Mama, I gotta pee."

"Then go find a goddamn bush!" Daisy shouted. "Have mercy."

The boy ran off.

"Then I looked over and there was this, this . . ." Daisy bit her finger.

"This what?" Charlene said.

"It was a nigger."

"Just standin' there?" Wheat asked.

"No, layin' there. Layin' there. He was dead too. All fucked up and swole up and deader than anybody I ever seen."

"My god," Charlene said. "Did Junior Junior kill him?"

"I don't know, I don't know. There's somethin' else. Oh Lawd. Junior Junior's balls were cut off."

"What the fuck!" Wheat paced away and came back. "His balls was cut off? His balls? You mean his nuts? Like down there?"

"He's dead, Wheat," Charlene said. "That's the least of his worries."

Granny C's face was blank, without emotion.

Daisy pulled back and looked at the old woman's face.

"Granny C? Granny C, y'all all right?"

"Granny C?" Wheat said.

"Did you recognize him?" Granny C asked.

"Who?"

"The nigger, you fool."

"No. Nobody could have recognized that man, the way his face was all beat up like it was. His own Black mama couldn't have knowed him. I can't see why it makes a difference who he is. Was. Junior Junior is dead."

"Shut up, fool girl," Granny C snapped. "Somebody roll me into the goddamn house."

Wheat did.

"What was that all about?" Daisy asked Charlene.

"I don't know, I don't know. I ain't never hear Granny C cuss." Charlene looked at the slate-gray sky, then at Daisy's simple face. "So, anyway. What a fuckin' day. The blood all cleaned up?"

6

Delroy Digby and Braden Brady leaned against a squad car and watched as Red Jetty parked his deuce-and-a-quarter several yards from them in back of the coroner's building. The sun was trying to break through.

"Well?" Jetty asked.

"We searched all around," Brady said.

"We found one set of tracks headin' away from the building and down into the creek bed."

"Can't tell how old the tracks is, but they was light. Couldn't a weighed more than a buck twenty," Brady said.

"At most," Delroy added.

"Well, that just don't make good sense. That body weighed at least a hundred and fifty by itself. Ain't no small woman or big child could have carried that body. Or ripped that door open like that."

"Don't know what to say, Sheriff," Delroy said.

Jetty looked back at the building. "Jethro finished dustin' the place?"

"Think so," Brady said. "He's still in there, though."

"You two clowns go find something to do."

"Right, boss," Brady said.

Inside, the sheriff found Jethro washing his hands at the sink in the examination room. "Tull, you done?"

"Yessir. I found prints all over the place in here. As you might expect. And everything between here and the back door was covered with dust."

"You're tellin' me there ain't no prints back there?"

"Well, no. I'm sure there are some prints back there, but, like I said, they're covered with dust. The dust has not been disturbed, so nothing's been touched in there since all that dust settled."

"Are you takin' a tone with me?" Jetty asked.

"No, sir."

"We all know you went to junior college."

Jethro sighed. "Anyway, I suspect the prints I found belong to the Doctor Reverend Fondle and to that Dill feller."

"Well, let me know," Jetty said. He shook his head. "What a fuckin' mess. A goddamn clusterfuck."

"Chief, is clusterfuck one word or two?" Jethro asked.

"What?"

"Never mind."

"Get back to the goddamn station."

"Yessir."

7

News of Junior Junior Milam's death spread like disease across the county. So did the story of the strange, missing Black corpse. Red Jetty didn't know if an APB made sense and so did not issue one, not officially anyway. He did tell his three deputies to take turns driving in widening circles around town. The photo of the Black man he gave them, as if one was needed, found its way into the local paper, the *Money Clip*. From there the wire services picked up the image, then the internet and cable news. It was a crazy story, and it made the people of Money, Mississippi, sound crazy, and that made Jetty upset. It also upset the mayor, Philworth Bass.

Bass paced the floor of Jetty's private office. "I don't understand how you could let this happen."

"Which part?" Jetty leaned back in his special-ordered swivel desk chair, his boots on his desk.

"Which part?" Bass asked. "The part where a dead man walked out of your custody. Obviously, he weren't dead."

"Fondle said he was dead."

"That quack? Didn't you check?"

"Ain't my job. Plus, if you had seen him, even you woulda known he was dead. You saw the picture."

"Yeah, I saw it. I saw it along with every gawddamn person in this gawddamn country. He looked plenty dead,

I'll give you that, but apparently he weren't."

"Yeah, well, ain't nobody seen him twitch or pass gas when they put him in the bag. Though he smelled something awful. Smelled like a squirrel what died in a wall. If that man weren't dead, then I'm a red-skinned Indian."

"I'm getting calls from the capitol," Bass said. "They seen him?"

"No, they keep asking if we need help, if the backwoods peckerwoods on the Tallahatchie need help. What should I tell them?"

"Tell 'em that the peckerwoods is lookin' everywhere but can't find the walking dead Negro man."

"This ain't no joke. We're a goddamn national laughin' stock. You, Sheriff, you're a clown in the eyes of state law enforcement—hell, national law enforcement. What do you have to say to that?"

Jetty smiled at the idle ceiling fan and pretended to blow smoke rings. "Mr. Mayor, this here is the sovereign state of Mississippi. There ain't no law enforcement, there's just rednecks like me paid by rednecks like you."

"Well, that nonexistent law enforcement is sending somebody to assist you in your investigation."

"The MBI?"

"Coming up from Hattiesburg. Be here in the morning."

Jetty put his feet on the floor, his elbows on his knees. "Well, that's just fucking dandy. City cops coming up here to the sticks to help the hillbillies. Don't worry. I'll be nice to the sumbitches."

8

Ed Morgan insisted on driving his personal car. The bureau's cars were full size, but they simply didn't accommodate his six-five, three-hundred-pound frame. Jim Davis sat in the passenger seat, his elbow jutting out the window. Though average in height, his knees were almost pressed against the glove compartment because his seat was broken and would not slide back. He opened his hand and let the air move it.

"You know, I've got the air-conditioner on," Ed said.

"Is that what you call this shit? My dog's breath is cooler than what's coming out these vents. I hate this fucking car."

"It's comfortable."

"You need to get this seat fixed so I can slide it back."

"It's comfortable."

"It's a ten-year-old Toyota Sienna. There's a picture of it in the dictionary next to the word *uncomfortable*. I feel like we should have a couple of kids in the back." Jim looked back and saw there was, in fact, a child's booster seat behind Ed.

"I don't like being cramped," Ed said.

"Then you need to lose seventy pounds. What about me?"

"Okay now."

Ed and Jim were not officially partners, but they were

often paired because they were both difficult for others to work with. They actually liked each other, though it was unclear if either liked anyone else. More important, they trusted each other. Each knew the other was not only a good cop but street savvy and quick to take action if a situation became dicey or dangerous.

Jim put a cigarette in his mouth but did not light it; he was trying to quit. "We're going to confuse the hell out of these crackers. Driving into town in your mom's car like this. You ever been to Money?"

"Fuck," Ed said, "I never even heard of Money, Mississippi, until this morning. And lay off my damn car. It's comfortable. I don't care what you say. This motherfucker's got three hundred thousand miles on it."

"A thousand miles for every pound of your fat ass."

Ed cut Jim an evil look. "Open up that damn file and remind me what we're getting into."

Jim pulled the thin blue folder from his hard-shell briefcase and opened it. "It appears the local yokels have lost a body. Murder. All pretty gruesome if these photos are real. A White man named Milam was killed in his home. Found by his wife. Body of a dead Black man found at the scene."

"Same person kill both of them?"

"Doesn't say. Does say that the White man's testicles were severed and clenched in the fist of the Black man."

Ed whistled. "Ouch. Kinky, though. Maybe they killed each other? Whose body is missing?"

"The Black man's. Or, as it says here, 'the Afro-American individual's body appears to have been misplaced.'"

"COD?"

"Not specified. For either. Both were badly beaten," Jim said.

"Do you think?" Ed said, looking from his driver's seat at the photographs on his partner's lap.

"Hey, I'm just reading the report, motherfucker. And keep your eyes on the road. The Black man's corpse from the city morgue. Apparently there was no sign of anyone breaking into the place."

"Obviously, the brother wasn't dead," Ed said. "Did he still have the cracker's nuts in his hand when he left?"

"Does not say."

Ed put down his window a bit. "You're right, it is just a little close in here."

"Goddamn, though," Jim said. "The Black dude was really fucked up. That is the deadest-looking motherfucker I've ever seen."

"God, I hope we don't have to spend the night in this little peckerwood village," Ed said as they rolled past a once-colorful sign that read *Welcome to Money, It's worth a visit!*

"Keep your fingers crossed."

The next sign was a billboard that read *Pull a catfish out of the Little Tallahatchie! They's good eating! Visit the Dinah!*

"Save me, Jesus," Ed said.

"You know you want you some," Jim said.

"Shut the fuck up." Ed glared at his partner and then they both laughed. "Yeah, you're right."

9

"Come on, Wheat, there is other folks in this house gotta use the toilet!" Charlene shouted at the closed door. "What you doin' in there?"

"Tell that fool to get out of there," Granny C said. She was on her walker now. The chair wouldn't fit through the bathroom door. "Tell that dang fool I gotta pee and go number two."

"Hot Mama Yeller, I gots to pee real bad," little Wheat Junior said.

"Go on outside and piss in them bushes," Charlene barked. She banged on the door again. "Wheat?"

"I don't hear nothin'," Granny C said.

"Somethin's wrong," Charlene said. "You children go on outside," she said to her three daughters. She then went to the closet by the front door and grabbed a wire hanger. "Wheat, I'm coming in there." She straightened the curve of the hanger and pushed the rod into the hole in the knob. Click.

"You got it," Granny C said.

Charlene pushed on the door, but it wouldn't budge. "What the hell?" she said. "It won't open."

"Push harder, girl," Granny C said.

"I only weigh so much," Charlene said.

"You weigh plenty."

"Bitch," Charlene let out under her breath. "What was that?"

"Never mind." Charlene put her feet against the opposite wall for leverage and was able to push the door open several inches.

"There's blood on the floor!" Granny C said. "Oh, Jesus!"

"Wheat!" Charlene shouted. "Wheat, baby." She managed a couple more inches and got her head inside to look. She screamed, "Oh, my fucking gawd!"

"Language!" Granny C said.

"Fuck you, old lady. Wheat is dead!"

"What? Oh, Lawdie!"

Charlene fell over herself getting to the phone on the wall in the kitchen. "My husband is in the shitter and he's dead," she said. "I live at the end of Nickel Road. I don't know what happened. He's just dead in there. I think he's dead. He looks dead, sho 'nuff. They's blood all over the place!"

Granny C was leaning on the bathroom door, one hand still on her walker. "Wheat? Get up."

"What's wrong, Hot Mama Yeller?" one of the daughters came in and asked. "Something wrong with Wheat?"

"Stay yo ass outside, Lulabelle!"

Charlene ran back to the bathroom door and pushed some more.

"Push harder, girl," Granny C said.

"Why don't you help me?" Charlene said.

Granny C let go of her walker and placed both palms against the door, but it didn't help. "Oh, Lawd Jesus."

10

Delroy Digby and Braden Brady hurried out of the police station. Brady ran into and bounced off Ed Morgan. He became momentarily angry and then regarded the size of the man who'd sent him sprawling.

"Come on, Brady," Delroy said. "We gotta go."

Ed and Jim walked on into the poorly lit station. They were greeted by a tall, small-shouldered woman with cat's-eye glasses on a chain. "May I help you gentlemen?" she asked.

"We're here to see Sheriff Jetty," Jim said.

"I'll see if he's in." She walked over to the open door of the sheriff's office and said, "Two men here to see you. Are you in?"

"Well, I guess I have to be now, don't I?" Jetty said. He stepped into the doorway. He was momentarily surprised by the appearance of the men, but recovered quickly. "You two from Hattiesburg?"

"I'm Special Detective Jim Davis and this is Special Detective Ed Morgan. We're from the MBI."

"Special detectives," Jetty repeated.

"And that's not just because we're Black," Jim said. "Though plenty true because we are."

This put Jetty off-balance. The receptionist, whose name was really and from birth Hattie Berg, spat out a sudden chuckle.

"Go on back to the phone, Hattie," Jetty said.

"Yes, Sheriff."

"Well, come on in." Jetty stepped aside to let the men into his office. "I wish I could offer you something, but I won't."

"What was all that excitement out there?" Ed asked. "Your deputies nearly ran us over, they in such a hurry."

"Don't know yet. Call just come in." Jetty gestured for them to sit.

"Let's just get to it," Jim said. "What do you have?"

"Nothing. That's why the big shots sent you two hotshots here. I assume you've read the file."

"We've read it," Jim said.

"Obviously, the African-American individual was not dead," Ed said.

"You didn't see him," Jetty said.

"I'll grant you he looked dead in the photo," Jim said. "But looking dead is not the same thing as, well, being dead."

"Thank you for that," Jetty said.

"You did fingerprint the man," Ed said. "Yes, and we come up empty."

"Anybody fitting his general description reported missing?" Ed asked. "You know, five-six Black man, blue suit, dead."

Jetty shook his head. "It seems everybody around here is accounted for, living and dead. Not that there was much of a general or normal description to report." Jetty looked at Ed and then at Jim. "Would you special detectives like to go out to see where these crimes took place?"

Jim looked at Ed. "Well, we've come all this way."

Jetty lit a cigarette. "You know, because you never can tell what us hillbillies might have missed."

Ed looked at Jim, said, "He does have a point."

"A good point."

"Smart-asses," Jetty said.

"He wanted to say *uppity*. Didn't he want to say *uppity*? I could hear it even though he didn't say it," Jim said to Ed.

"Yeah, he did," Ed said. "That's not all I heard him say. Sheriff, you didn't say what I think you didn't say, did you?"

"You guys got an attitude problem," Jetty said.

"At the very least," Jim said.

11

"He's in the bathroom," Charlene told the deputies.

Granny C was now sitting on her wheelchair in the front room, crying, shaking, rocking back and forth.

"You think he's dead," Brady said, following Charlene.

"He's on the floor blockin' the door, and I cain't budge him," Charlene said. "He was in there for so long."

At the door, Delroy tried to get his head inside for a look. "There's a lot of blood, but I can't see shit. Help me push, Brady."

The deputies put all of their weight against the door. There was stiff resistance at first, then the door moved quickly, almost like Wheat's body just broke and fell over. The room smelled of shit and toothpaste.

Delroy stepped fully inside. "Fuck me," he said.

"What is it?" Charlene asked, pressing forward.

"Don't let her come in here," Delroy said to Brady.

Brady held Charlene back.

"What is it?" he asked Delroy.

"Fuck me," Delroy repeated.

"Stop sayin' that and say somethin'," Brady said. "Is he dead?"

"Oh yeah, he's dead."

Charlene screamed. That caused Granny C to scream in the other room. "What happened?" Charlene cried.

"Jesus," Delroy said.

"Come the fuck out of there and let me look," Brady said. Delroy backed out and took Brady's place holding Charlene back. Brady took a deep breath, like he was going underwater, and entered the bathroom. "What the fuck?"

"What is it?" Charlene screamed.

"Call the sheriff, Delroy. Call him now."

12

Hattie called to the sheriff as he was leading the MBI agents out of the station. "It's Delroy," she said. "He says you need to get out to Wheat Bryant's place pronto."

"He say why?"

"No, but he sounded plenty excited."

"He gettin' shot at?"

"I don't think so," Hattie said. "Didn't say nothin' about gettin' shot at. I didn't hear no gunfire."

Jetty turned to Ed and Jim. "Why don't you boys go down the street and grab some lunch? I gotta tend to somethin'."

"You want us to come along?" Ed asked.

"No, that's all right, Special Detective, I think we bumpkins can handle our situation," Jetty said.

"He sound a little sarcastic to you?" Jim asked Ed.

"Little bit," Ed said. "I wouldn't mind eating."

Jim smiled at Ed.

"Here's my card," Ed said to the sheriff. "Cell number is on it. Call us when you're ready for us."

"You can believe I'll do that," Jetty said.

13

Behind the cash register in the Dinah at the near end of a long counter was a large photograph of a large White woman dressed in white pants and a white apron that looked like a tent. Her apron was embroidered with a big red letter *D*, and under that was embroidered *Fat and Happy*.

The place was fairly full. A Black couple nodded to the men as they entered. Ed and Jim sat at the counter and grabbed menus.

A slender, smiling waitress came to them with a pot of coffee. "Y'all want some of this?"

"Please," Ed said.

Jim pushed his mug toward her. "I take it that's Dinah," he said, nodding toward the photo.

"Naw, that there's Delores. She opened this Dinah a long time ago. Before I was born. She could fry a hell of a catfish, they say. Couldn't spell worth a damn."

"Understood," Ed said.

"So, what will you two sophisticates have?" she asked.

"I think I will have to have the catfish," Ed said. "Tell me, is it fried?"

"Fried? It comes with a side of angioplasty."

Ed and Jim laughed.

Jim looked at the waitress's name tag: Dixie. "For some

reason, I don't think that's your name."

"And you'd be right," she said. "Dixies get better tips than Gertrudes."

"Well, Gertrude, you seem appropriately out of place here," Jim said. "I'm hoping we seem out of place too."

"Well said," she said. "And what will you have?"

"How is the chili?" Jim asked.

"Do you like chili?"

"Yes, I do."

"Then you will hate the chili here. Catfish or burger?"

"Cheeseburger," Jim said.

"Do you like cheese?" Gertrude asked.

"Burger."

"Wise choice. And what about you?" she asked Ed.

"Catfish."

"Coming up." She turned and walked back into the kitchen.

"She's cute," Jim said.

"May I remind you that we're in Money, Mississippi. Maybe I should say that again: Money, Mississippi. The important part of that is the word *Mississippi*. You do understand what I'm saying?"

"This is the twenty-first century," Jim said.

"Yeah, well, tell that to those fuckers back there in Trump caps."

"At least there's some color in this joint. I mean besides us." Jim looked at the walls. They were covered with photos from the fifties and sixties and old tin product signs: Nehi soda, Blue Ribbon biscuit mix. There were also weirdly colorized photographs of Elvis Presley and Billy Graham.

"So, are we clichés too?" Jim asked.

"No, we're dinosaurs, but we're not clichés."

Gertrude came back with the food.

"That was fast," Ed said.

"Luckily we'd already caught the fish," she said. "So, what are you two doing here in Money?"

"I hate to tell you, but we're cops," Jim said.

"Why do you hate to tell me?"

Jim sipped some coffee and put down his mug. "Because people either love cops or hate them. It's been my experience that most interesting people hate them. Hell, I'm a cop and I hate them."

"Me too," Ed said. "I especially hate him. Hate myself too, on occasion."

"So you think I'm interesting?" Gertrude said to Jim.

Jim, caught, looked at Ed, then said, "I guess that's right."

"I'm going to get you some extra fries."

"I'm telling you to be careful," Ed said.

"I can't help it if I exude charm."

"Well, do me and yourself and maybe Dixie there a favor and try not to do so much exuding."

"I'll do my best," Jim said. "You just control your intake of fatty foods."

14

Delroy was waiting in the front yard when Jetty crunched to a stop on the gravel. The deputy was visibly agitated as he walked out to meet the sheriff.

"What's so damn urgent?" Jetty asked.

"Another one."

"Another what?"

"Another murder. Wheat Bryant."

Jetty shook his head and stared at the house like it was on fire. "What the freegone fuck is going on?"

"That's not all," Delroy said.

"What else?"

"You just have to see."

"Don't be playin' games with me, Digby."

"Really, Sheriff, you just gotta see this."

Jetty followed Delroy through the front door and past the stillwailing Granny C. Charlene leaned against the wall outside the bathroom.

"It's Wheat, Sheriff. Wheat is dead," Charlene said.

"I'm sorry," Jetty said. "Go on outside and tend to your babies. We'll take care of things in here."

"I reckon I'll do that. That's Wheat in there, Sheriff. That's my husband in there. I'm so cold." She folded her bare arms over her yellow halter top. "I'm gonna go get me a sweater and go outside with the babies like you said."

"You do that," Jetty said. When she was gone he stepped into the bathroom. His boot skidded just a bit in the blood, and then he froze.

"See," Delroy said.

"What kinda fuckin' pig shit is goin' on here?" Jetty said.

Wheat was certainly a disturbing sight, dead and bloody as he was, barbed wire around his neck just like Junior Junior. But in the tub, sitting back to faucet knobs, was the same Black man they had found with Junior Junior Milam. The same battered-beyondrecognition Black man in the same dirt-encrusted blue suit, holding another set of testicles in his bloody, stiff, Black fist.

"What's goin' on, Sheriff ?" Brady asked.

"I do not know." Jetty stepped out of the room and looked long at Delroy. "Get Jethro out here to dust for prints and take pictures again. And call Fondle."

"And tell him what?"

"Jesus, Delroy. He's the coroner. I think he'll know why we want him."

"I mean do you want me to tell him about the, you know, the nigger being back?" Delroy said.

"I guess don't mention that," Jetty said. "Well, I reckon we don't need them special detectives no more. We found our body."

"Is that who we run into coming out of the station?" Brady asked.

"City cops," the sheriff said. "Slicker than snot on a doorknob. Smart-asses. Think we're just rubes."

"Want us to show them the way out of town?" Brady asked. "Make sure they stay away?"

"Shut up, Brady."

"How did that dead guy get here?" Delroy asked.

Jetty didn't answer. "Damn it." The sheriff marched back into the house and to the bathroom. Delroy and Brady were on his heels.

"What is it, Sheriff ?" Brady asked.

"Did either of you check the nigger for a pulse?"

"I didn't," Brady said. "You, Delroy?"

"Nope. Scared to touch him."

Jetty kneeled next to the tub, his knee settling into the blood on the floor. He put his fingers to the Black man's throat.

"Nothing. This man is ice cold."

"He's really dead, then," Delroy said.

"He's really, really dead."

15

Jim Davis put away his cell phone. "That was Sheriff Red Jetty of Money, Mississippi, calling to tell us that they have recovered the missing Afro-American individual's body and that our help is no longer required."

"Did he say where they found him?" Ed asked.

"Nope."

"Did he say whether the man is dead or alive?"

"Nope."

"Do you want to swing by the station and check this out before we drive all the way back to Hattiesburg?"

"Yep."

Ed pushed his half-eaten pie away. "Me too."

Jim put down a generous tip. "Bye, Dixie. Thanks."

"Y'all never did tell me your names," Gertrude said.

"That's Ed. I'm Jim."

Gertrude nodded. "Come back."

"You're going to mess around and get yourself shot," Ed said once they were on the street. "She could have some crazy-ass husband or boyfriend. You know, a stupid redneck with a gun."

"That's redundant."

16

The Doctor Reverend Fondle fell to arthritic knees and leapt into prayer when he saw the second murder scene, especially the dead Black man. "Oh, Gawd Jesus, I knows you have a plan, but us poor White mortals is scared to death down here with this strange nigger you keep sending. Is he an omen, oh Lawd, a sign, or is he the devil, and should we dismember him and burn his body right away? Jesus Gawd Almighty, it's clear that you ain't aimed to take the best of us, givin' you chose to take Wheat and Junior Junior, but still we're all terrified down here. So, a clear sign would be greatly appreciated. Thank you, Lawd, for yer time and consideration. Amen."

"Are you done yet?" Jetty asked.

"Yeah, I'm done."

"Are you sure they're both dead?" the sheriff asked. "You did examine them this time, touch them?"

"Yes, I did. And yes, they are dead."

"Put them in the wagon so we can get out of here and leave this family to their grief," Jetty said.

Delroy and Brady covered Wheat's body, face and all, and zipped him up tight out of respect for the family. Still, Charlene, the four kids, and Granny C stood and sat on the porch and cried as he was carried past them. They had only the one body bag and saw no reason to cover the Black man, even though he was so gruesomely disfigured about his neck and head. The sight made the children and even Charlene scream in horror, but Granny C made no sound whatsoever. She froze there in her chair and stared off into nowhere like a mannequin, her lower lip slack, her fingers clamped around the cracked and split vinyl of her wheelchair armrests.

"Granny C, y'all awright?" Charlene asked.

"Granny C, Granny C," the children called to her.

Charlene shook her. "Granny C, snap out of it." She slapped the old woman across the face. Nothing. Charlene shouted out into the yard, "Reverend Doctor Fondle! Reverend Doctor Fondle!"

"Yes?"

"It's Granny C, there's something wrong with her."

Fondle climbed back onto the porch and examined the old woman, took her pulse, and looked into her eyes.

"Is she dead?" Charlene asked.

"She's alive. Unresponsive, but alive." He looked at her pupils. "What do you call her?"

"We calls her Granny C," Lulabelle said.

"Granny C?" Fondle said. "It's like she's in shock. But why wouldn't she be? Her son was just brutally murdered and castrated by a strange nigger who was not only presumed to be dead, but in fact was found dead just feet from her son's body." He paused and looked at Charlene. "You do see what I mean. Take her inside and put her in bed and see if she's better tomorrow."

"Thank you," Charlene said.

17

"I told you I don't need you boys," Sheriff Jetty said when he walked into the station to find Ed Morgan and Jim Davis. "We found our missin' dead man, and this time there ain't no question about him being dead."

"Just for the purposes of our report," Ed said, "can you tell us where you found the body?"

Jetty looked around the room. "Come into my office." Jim and Ed followed him in. "Close that door."

Jim did.

Jetty looked out his window, then closed the blinds. "We found him at the scene of another homicide. Terrible, just like the other one. He was grippin' the balls of this victim, just like last time."

"You know that this man is the killer?" Ed asked.

"Who else could it be? He was holding another man's testicles in his fist. This time it was in a bathroom in the family's house. One door, no window. Wife, children, and mother in the home at the time."

"Did anybody see him enter the house?" Jim asked.

"No. Ain't nobody seen shit."

"If no one saw him, why couldn't someone else have been there too, also unobserved?" Jim asked.

"I don't know, *Special Deeetective*."

"You know how this is going to go, Sheriff," Ed said. "We're going to drive all the way back to Hattiesburg just to have our superiors tell us to come back here and try to sort this out."

"Actually, I don't have any superiors," Jim said.

"You two are real funny," Jetty said. "So what are you telling me? You want to see the evidence?"

"And the scenes," Ed said.

"Why didn't you just say? One of the scenes has been cleaned up already, though none too good, I'm sure," Jetty said.

"We'll take a look anyway," Jim said.

"You're serious about this." Jetty lit a cigarette. "You know this here is Money, Mississippi?"

"What are you saying, Sheriff ?" Ed asked.

"This ain't the city. Hell, this ain't even the twenty-first century. It's barely the twentieth, if you know what I mean. It's your business, though. I'll have one of my deputies go with you." He picked up his phone. "Hattie, tell Delroy to come in here."

"We'd prefer not to have your man with us," Jim said. "No offense. We tend to work better alone."

"You do, do you?" Jetty stared at them. "Have you two been listening to me? This here is M-I-crooked letter-crooked letter-I-crooked letter-crooked letter-I-P-P-I."

"We don't need him," Ed said. "But I liked the song."

The door opened and Delroy poked his head in.

"Never mind," the sheriff said. "Go out and patrol something. Tell Brady to set up a speed trap at the bridge."

"Yessir."

Hattie opened the door immediately after it had been

closed. "Reverend Doctor Fondle on the phone. Sounds upset."

Jetty picked up the phone, listened, then put it down.

"What is it?" Ed asked, looking at the sheriff's face.

"That was our esteemed coroner," Jetty said. "Seems we've lost our Negro man again."

18

Charlene Bryant somehow managed to get her crying children to sleep that night. Granny C was still in her bed, staring blankly toward the cracked and peeling ceiling, muttering something over and over again that none of them could make out.

Charlene washed her face and brushed her teeth at the kitchen sink. She could not yet bring herself to use the one bathroom. She'd had the kids pee in the yard, and now they were buried under quilts. She prepared herself to go back and scrub the tiles and tub with bleach, though she already knew that the grout would be forever stained pink, not that it was clean, but at least it wasn't pink.

"Oh Wheat, what the fuck happened in there?" she said. Kneeling like she was on the porch, somebody might have thought she was praying, she imagined, but she was talking to Wheat, even though he was dead. He probably heard her just as well when he was alive. "Did that Negro man kill you? Did you kill him? Did you know him? Oh why did he have your nuts in his hand? That's what I really want to know. Were you secretly funny and he was your lover? I won't judge you, just let me know. That possibility makes you a much more interestin' person. I wish I'd knowed that side of you. Granny C looked like she knowed that man when they toted him out. She all froze up now. Did she know you was gay? She never let on iffen she did. It won't be hard carrying on without you, so don't worry none. I mean you never brought home a dime and you never cleaned a dish or changed a shitty diaper. But still, you was a warm body in my bed. Not one I ever touched lately, but still, you was in it. I should have suspected you was gay by the way you liked to watch that wrasslin' on the television. Is it true what they say 'bout them Black men? Don't answer that. Oh Wheat, where you at now? Oh Lawd, please take care of my Wheat, though I have my doubts whether he's even with you. And please don't let that blood stain the tub tiles. I don't mind the pink in the grout, but we gots to sit in that tub. Amen." Turned out it was a prayer. She stood up and slapped off her knees.

Bleach and brush in hand, she returned to the bathroom.

19

The Reverend Doctor Fondle paced the uneven sidewalk in front of his office, his head bobbling as he muttered to himself. He looked up to see Sheriff Jetty getting out of his car. The men from the MBI had followed the sheriff in their own car.

Fondle started talking immediately. "I examined that ni—" He checked himself. "I even listened to that man's chest with my stethoscope. Not a sound, not a goddamn—excuse me, Lawd—sound. Jetty, you saw me do it. Then we put him in the truck. Brady and Delroy put him in the back of the wagon. Jethro closed the door. I didn't stop once on my way here. Dill was driving and I was sittin' right beside him."

"Get to it, man," Jetty said.

"We opened it up, the wagon, Dill and me, and what do you think we found?" Fondle asked. "Well? What do you think?"

"Just say it," Jetty said.

"Just one bagged body. I even looked in the bag to see if they wasn't two of them inside it. But no, there was just one dead body, a dead White body. The ni—the Black man is missing. Again."

"And you didn't stop?" Jetty asked.

Fondle shook his head. "And your deputy was behind me the whole way. He can tell you we didn't stop."

"Jethro!" the sheriff called.

"Sheriff?"

"You was behind the van the whole way?"

"Yes, sir. Most of it, anyway. A freight train separated us for just a minute or so, but it wasn't a long one."

"All right."

"Fondle, these men are from the MBI," Jetty said. "They come up from Hattiesburg to help us find our missing body." Jetty looked at Ed and Jim. "They tell me they is special detectives."

"Well, I hope so," Fondle said.

"Show us the truck," Ed said.

"It's right there." Fondle pointed.

Ed and Jim walked away from Fondle and Jetty to the old Ford Econoline van. "This is some crazy shit," Jim said to his partner.

"You're right about that," Ed said.

"And I got to say these inbred redneck motherfuckers scare the hell out of me," Jim whispered.

They stared at the van, the inside of it, the doors, under it. Jim closed and reopened the doors, examining the mechanism and the hinges. The rear doors not only stuck and had to be yanked open but shook the whole truck, and were loud with creaking and clunking. "No way anybody got into this without the driver or passenger knowing."

"Plus the deputy was following."

"Sheriff Jetty," Jim called.

Jetty walked over.

"Did you get photos of the Black man at the second crime

scene?" Jim asked. "Are you sure it was the same man?"

"It was the same man," Jetty said, irritated. "Jethro, grab your camera and show these special detectives the pictures of the scene."

"Yes, sir."

Jethro trotted to his car, opened the rear door, retrieved his digital camera case, and brought it over.

"Show them the pictures," Jetty said.

Jim and Ed looked over Jethro's shoulder as he fumbled with the camera. "Sorry, that was my girlfriend."

"Congratulations," Jim said.

Jethro scrolled through the pictures. "That there is Wheat Bryant. You can see he's dead, throat's kinda ripped out by the barbed wire. That must hurt like hell, don't you think? Blood on the floor, the toilet."

"Very thorough," Ed said.

"Thank you," Jethro said. "And here he is right here."

Ed nodded to Jim. "Same man."

"What y'all thinking?" Jethro asked the detectives. "I just want you to know I ain't like a lot of folks around here."

"Is that right?" Jim asked.

"I went to junior college."

"Good for you," Ed said.

"Know what I think?" Jethro said.

"I should hope not," Jim said.

"What?"

"Don't mind him," Ed said. "Tell me what you think, Jethro. Jethro, right?"

Jethro looked back to see if anyone was listening in. "I think we're all suffering from mass hysteria around here. You see, there weren't no Black man at either crime scene.

We're just so afraid of Black people in this county that we see them everywhere. I mean there's Black men all around, but not dead ones. Not like this dead one."

"How do you explain the pictures?" Ed asked.

"I ain't ironed that out."

"Good theory, though," Jim said. "You keep working on it."

"Yes, sir."

The detective watched Jethro walk away and join Jetty and Fondle.

"What are we doing with our lives?" Jim asked.

"Beats me."

Inside, Dill had already learned who the two Black men were and seemed willing to help. He also didn't seem impressed one way or the other by the fact that they were Black or from the MBI. He appeared, more than anything, to be delighted to have someone not from Money to talk to.

"The son of a bitch is a fuckin' ghost," Dill said. "That's all there is to it, a fucking ghost."

"Why do you say that?" Ed asked.

Dill gave him an incredulous look and then deemed the question unworthy of any answer.

Jim pointed with an open hand down the hallway. "Why would a ghost need to push the door open?"

"You an expert on ghosts?" Dill asked.

"Point taken," Jim said.

"Did you go to junior college too?" Ed asked.

"Three years at Auburn. Jethro thinks that junior college is college. Hell, some people think that Auburn is college. I came back to this godforsaken shithole of a town because of my mother."

"Sick?" Ed asked.

"She's fat. Too fat. It takes a toll." Dill looked at Ed's girth. Ed cleared his throat.

"Have you ever seen a ghost?" Jim asked, sort of changing the subject. "I mean, in real life?"

"Yeah, yesterday and today."

"Before that?"

"Nope."

"Who discovered the body missing?" Ed asked.

"Fondle," Dill said.

"What do you think of Fondle?" Jim asked.

Dill looked back over his shoulder to see if anyone was in earshot. "Crazier than a one-winged fly."

"That's very poetic," Jim said.

"I was a creative writing major at Auburn. Poetry. I always wanted to be a Beat poet. Wrong generation. Now I stick dead people in drawers. I suppose it's the same thing once you get down to it."

Ed and Jim exchanged glances.

"Thanks, Dill," Ed said.

Dill left them in the hallway.

"Okay, no more catfish for me," Ed said.

"There's nothing to see here," Jim said.

20

When Jim and Ed parked in front of Daisy Milam's split-level house, the first thing they saw was a boy and a girl chasing a piglet. Daisy was sitting on the wooden steps of the front porch holding a Fig Newton to the mouth of her disinterested toddler. Her eyes were sunken, hollow. Her hair was a mess. She was wearing a blue halter top. She looked up at the two approaching men.

"Who the hell is y'all?" she said.

"We're policemen," Ed said. "Mrs. Milam?"

"Yeah?"

"We're sorry for your loss," Ed said.

Jim nodded and watched the pig and children run past.

"Ma'am, we'd like to ask you a few questions, if you don't mind. Would that be all right with you?"

"What the hell else I got to do?" she said. "My Junior Junior is dead. Kilt in his own home. Them people can say what they want, but Junior Junior was a good man. He was a good daddy to these here younguns." She watched the children tackle the piglet. "Don't y'all hurt that pig none." Then, to the detectives, "He didn't have no money or a lick of sense, but he was a good man."

"Yes, ma'am," Jim said. "Mrs. Milam, did you know the other man, the Black man they found in your house?"

"How would I know?" she said. "His face was all fucked up. He just barely looked like a person."

"Did your husband have any close Black men as friends or associates or enemies? Did he ever mention having problems or conflicts with anyone?" Ed looked at the rickety steps and the rickety screen door. "You ever have anybody doing work for you around here? A yardman or a handyman?"

Daisy shook her head no. "No, we let the gardener go when we hired the butler." She smirked.

"So nobody saw or heard the Black man or anyone else come into the house?" Jim asked.

"We wasn't here. We was at the swap meet in the Sam's Club parking lot. I keep tellin' everybody that, but no-fuckin'-body listens. I wanted me a lime-green halter top, but I got this blue one instead."

"Yes, ma'am."

"Why did that Negro man kill my husband?" she asked, sincerely.

"I don't know," Ed said. "Maybe he didn't. Maybe it was some-body else. It seems unlikely they killed each other."

"Did something happen over at Wheat Bryant's today?" Daisy asked. "Somebody called all hysterical, but I couldn't pay no attention because of the baby. Every time I go into the house I feel like I'm gonna lose my mind."

"Mind if we go in and take a look?" Jim asked. "We'll be careful not to disturb anything."

Daisy laughed. "Disturb anything? Disturb away. Won't make no difference. Funny, though," she said.

"What's that?" Ed asked.

"I ain't never had no colored people in my house, except

for the man from the satellite TV, and in two days three of y'all come in."

"Yes, ma'am," Jim said.

The screen door was every bit as loud as Ed imagined it would be. The house was clean, cluttered with bright plastic toys. Against the far wall of the front room were stacks of T-shirts, bright white.

"The report says it happened in a room way back off the kitchen," Jim said. He led the way.

There was no police tape, but an empty, yellow, five-gallon bucket sat in front of the closed door, as if put there as a barrier. Jim moved the bucket, opened the door, and they stepped inside.

"I hate murder scenes," Ed said.

Jim looked at the room, scanning slowly front to back. It appeared to be a spare bedroom that had become a catchall storage area, not a strange thing. The only thing truly out of place was what appeared to be a high-end racing bicycle turned upside down onto its seat, the wheels removed.

"Milam was right here," Jim said. "Our unidentified *colored* man was there. No weapons were found."

"There is another way in and out." Ed pointed to a sliding glass door. There were boxes stacked in front of it. Ed looked closely. "Except this door hasn't moved in a long time. Crud is all built up and undisturbed in the track."

"This is some weird shit," Jim said.

"We're not going to figure out anything here," Ed said.

"We're not going to figure out any of this," Jim said. "We're just going through the motions, partner. Crossing the t's and dotting the i's."

"What time is it?" Ed asked.

"After four."

"I guess I should call home and tell Joyce I won't be home tonight. My kid has a recital too."

"Oops." Jim pointed. "Just out of curiosity, what's in those boxes?"

Ed peeled back a lid. "T-shirts." He opened the one beside it. "Same here. All white."

"Do you believe any of these folks are lying to us?" Jim asked.

"That's the weird thing. I don't think so. I think they're all telling the truth. Even Jethro with his ghost theory."

Jim rubbed the back of his neck. "It always helps when somebody lies."

21

Braden Brady and Delroy Digby fell into the vinyl booth seats opposite the sheriff. The Dinah was busy because everyone was trying to beat the dinner rush. This happened every day. The restaurant was packed from five to six-thirty and then virtually empty until closing at nine, staying open that late only for the occasional trucker and a few regulars and those too late to beat the dinner rush.

"So, where are they?" Brady asked.

"Who?" Jetty asked.

"You know, Shaquille O'Neal and Samuel L. Jackson?" Brady said. "I don't know their fuckin' names."

Delroy laughed.

"Investigating, I guess," Jetty said.

"Are we just gonna let them two colored boys roam all over town like that?" Brady asked.

"What's wrong with you?" Jetty asked. "Did your mama drop you on your head or something?"

Brady gave Delroy a puzzled look.

"You mean you want them here?" Delroy asked.

"Have you found the body?" the sheriff asked. "That was rhetorical. Maybe they will. Then they can go back to Hattiesburg and feel all superior and laugh about them stupid peckerwoods up in Money. All I can say is that this is crazy. Scary. Dead bodies disappearing. What's next?"

The deputies stared stupidly at Jetty. The sheriff studied their blank faces and shook his head.

"What?" Delroy asked.

"Nothing," Jetty said.

Gertrude came to their table and stood there, pencil and pad ready.

"Chili for me," Delroy said.

"Me too," Brady said. "And sprinkle some of that crumbly cheese on it. I like that cheese."

"I'm good with coffee," the sheriff said.

"You got it," Gertrude said and walked away.

"You know, I don't like her much," Brady said. "I don't even think Dixie is her real name. She's kinda uppity."

"Delroy"—Jetty pointed his coffee mug at the man—"I want you to get in your private car and see if you can't keep an eye on them special detectives."

"You think they up to somethin'?" Brady asked.

"No, I don't think *they up to somethin'*. I just want to know what's goin' on. Try not to be seen."

"So, I'm like, goin' undercover," Delroy said.

"Yes, undercover, Delroy."

"Should I put on my regular street clothes?"

"Well, yeah."

"Want I should go with him?" Brady asked.

"No." Jetty finished his coffee.

22

The smell of skunk wafted over the property. Charlene Bryant was swearing a blue streak and telling her children to stay indoors. Three skunks were on the side deck scratching at the glass door.

"What are they doin' here, Hot Mama Yeller?" Lulabelle asked. She was frightened of the animals.

"Granny C didn't feed them like she always does, and now they lookin' for food," Charlene said.

"What's wrong with Granny C?" the child asked.

"Well, honey, your daddy was just brutally murdered. That kinda messed her up. You know your daddy was her son. Me? I'm upset too, but ain't nobody worrying over me. It's fucked up."

"Daddy was dead when they took him out?" Lulabelle said.

"Yes, baby."

"Is Granny C gonna die?" the child asked.

"No, baby."

Outside on the front porch, Jim Davis squeezed his nose shut. "Is that decomp?" he asked.

"I think it's skunk," Ed said.

"It's awful."

"I sort of like the smell."

"Just knock," Jim said.

Ed rapped on the screen door.

"Who you? What y'all want?" Charlene stood behind the screen. "I'm gonna call the police if you don't get off my property."

Ed flashed his badge. "Ma'am, we are the police."

"I ain't never seen you before," she said.

"I'm Special Detective Morgan and this is Special Detective Davis. We're Mississippi State cops."

"Well, what y'all want? Let me see that badge again. Anybody can get theyselves a badge."

Ed showed her his badge and his ID. Jim held his up also.

"Okay," she said, hardly looking at them. "What you want?"

"We're sorry for your loss," Ed said.

"You know it was a nigger who killed him. I got every right to be scared of you. I could shoot you if I wanted. Could say you scared me real bad and I had to shoot you. You hear what I'm sayin'?"

"I wish you wouldn't," Jim said.

"Don't you think there's been enough killing around here?" Ed asked.

"Enough killin'? What kinda crazy talk is that?" Charlene looked past them into the yard to see if anyone else was there. "How come the sheriff ain't with you?"

"This is a state investigation now, Mrs. Bryant," Ed said, though it was not technically true.

"Ma'am, can we come in and ask you a few questions? The skunk smell is pretty bad out here."

Charlene gave him a hard look. She unlatched the door and let them in. "We can sit in here."

The men sat side by side on a love seat. Lulabelle came

running into the room and stopped at the sight of them.

"Who they, Hot Mama Yeller?"

Jim looked at Ed and, while Charlene was tending to the child, mouthed the words *hot mama yellow*?

Ed shrugged.

"These men come to ask some questions about your daddy," Charlene said. "Now you go on and play."

"My daddy dead."

"We're very sorry about that," Ed said. "You know, I have a daughter about your age. She pays attention to almost everything. How about you?"

"Mama say I'm nosy."

"Did you see anyone you didn't know this morning?" Jim asked.

"No."

"Did you hear any voices other than your family's?"

"No." The girl looked to her mother. "I think them skunks is givin' up."

"Good," Charlene said.

Jim said to Charlene, "Ma'am, did you see the stranger enter your house. Or hear him?"

"Nobody seen or heard nothing. I needed to pee, actually more than pee, Granny C too, and Wheat had been in the bathroom for a real long time. That's when I tried to get in. We only got one bathroom. Wheat kept saying he was gonna put another toilet on the back porch." She started to tear up. "He was on the floor blockin' the door. I feel bad for yelling at him. I thought he was in there with a magazine or somethin'."

"It's okay, Hot Mama Yeller," Lulabelle said.

"May I ask why she calls you that?" Jim asked.

"That's my CB handle," she said. "All the children call me that now. Hot Mama Yeller, ten-four."

Jim nodded.

"The other man in the room, had you ever seen him before?"

"Not lookin' the way he did. I didn't recognize him. I know he ain't never been around here, not looking like that."

"Could your husband have known him?" Ed asked. "Worked with him or had some other business with him away from here?"

"Wheat never left the house. And he sure as hell never went to work. So no. I don't see how Wheat coulda knowed him."

"Has anything seemed strange or different lately?" Jim asked. "Anybody been hanging around?"

Charlene shook her head. She seemed much more relaxed now, though, showing more grief. She inhaled deeply and sighed. "Do you want to see where we found him? I already done cleaned up the mess."

Ed looked at Jim. Jim said, "I don't think that will be necessary. Who else lives here in the house?"

"My other babies. They's younger than Lulabelle here. And Wheat's mama. We call her Granny C."

"You think we could talk to her?" Ed asked.

"You can talk at her, but you ain't gonna learn nothing. She got all froze up when she seen them takin' Wheat and that nigger out. Sorry, no offense."

"None taken," Jim said.

"Granny C was here all morning?" Ed asked.

"She was."

"We'll try not to upset her," Ed said.

Charlene led the men down the hall and into Granny C's bedroom. She was lying on her back, a heavy crazy quilt pulled to just under her chin. "She ain't said a single word since she seen that Black man."

Granny C's eyes found Jim or Ed or both. Her mouth opened as if she was about to say "egg" and let out a wild scream. Her body shook, and spittle spilled from the corner of her crooked lips. Charlene tried to settle her down. The old woman's arms flailed, and her screaming became the word *sorry*. She repeated it, holding the last sound for several seconds.

"We'd better leave her alone," Jim said.

As soon as they were out of the room, the old woman became quiet. Charlene came out to them. "That was just weird," she said. "Didn't you think that was weird? She always been crazy, but not like this."

"I think we've taken up enough of your time," Jim said.

Ed knelt to address Lulabelle. "You keep on being nosy, okay?"

"Okay."

23

Delroy Digby's '97 sky-blue Nissan Sentra was the only car parked on the curbless Dime Drive. He was parked in front of the unoccupied shotgun house across and just down the road from the Bryant house. The house was slated to be razed, but it also had possibilities as a meth-making lab, so it remained. Delroy held a newspaper in front of his face, peered around the edge of it at the two Black men climbing into the dark-green Toyota Sienna. He called Sheriff Jetty.

"Sheriff, it's me, Delroy Digby. I'm calling from undercover."

"Yes, Delroy? I know your last name."

"I'm parked outside Wheat Bryant's place. Or what used to be his place. Is it still his place? I mean, given that he's all dead and stuff? I guess I should call it Charlene Bryant's place. You know?"

"Why are you calling me?" Jetty asked.

"I just seen the subjects exitin' the house. They just got into their van. They ain't seen me. I'm parked across the road."

"Are there any other cars parked around you?"

"No, but don't worry," Delroy said.

"Pray tell why not?"

"They couldn't see me cause I was makin' like I was readin' the newspaper."

Jetty sighed. "Delroy, when's the last time you actually saw somebody readin' a newspaper?"

"I dunno."

"Just stay with them," the sheriff said. "Don't call back."

24

Jim and Ed decided to stop at the diner called the Dinah for an early dinner. Gertrude waved to them and gestured for them to sit in a window booth. The vinyl seats were that avocado green from the sixties, cracked and repaired with tape that almost matched the color. A couple of names were carved into the table.

Ed took out his phone. "First things first, I'll call and get us a room at the Motel 6 we saw coming into town."

"Eight," Jim said.

"What?"

"It's a Motel 8."

"You're crazy," Ed said. "There's no such thing."

"It's a Motel 8."

Gertrude came to their table with coffee. "You men want coffee?"

"I do, he doesn't," Jim said.

Ed looked at her. "Motel 6 or Motel 8?"

"It's a Motel 8," she said.

"What the hell does that even mean?" Ed muttered. "What's the eight for?"

"What's the six for?" Jim asked.

Ed froze. "Well, okay, you've a got a point. I'll call and

make a reservation at the Motel fucking 8."

"How has your day been?" Jim asked Gertrude.

"The same as yesterday, the day before, and the same as tomorrow will be. What about you? I heard about those murders. Is that why you're here?"

Jim nodded. "Not that we're doing much."

"Somebody said there was a Black wizard or ghost running loose around town," she said.

"It appears so."

"What?" His lack of irony confused her.

"You don't mind if I say this a fucked-up town."

"It would be weird if you didn't say it," she said.

"What are you doing here?" Jim looked at her eyes. They were brown, like his. She had a few freckles around the bridge of her nose.

"Excuse me for asking, but are you Black?" Jim asked.

"Why yes."

"I knew it," he said. "I didn't know that you're Black. I didn't know that, but I knew there was something. Does Whitey know?"

"They know," Gertrude said. "They forget." She had to go check on another patron who was calling to her from the back. "Be back."

Ed got off the phone.

"She's Black," Jim said.

"You didn't see that?" Ed said.

"You knew?" Jim asked, incredulous.

"I'm telling you I knew. I knew she was Black just like I knew it was a Motel 8."

Jim laughed.

"That doesn't change anything, does it?" Ed asked.

"Of course not."

Ed pushed his phone to the side. "We got the last room. Why anybody is staying in Money, Mississippi, I don't know. Truckers, I guess. I called Joyce and told her we're stuck in Money. She said she wished that was true."

Gertrude returned. "What will it be?"

"I think I'll pass," Ed said.

"Very funny," Gertrude said.

"I will have the chicken-fried steak," Ed said.

Jim looked at him.

"Baby steps, little brother," Ed said. "And a salad."

"I'll have the club sandwich," Jim said.

"Am I to understand that you're staying overnight here in Money?"

"Afraid so," said Ed.

Jim pointed to the man seated at a two-person table in the far corner. "There's our friend," he said.

"Which Keystone Cop is that?" Ed asked.

"That is one Delroy Digby," Gertrude said. "Nephew-in-law of the esteemed Sheriff Jetty."

"He followed us from the last crime scene," Jim said.

"He's harmless," Gertrude said.

"I've heard that before," Ed said. "Tell me, just what do you think of the esteemed sheriff?"

"He's okay. He tries to not be the racist asshole he can't help being. It's a sincere effort, I think. Sometimes he's a racist, sometimes he's an asshole, and every now and then he's both," Gertrude said. "So what's the Black wizard story? Or ghost."

Jim shrugged. "Could be true. Have you seen anybody new around?"

She shook her head.

"Black or White," he added.

"Nope." Gertrude tapped her pad with her pencil. "I'll put this order in. You want any bread?"

Ed said yes while Jim said no. "No bread," Jim said. "For him either."

Gertrude put in their orders and poured coffee for an oversized trucker seated at the counter. Jim looked at the television above the counter. "Dixie, would you turn that up, please?"

Gertrude did.

A reporter stood on a city street, CNN emblazoned on the screen. The scroll said Man Found Beaten to Death in Chicago Apartment. Ed tuned in with Jim.

The reporter braced himself against the November wind. "In a unit of this multifamily dwelling in the Brighton Park neighborhood of Chicago, a man was found brutally beaten to death. The beating was so severe that authorities became alarmed. Police have determined the identity of the victim. He is Lester William Milan, in his midfifties, and he is listed as the sole resident of the one-room apartment, in this depressed community in the middle of Chicago. The man's head was nearly severed from his body. And he was wrapped in wire. He was discovered by the building manager, who said he had received complaints about the smell. Again, the sheer brutality of the beatings has prompted serious concern for public safety, and residents of the community are being asked to be extra vigilant. Right here we have Anthony McDougall, the building manager. Mr. McDougall, can you tell us what you saw?"

"It was horrible," McDougall said. "I mean, this is a quiet

building, a quiet neighborhood. We ain't got no gangs or nothing, if you know what I mean. That smell was strong, and when I opened that door it about knocked me over. It ain't but one room, so I seen him immediately, lying there on the floor. I think some of the blood was still wet. I never seen anybody beaten like that in my life. Hope I never see it again." McDougall smiled at the camera.

"A terrible scene here in Chicago," the reporter said.

An advertisement for Coke Zero came on.

"Thanks," Jim said.

Gertrude lowered the volume.

"What are you thinking?" Ed said.

"Beating death," Jim said, absently. "I'm seeing ghosts everywhere."

"Paranoia is a good thing," Ed said.

25

Sheriff Red Jetty sat behind his metal desk. He rested his elbows on the cluttered surface and his face in his hands. He looked up when Delroy Digby walked in. "What is it?" the sheriff asked.

"I'm here to make my report," the deputy said.

"Go ahead."

Delroy pulled out and flipped open a little notebook. "I observed the two subjects leaving the Bryant house at five twelve. I then followed them, at a safe distance so they wouldn't see me, to the Dinah. Dixie waited on them and they ordered food. The big one had the chicken-fried steak, and the other one, well, I don't know what he had. They ate and then went to the Motel 8."

"So, you're here to report that you ain't got nothing to report?"

Delroy said nothing.

"Let me see that little notebook," Jetty said.

Delroy handed it to him.

The sheriff, without looking at it, dropped it unceremoniously into the waste can beside his desk.

"You want me to wait outside the motel?"

Jetty regarded him for a second. "Yeah, sure. You can wait there in case they leave in the middle of the night."

"Really?"

Jetty nodded. He watched the man leave.

Hattie came in. "You really gonna make him spend the whole night in his car?" she asked.

"I don't know," he said. "Maybe I should. I'll call him in a while and tell him to go home."

"You okay, Red?"

"No. I hate this crap. I hate this job. I hate them fancy state police. I hate my dumbass deputies. I hate this dumbass town."

"Do you hate me?" Hattie asked.

"Not yet, but you're next."

"It's nice to be included."

"How can a dead man just get up and walk out and then show up someplace else? It might even be amusing, if there weren't no other dead bodies. Did I mention that I hate dead people? Especially dead, disappearing Negroes."

"Lots of people talkin' about a Black ghost," Hattie said.

"Who?"

"Just about everybody in town."

"Jesus."

"Should I be scared?" the woman asked.

"Who the fuck knows, Hattie? I got me two dead crackers in the morgue and a dead nigger running around maybe killin' people and gettin' hisself killed over and over again. What is anybody supposed to think?"

"Will you drive me home?"

"Yes, Hattie."

26

Jim and Ed asked the desk clerk at the Motel 8 where they might hear some Black music. Well, they started by asking about mere music. After a couple of recommendations, the question became more specific. The man stroked his little Pekingese dog while he considered the question. He directed them to a juke joint in the Bottom. "It used to be called Black Bottom," the man said. "Now we just call it the Bottom. Anybody will know what you're talkin' about. Nobody ever heard of no place called White Bottom."

"I think that's fair to say," Jim said. "What's your dog's name?"

"Oh, he ain't got no name."

"Why's that?"

"I don't like names," the man said, looking down at his pet.

"How do you call it?" Jim asked.

"Call it?"

Now, the two detectives sat outside the juke joint, constructed of cinder blocks and noise.

"Signs of life," Jim said.

"Got the photo?"

Ed asked.

"Yep."

They walked across the gravel parking lot to the bar. They had shed their blazers but still looked alarmingly like police.

"Did we start looking like this before or after we became fucking policemen?" Jim asked.

"Got me. But it's damn hard to wash off, that's all I know."

They walked in to find Earth, Wind & Fire blasting from an actual juke box. The lighting was fairly bright, brighter than taverns are usually. Several couples danced in the middle of the floor, others sat at tables, and several men and a couple of women sat at the bar. Everything stopped when they entered. Everything except the music. Jim and Ed stared back at the staring faces.

"Yes, we're cops," Jim said loudly. "And we don't like it either. Everybody carry on. Have fun. Break the law, if you like."

A couple of people laughed, then others. There was the sound of someone breaking a rack at the pool table in back. The dancing and chatting started up again.

At the bar, the tender, who looked very much like Isaac Hayes, said to Jim, "Hey, that was pretty good."

"Nice crowd," Ed said.

"This ain't nothing," the man said. "You should see us when we're open. What do you want to drink?"

"Beer," Ed said. "Any kind."

"Jameson for me," Jim said.

"Ice?"

"Sure."

"Have you heard about the murders?" Jim asked.

"Yep."

"Nobody seems too broken up about it?" Jim said.

"Hell, that's why we havin' a party. Ain't nobody gonna miss them racist motherfuckers. Their own families won't miss them."

"You heard about the Black man found with them?" Ed asked.

"You mean the Black Angel? That's what folks is callin' him."

"You got an idea who this angel is?" Ed asked.

The bartender shook his head.

"You know we don't even know if he killed those White boys," Jim said. "Same person could have killed him as killed the White men."

"All I know is what people been sayin'."

Jim pulled the picture from his pocket. "This is kind of hard to look at, but tell me if you recognize this man."

The man cringed at the sight. "Ain't nobody gonna recognize him. What the fuck happened?"

Jim shrugged. "If this man is alive, we want to find him before that cracker sheriff and his deputies do."

"How can that man be alive?" the bartender asked.

Jim shrugged again.

"Franklin, come here and look at this."

The other bartender came over. Jim held up the photo for him to see. "Lord, have mercy. What's that?"

"That's a human being," Ed said. "Somebody did that to another human being. Do you recognize him?"

The second man shook his head. "He must be dead. Is he dead?"

"On and off," Jim said.

The man offered a puzzled look.

"We don't know," Ed said.

Though people carried on their conversations and dancing, they were tuned in to the discussion at the bar even without hearing it.

"Have there been any strangers around lately?" Ed asked. "Small man, about five six, slight build."

"Nobody new around at all," the first bartender said. "Of course, we seldom see the truckers. Most of them stop at the diner in town. Even the Black ones. They can park in back of the motel. We ain't got room like that. They wouldn't stop here anyway."

Ed and Jim listened.

"So, was them cracker boys fucked as bad as this brother?" the second bartender asked.

"Oh yeah," Jim said. "Somebody put a real beating on them. Wrapped barbed wire around their necks."

The men were silent for a few seconds.

"Cut off their balls," Jim said.

"Say what?"

Jim didn't repeat himself.

Then the first bartender whistled. "As long as the brother weren't the only one. Barbed wire."

"Maybe baby boy got him some," the second man said. He and the other bartender bumped fists.

"You know anybody who hated Milam or Bryant enough to do something like that to them?" Ed asked.

"Oh, everybody," number one said. "I don't even know of any White people what liked Milam. The one they called Junior Junior. Ain't that some stupid shit? Junior Junior. Imagine that."

"To be hated by your own people?" Ed asked.

"No," number one said. "That name. Junior fucking Junior."

"It's a fact," number two said. "Nobody liked him at all."

"What about Bryant?" Jim asked.

"Asshole. Don't know much about him. He was on the news once a while back," said the one who looked like Isaac Hayes. "Remember that shit? His truck was hanging off the bridge. Looked like a big Piggly Wiggly dick."

"Oh yeah," number two said. "Nobody paid him much mind after that. He never come around here at all."

"Why did everybody hate Milam?" from Ed.

"He cheated people. Would say he was gonna pay one thing, then change up on you. He would steal livestock too," number two said.

"Especially pigs," Hayes said.

"Loved him some pigs," number two said. "People down here in the Bottom, they don't tag or brand their cows and pigs and what have you. So if somebody steals them, who can tell one pig from another? And that Junior Junior would come hanging around, looking to break off a piece."

"I get it," Ed said.

Hayes looked at number two and said, "I don't think they know."

"Don't know what?" Ed asked.

"About those two families," Hayes said.

"What are you talking about?" Ed asked.

"Long time ago. It was their daddies who killed Emmett Till back in the fifties," Hayes said.

"You're shitting me," Jim said.

"True," number two said.

Jim and Ed, of course, knew the case. It was famous. It was a part of American history. A White woman in

Mississippi claimed that a fourteen-year-old Black boy had said something suggestive to her, and then her husband and brother beat the boy, wrapped barbed wire around his neck, shot him in the head, and threw him over the bridge into the Little Tallahatchie. The image of the boy in his open casket awakened the nation to the horror of lynching. At least the White nation. The horror that was lynching was called life by Black America. The killers, Roy Bryant and J. W. Milam, were acquitted by an all-White jury.

"Does that mean that the old woman is—" Jim started.

"The crazy bitch who accused him," Isaac Hayes said.

"Years later she finally told everybody that the boy didn't say nothing to her, didn't even whistle. Can you believe that shit? She didn't say a word then, but all them years later. Too late for that boy."

Jim nodded.

"Wheat Bryant's father, that Roy Bryant, owned a store way back when, but he lost it," number two said. "He was bitter as hell after that. You'd think he was the one got lynched the way he hated us. That was a bad man. But the real bad one was that J. W. Milam. Klan through and through. We know that boy weren't the only one he killed. Know what he said years after the trial?"

"Tell me," Ed said.

"'That nigger boy is dead, I don't know why he can't stay dead.' Can you believe that shit?"

Number two said, "My granddaddy told me that back in the nineteen tens, you could find a hanging Black man at the end of every turned row."

Jim studied the photograph and then looked at his partner. "Man, this just keeps getting better."

27

At the funeral home, a rather new establishment named the Easy Rest, occupying a building that used to be a Dairy Queen, Charlene Bryant waited while Daisy Milam took care of business with Otis Easy, the mortician. Charlene thumbed through the *Popular Mechanics* magazines and tried to eavesdrop. She looked at the science magazine instead of *People*. She hated them intellectual elites in *People*. She strained to hear Daisy's voice. She could hear only the deep rattle of Otis Easy's baritone.

Easy sat behind his massive oak desk and smiled with all the teeth a person is supposed to have and then some. Daisy was seated opposite him in a chair that was noticeably lower than the man's. Though she was nearly five ten she looked like a child sitting there. Her side of the desk was lined with ornate tissue box covers. The oak paneling made the room dark, in stark contrast to the thin, pale man with the deep voice. He looked every bit the part of a funeral director, with his long fingers that seemed to caress the air as she spoke. If he walked into a strange house and no one was yet dead, someone soon would be, Daisy imagined.

"What an awful thing to find your loved one like that," Easy said. "It must have been terrible, horrible, saddening."

"Oh it was, Mr. Easy," Daisy said.

"We're going to do everything we can to make all of this as manageable and as easy as possible," he said. "Oops, I just said my name, didn't I? I didn't do it because I'm vain, I promise."

"Didn't this used to be a Dairy Queen?" Daisy asked. "The building, I mean. Wasn't this the Dairy Queen?"

"Yes, it was. It's worked out quite nicely for us. The kitchen became our embalming room, and of course there was already a giant freezer. Can't have anybody going bad." Easy looked around the room and smiled.

"I came here when it was a Dairy Queen," Daisy said. "All the high school kids came here." She looked out the partially stained window behind Easy. "The soda fountain was right up against that wall behind you."

"Yes, it was. What a wonderful memory you have."

"You ain't from Money, are you?"

"I wish I was," Easy said, but Daisy didn't bite at his joke. "But no, ma'am, I'm from Biloxi. Your little town needed a mortician, and here I am to fill that need, and a few holes. That's an industry joke. And I prefer mortician to funeral director. It sounds more professional and, well, it is more precise. I deal with more than mere funerals; I deal with death, passing on, the transition."

"Uh huh."

"What kind of service are you imagining for the departed?" Easy asked.

"For the who?"

"Your husband."

"Oh."

"Most people think they want something simple, but then I remind them that this is the last thing they're ever going to do for the deceased."

"The deceased?"

"Your husband. The dead man."

"Junior Junior?"

"Yes, Junior Junior. That is an interesting name, isn't it? Repeated like that, I mean. Junior Junior."

"Ain't it?" Daisy said. "I always thought so too. That's why I named my boy Triple J." She adjusted her blue halter top. The back of the wooden chair was pressing the blue fabric knot into her spine. She sat up straight.

"I think our gold package is rather nice. We do offer a platinum package, but even I have to say that it's a bit pricey. Still, some folks just can't do enough for their beloved. The gold package is very reasonable."

"What does it come with?" Daisy asked.

"Let me describe it to you. Your husband, Junior Junior, will be laid out in his coffin. I will personally look after all the embalming and cosmetic work. He will look just how you remember him."

"You know his face was beat to shit, don't you?"

"What?"

"Oh, his face is a mess. Right now that's how I'm rememberin' him, and it ain't pretty. Not that he ever was."

Easy leaned back. "I haven't seen him yet, but I'm certain I can make him look like he used to. You have photographs."

"Sure I do. But, like I said, he wasn't no great shakes to start with.

Nobody ever called him handsome," Daisy said.

"It may take me a little extra time, if what you say is true. But, believe me, I can do it," Easy said.

"Junior Junior used to always say that time is money. So, what is this extra time gonna cost?"

Easy sighed. "It may cost you a little more."

"Just how much is this gold package?"

"Let me finish describing it for you. You and your children will come into the chapel and walk down the center aisle, escorted by my ushers, of course, and then you'll see him, Junior Junior, lying there in his elegant casket, and he will look alive. He will look like he might just sit up."

"That might scare the kids," Daisy said. "I mean, I done told them they daddy's dead. They seen death before—pigs, skunks, dogs—and ain't none of them looked like they was gonna rise up or nothing."

Easy took off his glasses and rubbed his temples. "What I mean to say is they won't be able to see that he's been beaten."

"Well, that sounds all right."

"Anyway, the organist will be playing sweet church music. You can even choose the songs he loved in life."

"Junior Junior just loved 'Sweet Home Alabama.'"

"But this is Mississippi," Easy said, wishing he hadn't.

"Yeah, and Junior Junior hated Alabama, but he loved that song. How come there ain't no 'Sweet Home Mississippi' song?"

Easy went on. "Then everyone else, family and friends, will be seated behind all of y'all. I will get up to the lectern and say a few words, and may I say I am very, very good with words, and then some other people will speak—your pastor, you, relatives, friends, whoever you want to say something."

"You think we could get Archie Manning to say something? Junior Junior loved Archie Manning."

"The football player?"

"Yes."

"Did your husband know Archie Manning?"

"Not a bit."

"Mrs. Milam, it has to be somebody you know."

"I don't know you and you gonna talk," Daisy said.

"I suppose that's true."

"Forget all this describin'. How much is this gonna cost?"

"The gold package is eight thousand."

"Dollars?" Daisy asked.

Easy nodded. "We do offer financing."

"What else you got?"

"We have a silver package," he said.

Daisy shook her head. "Somethin' that ain't metal. Or that kind of metal. What about tin? You got a tin package? Aluminum? Wood?"

"How much are you looking to spend?"

"A thousand dollars."

"One thousand dollars," Easy repeated. He looked at her. "Okay, we'll make it happen. Now, the casket."

"What? You mean the box ain't included?"

"No, ma'am."

"How much is your cheapest one?"

"May I remind you that the dearly departed is going to be in this box for eternity," Easy said. "By eternity I do mean forever."

Daisy stared at him.

"We do have a pauper's coffin. We sell them to the county for unidentified and unclaimed corpses."

"How much?"

"Four hundred." Daisy whistled.

"Three hundred dollars."

"I can live with that."

"I guess Junior Junior will have to as well," Easy said.

"Damn straight," Daisy said.

"I have someone waiting, Mrs. Milam. I am very pleased that the Easy Rest is going to see you through this." He stood up.

"Yeah, right," Daisy said.

"Sylvia out there will help you with the paperwork."

Outside Easy's office, Daisy looked at Charlene in her yellow halter.

"What was it like?" Charlene asked.

"Creepy," Daisy said. "Good luck."

28

Red Jetty took a bite of toast and put it back on his plate. He sat at the table with his wife, Agnes. His dog, an American foxhound, stood beside him, his long snout resting on Jetty's leg.

"You okay, Red?" Agnes asked.

"I'm okay."

"The only time Wallace puts his face in your lap like that is when you're upset," she said.

"It's these murders," he said.

"Gruesome," Agnes said. The back door was open, and a cool breeze blew in. She pulled her housecoat closed.

"Want me to close the door?" Jetty asked.

She shook her head.

"I like it."

"Two men in two days," the sheriff said.

"I hate to hear about anybody gettin' killed," Agnes said, "but nobody liked them boys very much. Still, I don't know who would up and kill both of them."

"It's so strange," Jetty said.

"What is?"

"Their names. Them families is all tied up together."

"Maybe it was one of them domestic squabbles," Agnes

said. She looked up at the sound of a car pulling in to the yard. "Who could that be?" she asked.

"I have a feeling that's my undercover man."

Delroy appeared on the other side of the screen. "Morning, Aunt Agnes."

"Come on in, Delroy," she said. "Want some coffee?"

"Yes, ma'am."

"There's some bacon on the table. If you want eggs, you're gonna have to make them yourself."

"Coffee is enough, Aunt Agnes, thank you."

"You sure are polite," Agnes said. "Your mama done a good job. Then she oughta have. She's my sister."

"And the air force."

"What is it, Delroy?" the sheriff finally spoke.

"I followed them boys to the juke joint in the Bottom. I sat outside for an hour and I fell asleep. When I woke up the place was closed, and this note was on my windshield." He handed a piece of paper to Jetty.

Jetty read it aloud. "'We'll be at the motel if you need us.'"

"Sorry, Sheriff."

"Who are you two talkin' about?" Agnes asked.

"State sent up a couple of real hotshot special detectives to help us bumpkins out," Jetty said.

"Colored detectives," Delroy added.

Agnes gasped. "Red, you must feel just plumb awful."

"I do."

"I got to thinkin'," Delroy said.

Jetty looked at him.

"What if there was two different Black men? Not the detectives, but the one we keep finding dead. What if there

97

was two of them? Twins. They was so beat up, who could really recognize them?"

"Two different disappearin', dead, Black men," the sheriff said. "How is that any better, Delroy? How does that help? Hell, that's worse. That's two dead men we can't keep track of. But you keep on thinkin'."

"Should I keep followin' them boys?" Delroy asked.

"No. Go on back to the office. Tell Brady and Jethro that I want the three of you to increase patrols through the Bottom. Maybe one of you will see our missin' Negro crossin' the road or something."

"Yes, sir."

"What are you going to do, Red?" Agnes asked. "Is there a killer roamin' round Money?"

Delroy looked at Jetty, waited for his answer.

The sheriff sighed. "Keep the doors and windows locked."

"You coming to the station, Sheriff?" Delroy asked.

"I'll be in later. First, I'm gonna go talk to an old lady."

29

Ed stood at the washroom sink staring at his lathered face. He didn't like the razor he'd bought at the little store just outside town, but he used it anyway. Jim sat at the tiny desk beside the small television and studied the screen of his laptop.

"There might be another body in this town if I slip with this razor," Ed said. "How can something be sharp and dull at the same time?"

"The Wi-Fi in this place sucks."

"What do you expect from a Motel 8?"

"I don't know. Two better than a Motel 6?"

"Nice."

"You need to see this," Jim said.

"Ouch." Ed cut himself again.

"Ed, you need to see this."

Ed came from the washroom, wiping his face and looking at the blood on the towel. "What am I supposed to see?"

Jim leaned away from the screen. There was a photograph of a face that just barely appeared human attached to a body in a coffin.

"That's Emmett Till," Jim said. He then held up the photograph of the missing or disappearing Black man.

"Fuck me," Ed said.

30

Charlene was out. The children were somewhere, but not at home. And so Granny C was in the house all by herself. She managed to come out of her comatose state while the family was away at the swap meet. As she came back to consciousness, she found grief for the passing of her son. Wheat had been no prize by any stretch, but he was her only child. *No parent should have to bury her child*, she thought, and then she thought back to long ago. There was another mother in Chicago who had buried her child, and Carolyn Bryant knew all too well that she herself was to blame for that loss. She felt the emptiness of her house change, perhaps starting with an odor, a sickly sweet smell. She pulled herself up and leaned against her cheap walker. Outside the sunny day had become overcast. She felt something blow through the house, not a normal wind. Something small, a fork, a spoon, maybe a knife fell on the floor in the kitchen.

"Who's there?" she called out. There was no answer. She inched her walker forward toward her bedroom door. The door was not closed. It was never closed all the way. It wouldn't close all the way. The wood had swollen and was so tight against the jamb at its hinges that there were three final inches the door could never cover. She thought she saw something move past those three inches. A shadow?

"Who's there?"

She pulled the door open. The hinges complained.

Wheat was always saying he was going to spray some WD-40 on the hinges, but he never did. Where was Charlene with the children? Lulabelle and Tammy were in school, but the younger ones should have been left there with her. But she had been all comalike in bed. Another sound. From the kitchen again. Carolyn Bryant moved as quickly as her eighty-five-year-old legs and walker would take her across the front room to Wheat and Charlene's bedroom. She got inside and closed the door, locked it with the eye hook that had been placed high enough for the kids not to reach. She could barely reach it herself. She paused to catch her breath. She reached behind the armoire and grabbed Wheat's double-barreled twelve-gauge, pulled a couple of shells from the top drawer of the bureau, and loaded it. The clack of the barrels engaging made her feel better.

Now there were footsteps out there. They moved from the kitchen and down the hall toward her. She rested the cold barrel of the shotgun on the cushioned crossbar of her walker and leaned her back against the windowsill. "I don't know who you is, but if you come through that there door, there's gonna be two of you. You gonna be sorry as hell!" she shouted. Her gown was soaked with sweat and maybe urine. She took a long, deep breath and prayed, "Lawd, Lawd, please forgive me for what I done. I tried to be good all my life since I lied on that Black boy. I knowed I was gonna have to pay for it someday, but why my Wheat, my sad, dumb baby? I been havin' them dreams again, so I just knowed he was comin'." There was a loud crash in the front room. She pulled back one hammer and then the other. "Is that you, Charlene? I don't want to shoot you, whoever you are, if you don't need shootin'. But if you do, I will, I swear on the blond head of the little baby Jesus!"

The front screen door opened and slammed. She knew the sound well. Was it someone leaving or arriving?

"Charlene?" Her liver-spotted finger trembled against the trigger. She had never seen or heard this weapon fired, but she believed it would work. It stank of gun oil because Wheat used too much and cleaned it every night while he watched *Wheel of Fortune*. He loved shouting, "Buy a vowel, you stupid bitch!"

The footsteps approached the door of the room. She pressed her finger more firmly against the trigger. The doorknob wobbled and started to turn. "Who's there?" The door strained against the latch.

"Say somethin'!" she shouted. "I know who you is! I know who you is!"

"Mrs. Bryant! It's me, Sheriff Jetty!"

"Thank Jesus," Granny C said. "Thank you, Jesus."

Red Jetty sat at the kitchen table while Granny C stood at the electric stove heating water for Sanka. "You know what they say: a watched pot never boils." She looked away from the pot and out the sliding glass back door at the empty pool. Half a mermaid's face stared back at her.

"I'm glad you didn't shoot me," Jetty said.

"I'm glad too," she said. "More mess to clean up. Enough people dead 'round here anyway."

"Where's everybody?"

"How the hell should I know? I was pretty out of it. I'm surprised they left me like that though. What you make of that?" She poured water into the mugs over the powdered coffee, handed one to the sheriff.

Jetty looked at the face of Dolly Parton on his mug and stirred the coffee. "She probably had some funeral business to take care of," he said. "Couldn't leave the young ones here unsupervised."

"I suppose that's true. But to leave an old woman in a big old house all by her lonesome."

"Why was you holdin' that shotgun, ma'am?"

"Because I was scared, of course. My son just got murdered in this very house." She eased herself from her walker into a chair.

Jetty couldn't argue with that. "You yelled out that you knew who I was before you saw me. Who did you think I was?"

Granny C said nothing.

"Mrs. Bryant? Just who did you think I was that you would want to shoot?"

The old woman sipped her coffee. "That Till boy," she said.

"Ma'am?"

"I killed that boy, and now he done come back for all of us."

"Mrs. Bryant, that was sixty years ago, more than sixty."

"That don't matter none," she said. "The dead cain't tell no time, cain't read no calendars. They ain't got calendar watches, is what I'm sayin'. He who digs a pit will fall into it, and he who rolls a stone, it will come back on him."

"What?"

"That's from the good book, and that book is always right, ain't it?"

"Yes, ma'am."

"I know my Bible."

"Are you tellin' me that you believe that some relative of that boy is killin' folks?" Jetty asked.

"Relative? That's the boy hisself."

"Mrs. Bryant, that boy is dead and buried."

"All I know is what I seen. I looked at that picture of that dead boy a million times, and then I saw him carried out of my house big as day, plain as the nose on my face. How do you figure that?"

"You know, when we get older our memories do funny things."

"You think I'm a foolish old woman."

"No, ma'am, I don't think that at all. I think your son is dead and you're scared. That's all I think."

"Y'all watch. There's gonna be more dyin'," Granny C said. "Just watch and watch out, too."

"Yes, ma'am."

"Drink your coffee before it gets cold."

"Yes, ma'am."

"You know that old story about the vulture? Man walks into town and sees a vulture land on a statue not five feet from him. The vulture looks right at him. He eats him some lunch and comes out and the bird is gone. He leaves town and his car breaks down on the road. He looks up and there's that turkey buzzard, starin' right at him. He say, 'How come you followed me to town and now here you is?'

"The vulture looks him up and down and says, 'I didn't follow you. I just happened to be in town. I was on my way to this spot to wait for you.'" Granny C nodded to punctuate the story.

"That's some story," the sheriff said.

"I'm that man, don't you see?"

Jetty nodded.

"That buzzard been waitin' on me."

"Yes, ma'am."

They sat through a couple of minutes of silence.

"I hate to leave you alone here, Mrs. Bryant, but I gotta get back to work."

"Don't leave me. He's here, I just know it."

"I'll look around before I leave. Then I'm gonna go on. And don't shoot nobody, you hear me?"

"I won't shoot nobody who don't need shootin'."

31

At the Dinah, Gertrude poured coffee for the two special detectives. They sat in the same booth as before. The men thanked her and she studied them for a long moment.

"Everything okay?" she asked.

"Dandy," Jim said.

"I'll be back for your order in a couple minutes." She went to the register to ring up a customer.

"Maybe Jethro is right," Ed said.

Jim laughed. "Yeah, right. You call the office and tell Captain Fat Face there's a ghost up here. A Negro ghost."

"Somebody *is* running 'round here killin' folks. There is definitely a connection. You can't deny that."

"Maybe it's some kind of Black ninja," Jim said and laughed. "You know, some kind of vigilante motherfucker with a spool of barbed wire. Like Bruce Lee or some shit. Jamal Lee swinging lengths of barbed wire in Money, Mississippi."

"That would be *bob wire*. That how they say it around here. Bob wire. Bob wire will keep the cattle in."

"Are you finished?" Jim asked.

Gertrude returned and they stopped talking.

"Oh, it's like that, is it?" she said.

Jim looked at her, said nothing, and sipped his coffee.

Gertrude sat next to Ed and looked across at Jim. "All right, so tell me: What the hell is going on?"

"Nothing," Jim said. "Except for a couple of murders. Gruesome, unsolved, messy, disturbing murders."

"And a disappearing body," Ed said.

"Aside from that, nothing is going on. Anyway, it's an active case and we can't talk about it." Jim put down his mug and watched a dually pickup bounce by. "Gertrude, who knows everything that goes on in this town?"

"Everybody knows everything that goes on in this town."

"No, I mean somebody special. Somebody who knows the history, the gossip, everything."

"I don't know what you mean?"

"Neither do I," Jim said. "I don't know what I'm asking."

"Is there a witch in town?" Ed asked. "He's just afraid to say it. A witch. A root doctor."

Gertrude laughed. "I knew that's what he meant. I just wanted to hear him say it. You're looking for Mama Z."

Ed looked at Jim. "Really a root doctor?" he asked.

"That's what I've heard. That's what she says."

"What can it hurt to talk to her?" Jim said.

"I have to go with you," she said.

"It's better if you just stay out of this."

"You're not going to find her without me."

32

In the basement of the defunct Bryant General Store, the Reverend Doctor Fondle stood before ten White men. They all shared the same flinty look. They were, almost to a man, fat. A tall, extremely skinny man sat by the door.

"Okay, let's say the oath," Fondle said. "Together now."

Standing, all: "I have done passed the Yellow Dog and stand here a member of the Grand Invisible Empire. I vow to protect the Godgiven rights of the White race from all aliens, be they Black, yellow, red, or Jew. I pledge to follow to the letter the orders of my superior, the Grand Dragon of the Majestic Order of Knights of the Ku Klux Klan, as passed down through the duly elected Grand Kleagle of my chapter. Rocka rocka shu ba day! We is the Klan of the USA!"

They sat at Fondle's gesture.

"I pronounce this meeting commenced," said the skinny sergeant of arms.

"We got ourselves a situation, White brothers," Fondle said. "I'm afraid what we're lookin' at is a real nigger uprising. Two of our own brothers lay dead, and a killin' nigger is on the gawddamn loose. I seen him, seen him close up, scarred up by Satan hisself. A nigger that's as good at fakin' death as anybody you will ever find. I seen him dead, and then he weren't."

"What do we do?" a man in front asked.

Fondle looked at all of them in turn. "We go back to the old, tried-and-true ways of our KKK forebears, the sacred ways, the ways of fury, fire, and the rope. First we gonna burn us a great big cross tonight, right out there in Smithson's Field, right where all them Black faces in the Bottom can see real good."

"What about them nigger police?" the thin man in back called out. "What the hell are they doin' here?"

"The state of Mississippi thinks we're just a bunch of rednecks can't take care of ourselves or our business," Fondle said.

"Well, we *is* just a bunch of rednecks," one of the men said, and the others chuckled. "Peckerwood Power." He raised his fist.

"Shut up now, Donald," Fondle said. "I'm thinkin' on what to do about them detectives."

Donald said, "You know, we ain't had no elections in this chapter in a long time. How come you still the Grand Kleagle? How come you decided you can just camp out in office like that? Other clubs have elections and other people run. Why we ain't had no elections? Why is that?"

"That's simple. It's because we ain't had us an election since I was elected," Fondle said.

"That was twelve years ago," the thin man said. "Ain't supposed to be no life term, is it?"

"No, it ain't," from another man.

"We ain't had no election because we ain't had no goddamn meetins," from still another.

"That's true, Jared," Donald said.

"Used to be back when my daddy was alive, we had

meetins all the time, every week," Jared said.

"Elections too," another man said. "They was always votin' back in them days. Right?"

"And they used to have cross burnins a lot more and family picnics and softball games and all such," said Donald. "I remember eatin' cake next to that glowing cross. I loved my mama's cake."

"Yeah," several voiced their agreement.

"We don't do nothin' now," a man complained. "I don't even know where my hood is. I don't even own a rope."

"Are you saying you want to have an election now?" Fondle asked.

"Yeah, yeah, election, election," they all chanted.

"No speeches, though," Donald said. "No speeches, no speeches."

"I move we have an election for Grand Kleagle of the Money, Mississippi, chapter," Donald said.

The thin man seconded the motion.

"In favor?" Fondle asked.

"Aye," from all of them.

"Opposed?"

Nothing.

"The ayes have it," Fondle said.

"Wait, who's taking minutes?" Donald asked.

"Oh hell, Donald, you take them," Fondle said.

"Nobody can read his goddamn scrawl," another said.

"Just do it, Donald," Jared said.

Donald pulled a pen from his pocket. Fondle gave him the little notebook he used for work.

"I nominate the Reverend Doctor Fondle for Grand Kleagle of the Money, Mississippi, chapter of the Supreme

Order of the Knights of the Majestic Ku Klux Klan of these United States of America," Jared said.

"Second," from the thin man.

The others looked back at him.

"I like to second things," the thin man said.

"All in favor?" Fondle asked.

"Aye," from them all. "Opposed?"

Nothing.

33

Jim and Ed picked up Gertrude at the Dinah after the lunch rush, such as it was. She sat in the middle of the rear seat and leaned forward.

"Sit back and fasten your belt," Ed said.

"So you're the one with kids," she said.

"Kid," Ed said. "She's seven."

"Turn left at the flashing light," Gertrude said. "Stay on this until it becomes a dirt road. Wake me up then." She leaned back and closed her eyes.

"Is her belt fastened?" Ed asked Jim.

"Yes, it's fastened," Gertrude said.

"I talked to the captain," Jim said.

"What did you tell him?" Ed said.

"Only what he already knew. I know what pilots who see UFOs feel like now. If you tell everybody, they're going to think you're crazy. If you don't say anything, well, you're not saying anything. Then the aliens invade, assume human form, start working in grocery stores, kill everybody you know, and take their places. You could be one."

"You'll have to excuse him," Ed said.

When there was no response, Jim looked in the back. "She's asleep."

"I wish my kid would go out like that."

"She'd be faking," Gertrude said. "I just like to close my eyes."

"Who doesn't?" Ed said.

"Will one of you tell me what you saw?" she asked.

"The fact is we didn't see much of anything. But if you believe the people around here, then there's a crazily battered and likely dead Black man running on the loose, maybe killing White boys with shady histories."

"Oh."

"See what happens when you ask questions?" Jim said.

"Anything we need to know about this Mama Z?" Ed asked.

"She calls herself a witch. What else do you need to know? She's kinda odd, kinda scary."

"How do you know her?" Jim asked.

"She's my great-grandmother."

The small house was set back in a tangle of tree branches, away from the wide expanse of yard, as if intentionally and effectively camouflaged. Gertrude trotted ahead and knocked on the screen door.

"You knock like a cop," Jim said.

"So I've been told."

She knocked again. "Mama Z!"

"Stop knocking and come in!" the woman shouted.

The front room was filled with books, floor to ceiling, wall to wall, but neatly, cleanly. A thick-legged wooden table sat centered on a jute rug in the middle of the floor. Mama Z was a broad-shouldered but not heavy woman, tall. She greeted them with a thousand-yard stare, looking at none of them as she reached out to shake their hands. Jim and Ed took her hand in turn, both coming to believe she was blind until the old woman let out a laugh.

"I'm just fucking with you," she said. "I can see better than both of y'all put together."

"Mama, these men are detectives from—" Gertrude started.

Mama Z interrupted her. "From Hattiesburg. Morgan and Davis. How come your office ain't in the capitol? I find that odd."

Jim and Ed were thrown a bit.

"Oh, Mama Z knows everything," the old woman said. "I know you're sleeping in the Motel 8, and I know you're driving a family van, a Toyota something or other."

Jim shook his head. "You know a lot, Mama Z."

"And I know how to use a police scanner," she said. "I listen to them crackers all day and all night. I know what's going on because I listen. It pays to listen. Them idiot deputies don't burp or fart unless they talk about it over the radio. They like talking on the radio. Sit down."

They sat at the table with Mama Z.

"Make some tea for our guests, girl," she said to Gertrude and slapped her rump as she walked by. "I got to feed her and put some meat on those yellow bones. She's my great-granddaughter so I can boss her around like that. Lord knows nobody else can. She's a damn pistol."

"So, you know why we're here," Ed said.

"You're looking for whoever killed those White boys."

"Pretty much, ma'am," Ed said. "We're trying to figure out what's going on with a certain seemingly dead Black man who keeps showing up and disappearing. Do you know who he is?"

"I have no idea," Mama Z said. "But I know what's troubling you, and I didn't hear that on the scanner."

"What's that?" Jim asked.

114

"The connection between Wheat Bryant and that Milam."

"That's right," Ed said.

"You've already figured out about their daddies," she said. "Roy Bryant and Robert Milam were the worst of the worst. They were Klan all the way through to the bone, and so was them stupid boys of theirs."

"Do you know anything about this Black man who keeps showing up and disappearing?" Jim asked.

Gertrude came from the kitchen with a tray of cups and a teapot to hear her grandmother say, "I don't believe in ghosts."

"I didn't know that," Gertrude said.

"Very funny," Mama Z said.

"I thought you were a witch," Jim said.

"Yeah, but not that kind." She poured tea for herself and sipped it. "I saw on CNN that a White man was killed in Chicago."

"We know about that," Ed said.

"They say the man was killed last week," Mama Z said.

"Okay," Jim said, leaning forward.

"They got his name wrong on the television, said it was Milan, but I'm suspecting it was Milam. That would be Junior's brother. I know because Robert had a son named Lester, Lester William. They called him L. W."

"Shit," Jim said.

"You got that right," the old woman said. "Somebody is exacting revenge."

"I wonder, why now?" Gertrude asked.

"That poor boy was lynched sixty-five years ago. Maybe the spirits have had enough," Mama Z said.

"You just said you don't believe in ghosts," Ed said.

"I have never claimed to always be right." The old woman put down her cup and tapped her fingers on the table. "I'll tell you what, though: if the spirits are out for revenge, there's going to be a lot more killing around here. Those spirits are going to have a field day around here. Every White person in this county, if they didn't lynch somebody themselves, then somebody in their family tree did. If you believe anything, you can believe that."

"How do you know that?" Jim asked. "The police scanner?"

"Come with me," the old woman said and stood, pressing against the table to find her full height.

They followed Mama Z down a short hallway lined with family photos and into another room. The room was filled with chesthigh file cabinets all the way around, shorter ones under the single window.

"What's this?" Ed asked.

"The records," Mama Z said. "These are the records. Tell them, child," she said to Gertrude.

"This is almost everything ever written about every lynching in these United States of America since 1913, the year Mama Z was born."

"Wait," Jim said. "That would make you—"

"One hundred and five," she said.

"Every lynching?" Ed asked.

"Damn near," Mama Z said. "I used to go to the libraries all over the state and read every paper. Now, I use the internet. You should know I consider police shootings to be lynchings. No offense."

"None taken," Jim said.

"Why do you do this?" Ed asked.

"Because somebody has to. When I die and this place is made known, I hope it will become a monument to the dead."

Gertrude's eyes welled up.

Jim Davis and Ed Morgan, who had seen nearly everything, been shot at, shot, seen death and pain, had killed in the line of duty, fell silent. They stood there and looked at the gray fronts of the cabinets. Jim counted in his head. There were twenty-three of them. The drawers were like those in a morgue.

Ed put his hand on the cabinet near him. "Are there any more relatives of Bryant and Milam?" he asked.

"I think I heard of another Milam boy, but I don't know for sure, and I certainly wouldn't know where he is," Mama Z said. "Of course, there is Carolyn Bryant. Though she doesn't look it, she's still alive."

"Yeah, we met her," Jim said. "That didn't go well. She was a little, shall we say, distraught. Of course, her son had just been murdered in her house. That makes even a racist distraught."

"Have you seen or heard about any strangers around town?" Ed asked. "Black or White."

Mama Z shook her head. "Wrong question," she said. "Death is never a stranger. That's why we fear it."

"Is that supposed to be some kind of witchy thing to say?" Jim said. "I ask because it sounds important, but I don't get it."

"I like this one," the old woman said to Gertrude. "You might talk to Deacon Wright. He was a boy then, and he was with Emmett Till in that store. I doubt he knows anything. And then there's Betty Smith."

"Who's she?" Jim asked.

"Her older brother, Lamar, was shot dead in front of the Brookhaven courthouse just before Emmett arrived here in Money. There was a lot of hate in this state back then. Maybe more than there is now. Lamar was a farmer, and he was already working for civil rights around here. Nobody ever talks about him. Shot dead. My daddy took me down there, and I saw where his blood had soaked into the ground. New sidewalk there now."

"Why do you think we need to talk to her?" Ed asked.

"If you want to know a place, you talk to its history," Mama Z said.

34

Red Jetty pulled over and turned off the engine of his squad car. He was on the Tallahatchie Bridge. From there he could see the burning cross. He remembered the cross burnings from his youth. His father had taken him to a few Klan rallies, but his Catholic mother had protested. He had never seen an actual lynching, and he was glad of that, but his father had either seen or participated. That thought made him sad, but also made him understand, as much as he could, why there was such tension and friction between him and the man. His mother finally ran away to Detroit with a man he never got to meet. He knew only that he sold meat saws. The flames sent black smoke into the dusk sky. Even from that distance the cross looked sad, not for political or social reasons, but because it was so obviously poorly constructed. The crossbeam was already collapsing, and the flames lost all enthusiasm, lapped at the air around as if exhausted. All the kerosene in the county wasn't going to keep that fire burning. Sadder than any of it was the fact that not a single masked member of the terrorist exercise was unknown to anyone in the town. It was a long-running joke in Money, Mississippi, that the way to discover who belonged to the Klan was to wait at Russell's Dry Cleaning and Laundry.

35

The children were finally tucked into their beds in the Bryant house. They had taken turns crying themselves to sleep, but not one of them understood what had happened. How could they? Charlene's CB radio sat on the sill above the kitchen sink. She sat on a high stool in front of it, the receiver near her mouth when she was speaking and nestled in her lap when she wasn't.

"This is Big Ten-Forty, I'm on that Five Eighteen headed north toward Money. Hot Mama Yeller, you out there so I can holler at you, baby girl? Come back," crackled through the speaker.

Charlene fumbled with the receiver, pressed the button, and said, "Here I am, Big Ten-Forty. Come back."

"How you doin', baby doll? I was sure sorry to hear about yer man. Just awful. Come back."

"Yeah, it's been just terrible. There was a lot of blood, but I got most of it cleaned up. You still driving that anteater? Come back."

"I'm a Kenworth man to the b-b-bone. I sure wish I had time to stop and pay my respects, Hot Mama Yeller, but I'm hauling a load of farm-fresh eggs and milk and the Frigidaire is dicey. Come back."

"Next time, next time. Where you been? Come back."

"Lord, I had me a good time down in Yazoo City. I went to one of them Trump rallies and scared me some fake news folks. Whooeee! That was fun. You know that man is just like us." Big Ten-Forty laughed. "I mean he ain't got no more smarts than a porkypine, but he knows how to put them liberal e-lites in their place. Come back."

"Damn. Is he as orange as he looks on TV? Come back."

"Oh, he's orange all right. Natural orange. I couldn't believe it. That Melangia was there too. She looks just like one of them Barbie dolls, got eyes just like one of them Barbies. Come on back."

"Hey, Big Ten-Forty, I got to sign off now and clean out my back porch freezer. Come back."

"Awright there, Hot Mama Yeller, I hope to catch you on the flip side. Y'all be good. Over and out."

"Cleaning the freezer" was their code for switching over to their private channel. They did.

Charlene whispered into the receiver, "This is Hot Mama Yeller lookin' for that Big-Ten Forty. Come back?"

"Hey there, baby doll. Whatcha wearin'?"

Granny C was lying in her bed. She had gone to sleep with her overhead light on and also the lamps on either side of her bed. She hadn't wanted to fall asleep, but she had, on her back, propped up slightly, a really vulnerable position, she thought. She snorted a little and found herself awake, more startled by the fact that she had been asleep. Across the room, sunk down into the chair she never used because it was too soft, she believed she saw the beaten Black man, the one who had been pronounced dead and carried from her house, the man who must have killed her son. The old woman looked at the face, believed she saw beyond the scars, past the dried blood, past the years, into the brown eyes closed by swollen flesh, back into the little store on that late August day. She didn't say anything, she didn't think anything, she simply died.

36

Ed Morgan's cell phone vibrated across the desk on the other side of the room. Ed was in the washroom shaving with a different brand of razor. Jim picked up and looked at the phone. He recognized the Money Sheriff's Department number.

"Davis here," he said. He listened.

Ed stepped into the room as his partner put down the phone. "What's up?" he asked.

"Gotta roll," Jim said. "It appears the yokels have found our dead man."

Ed wiped his face with a towel. "Oh yeah?"

"The Bryant house."

The Bryant house was teeming with people, deputies, Fondle and Dill, the Bryant children, the Milam children, Daisy Milam, and, of course, Charlene. The children sat like a choir on the ground next to the derelict Pontiac GTO beside the house. Charlene paced up and down the porch steps. Sheriff Jetty stood in the center of things and watched the road as if waiting for the special detectives.

His face did not change expression as the two men approached him. His mouth was a flat line, as were his eyes.

"What you got, Sheriff?" Ed asked.

"You tell me," Jetty said. "Come on." He led them up the steps past the pacing Charlene. She didn't register them at all. Jethro stood in an interior doorway. He was staring at something in the room. He didn't turn his head as they approached.

"You can go outside now, Jethro," Jetty said.

"Okay, Sheriff."

"I told him to watch without lookin' away. We're gonna keep eyes on him at all times," Jetty said.

Ed and Jim stopped cold. In an upholstered chair sat the battered Black figure from the photographs. Photographs from the recent crime scenes and a funeral sixty-plus years past. Ed and Jim stepped closer.

"He's dead," Jetty said. "Of course, he was dead the last two times I seen him also. How long you reckon he'll stay dead this time?"

Jim reached over and placed his index and middle fingers against the man's neck anyway. His skin was ice cold. There was no life there.

Jetty gave Jim a look as if to say, *See?*

Ed looked across the room and then pulled Jim's sleeve. There was Carolyn Bryant. Jim looked at Jetty.

"You might as well feel her neck too," the sheriff said.

"What did the coroner say?" Ed asked.

"He said she's dead. He don't know why. We expect her to stay dead. It seems White people know enough to die and stay dead."

"I'll call the office," Ed said and left the room.

"So, what do you want to do?" Jetty asked. "I can't keep a man starin' at this boy all day."

"What else does he have to do?" Jim said.

Ed came back into the room. "We're going to take custody

of the male deceased," he said.

"The male deceased?" Jetty repeated. "You mean this here Negro boy?"

"Yes," Ed said. "Give us a bag. We'll seal it as evidence and it will be picked up later today or tomorrow."

"Maybe."

"I'm not worried," Jim said. "That's a dead human being. He can't run. He can't walk. He's not going anywhere unless somebody takes him."

"Okay," Jetty said.

Ed looked at the Black man's face again. "I need to print him and take some samples for DNA. I'll go out and get the kit."

Jim looked over at the dead woman. "What do you think, Sheriff ?"

Jetty looked, but said nothing.

"She caused a lot of pain," Jim said.

"What are you talking about?"

"You know what I'm talking about," Jim said.

Red Jetty looked out the window, sighed slightly. "Did you see the cross burning last night?" he asked.

"That was a cross?" Jim shook his head. "I didn't know what that was. I thought it was a car fire or something."

Ed returned with his kit.

"Ed," Jim said, "that fire last night was a cross burning."

"No shit?" the big man said. "You mean like a KKK cross burning?"

Jim looked to Jetty for an answer. The sheriff nodded.

"I wish I had known," Jim said. "I forgot to be scared."

"Yeah, that's too bad," Jetty said.

Jim smiled. "Maybe next time."

37

Damon Nathan Thruff was an assistant professor at the University of Chicago. He held a PhD in molecular biology from Harvard, a PhD in psychobiology from Yale, and a PhD in Eastern philosophy from Columbia. He was twenty-seven years old. He had published three books on cellular regeneration, all issued by Cambridge University Press, and a two-volume work on the biological and philosophical origins of racial violence in the United States published by Harvard University Press. On this particular day, he was sitting at the desk in his tiny university office in the Department of Ethnic Studies (because they *didn't know where to put him*), trying to compile a list of names of people who might write letters in support of his tenure bid. He had been denied tenure the year before but was being given a *second chance*, what the university administration was calling an affirmative reconsideration. The reason given for this denial of tenure was his productivity. The dean told him, flatly, that no one really believed that he was capable of so much work of such quality so quickly. And so he was stuck with a one-year appointment called the Phillis Wheatley Chair in Remedial Studies. Part of his second (gift) bid for tenure required that he not publish anything for a year. Such restraint from active scholarship might show the proper commitment to his proper place, was what the dean told him. His phone rang.

The phone rang seven times before he finally picked it up. It was his old college friend, Gertrude Penstock. She had been an undergraduate at Cornell while he completed his law degree. "Gertrude, I'm really glad to hear your voice," he said. "I'm glad to hear any friendly voice."

"Sorry I haven't called in a while," Gertrude said. "How are you?"

"Fine. Jumping through hoop."

"You mean *hoops*?"

"No, just one hoop. What's up with you? How's your family down there in . . . where are you?"

"Money, Mississippi."

"No shit?"

"You need to get your ass down here," Gertrude said.

"Is that so? Is there a beach?"

"No beach. Just rednecks and the body of a dead Black man."

Damon sat up straight. "What are you talking about?"

"Somebody is killing White people down here, and the same Black man has been found dead at each scene."

"Have you been drinking? I'll come down and be your drinking buddy, but just say that's what you want."

"I'm not joking. Two White men and one old White woman. Dead," Gertrude said. "Really gruesome dead. Well, the men, anyway. Not only really dead, but truly and sincerely dead. The woman, I think she was frightened to death."

"Frightened to death sounds intriguing," Damon said.

"I thought you would think so."

"And what's this about a Black man? Is he being accused of the killings?"

"The Black man is dead, Damon. He was found dead with each of the bodies. In different places, at different times."

"Pardon?"

"It's complicated."

"Okay."

"I've made friends with a couple of brothers from the MBI, and I'm telling you this stuff is crazy, scary crazy."

"The MBI?" Damon asked.

"The Mississippi Bureau of Investigation," Gertrude said.

"I'll be hanging up now."

"There really is such a thing," she said. "The dead woman was the woman who accused Emmett Till of making a pass at her. The White men were sons of Till's killers. I want you to come down here. Something is going on. I can't say what, but it's something, and it's weird."

Damon looked at the desk he hated so much. "How does one get to Money, Mississippi?"

38

She could have been angry that her parents, Barry and Bertha Hind, had named her Herberta. It shouldn't have taken much imagination to imagine the possible nicknames that would crop up. The name confused everyone because there was no one named Herbert on either side of the family, and certainly there were no other Herbertas. Regardless, Berta would have been a fine nickname. Or Bertie. But her parents found and settled on Herbie, they said because they loved the jazz musician Herbie Hancock, though Herberta Hind believed it was a cruel attempt to make her a tougher person. It worked. She became a special agent with the FBI, much to the surprise and dismay of her parents, who had, in their Berkeley youth, been marked as individuals of interest by the Federal Bureau of Investigation. Herbie sat now in the wellappointed office of Supervisory Special Agent Ajax Kinney in the Southeast Regional Offices in Atlanta.

"I need you to go to Money, Mississippi," Kinney said.

Special Agent Hind laughed.

"No, I'm serious," Kinney said.

"There's no such place," Hind said.

"There is, Herbie, and you're going there. There have been four, possibly more, homicides that might be hate related."

"Hatred is often a factor in homicide," Hind said.

"Not that kind of hatred," Kinney said. "Racial hatred. You know, when one group really doesn't like another group. Sometimes they dislike them to death. You're going to Mississippi to check it out. It's a messy one. Seems there's a disappearing dead Black corpse. Actually, disappearing and reappearing."

"Come again?"

"I'm not sure what the story is. Whatever it is, I know you're expert in it. That's your job. Go do it. Be your usual charming self, set the local clowns straight, then come back here and do the requisite paperwork that proves we were there." Kinney pushed the case file across the desk to Hind.

"Money, Mississippi," she said.

"Money, Mississippi," Kinney repeated.

"I hate you, Ajax," she said. "I think I've always hated you. Sometimes at night I wake up just to remind myself how much I hate you."

"I know you do. Now, go home, pack a bag, get your ass to Money, Mississippi, and get to work."

"How does one get to Money?" Hind asked.

"First you go to Hattiesburg," Kinney said. "That should be fairly easy. It's written big on the map."

"What's there?" she asked.

"The MBI. The Mississippi Bureau of Investigation."

"And she was never heard from again."

Kinney watched Agent Hind walk to the door. "And don't scare the hillbillies too bad. They're not used to a Black woman with a Glock."

"I'll do my best. When I come back here I want *you* to remember that I carry a weapon."

"I never forget," Kinney said. "Sometimes I wake up in the middle of the night just to remind myself that you carry a gun."

"And it's a Sig, not a Glock."

Hind cracked the dossier and stopped cold, turned back to Kinney. "Did you see this picture? The one of the Black man?"

Kinney nodded.

"This is horrible."

"Yes, it is."

"Does he look familiar to you?" she asked.

"Yes, he does."

39

Jim Davis and Ed Morgan parked in a diagonal space in front of the coroner's office. The Reverend Doctor Fondle was standing in front of the building conversing with Sheriff Jetty. Deputy Brady smoked a cigarette just yards away. He gave the two Black men as hard a look as he could manage as they approached. The look was such a cliché that Ed and Jim looked at each other and laughed. Brady spat out his cigarette, stomped on it, and stormed off toward his patrol car.

"Good morning, Sheriff," Jim said. "Is our suspect still in custody?"

"As far as I know," Jetty said. He looked to Fondle. "Is that Black fella still in his drawer?"

"As far as I know. I ain't looked," Fondle said.

"Well, let's go have a little look-see," Jim said.

The three men followed Fondle through the lobby, past Dill at his desk, and into the examination room.

"He's in three," Fondle said.

Ed stepped to the drawer and put his hand on the handle, paused. He looked at Jim. "Do I open it?"

Jim looked at Jetty's face. "Yeah, open it." Jim stepped close, leaned over to peer into the drawer. "Go ahead."

When Ed pulled the door, he and Jim let out screams.

Fondle ran for the door. Jetty's hand slapped onto his pistol. Ed and Jim laughed.

"Just fucking with you," Jim said. "He's right here. And still dead, you'll be happy to know."

"Do you know more about who he is?" Jetty asked.

"Not yet," Ed said. "The office sent a courier up here to collect the evidence, but he hasn't arrived yet."

Jetty sighed.

"Yep," Jim said. "We're going to be around here for a while. Believe me, it doesn't make us happy either. Nothing personal."

"Okay," Jetty said. "Reverend Doctor, what do you know about the Bryant woman? What are you putting down as the cause of death? Was she, you know?"

Fondle shook his head.

"Whew, I'm so glad she wasn't you-knowed," Jim said.

"I don't know what kilt her," Fondle said. "There wasn't a mark on her. Not a cut or a bruise. She was old."

"That's been known to kill a person," Ed said.

"Thank you very much," Fondle said. "I'm thinkin' the old lady was simply scared to death."

"Blood test shows that?" Jim asked. "Gentlemen, for all we know she died before the walking dead man here showed up and, well, died again. I can't believe I just said that."

40

The Greenwood-Leflore Airport was a shining model of obsolescence. Despite its name, the airport was in Carroll County, a fact that the people of Carroll County both hated, it being a service to Leflore County, and loved, their being able to lord it over their neighbors. This was manifested in a practice that persisted even still. A woman, far too old for high school, though clad like a cheerleader, would greet the planes as they landed, *Hawaiian* style, lei and all, and say, "Welcome to Carroll County, Mississippi, the setting for Porter Wagoner's hit song 'Carroll County Accident,' six hundred and thirty-five square miles of Southern hospitality."

Damon Thruff was both amused and confused by the red-and-white lei and the strangely old cheerleader who had handed it to him instead of hanging it around his neck. He was met at the gate by Gertrude Penstock. They hugged awkwardly, as they always hugged awkwardly. Gertrude often said that hugging Damon was like embracing an Adirondack chair.

"I'm parked right over here," Gertrude said.

"Tell me again why you're living here," Damon said.

"To be near my great-grandmother," she said.

"I thought you were from Baltimore."

"Well yes, but my great-grandmother is from here."

"How is she? Is she really old? I'm fascinated by old people," Damon said.

"She's over a hundred."

"You're kidding me," Damon said. "I really want to talk to her. And she's from here? The things she must have seen."

"She's seen a lot," Gertrude said.

"What about these cops?" Damon asked.

"Oh, they're cool. Smart."

"Why am I here? Tell me again. In fact, tell me for the first time."

"What's happening here is really strange. If anybody can explain to the world what's going on, you can."

"That's very flattering, but why don't you tell me what's going on."

Gertrude filled him in during the drive up to Money. Damon stared out at the passing landscape, the tarpaper shacks, the dirt lanes that branched off the highway, the skinny cows.

"I'm hungry," he said. "I wonder what that cow tastes like?"

"Since when do you eat meat?" Gertrude asked.

"I figured, what's the difference? I was probably only going to prolong my life for a few minutes at best. And also, how many cows would I be saving? In fact, when you think about it, since no one's going to raise domestic cows for fun, and since they're too stupid to exist in the wild, then I'm really helping to save the species from extinction."

"That's warped reasoning," Gertrude said.

"But reasoning nonetheless."

"There's a place up ahead where we can eat," Gertrude said. "It will give you an idea of where you are."

"I think I can see where we are. I've been in the middle of fucking nowhere before and it looked just like this." Damon looked at the rundown, roadside food shack as Gertrude skidded to a stop on the gravel. "Maybe I'm not hungry."

"Shut up," she said.

The sign read Bluegum's. It was a cinderblock structure with no windows in the front. Smoke rose from a chimney. There were three other cars, nondescript like Gertrude's.

"This is a restaurant?"

"Trust me."

41

At MBI headquarters in Hattiesburg, Jim Davis and Ed Morgan sat at a conference table in a room with big windows. They looked down on the Confederate monument across the street next to the courthouse.

"Look at that piece of shit," Jim said. "Looks like a big White dick."

"Now that's funny," Ed said.

"You think so."

"Stop making fun of White people," the director of the agency said as he entered the room. His name was Lester Safer. He was born in Mississippi, educated in Washington, DC, and truly believed that Mississippi didn't have to be Mississippi. With him was a tall woman with a serious demeanor. "Men, this is Special Agent Herberta Hind of the FBI. It seems ghosts are the business of the feds."

Ed and Jim nodded hello.

"As far as I know the Bureau has no interest in ghosts," Hind said. "We are, on the other hand, interested in possible hate crimes." She looked at Ed and Jim. "Good morning, gentlemen. What can you tell me about Money, Mississippi?"

"Well, it's chock-full of know-nothing peckerwoods stuck in the prewar nineteenth century and living proof that inbreeding does not lead to extinction," Jim said. "No offense, chief."

"I'll take your word on that," Safer said. "I do want to point out to you that I'm from the state of Mississippi and that I grew up with these know-nothing, pre–Civil War, inbred peckerwoods."

"So, you don't agree that they are stupid miscreants?" Hind asked.

"Oh no, I agree," Safer said. "You know, it's just that it's okay if I say it since they're sort of my people. And I guess I don't agree completely."

"What don't you agree with?" Hind asked.

"The extinction part. They're pretty much on the way out."

"So, who killed whom?" she asked.

"I'm sure you've read the file," Ed said. He paused. "I'm assuming you've read the file."

"Yes," Hind said.

"Then you know what we know," Ed said. He tossed a glance toward Jim.

"The good folks of Money want to believe our dead Black man killed the two White men," Jim said.

"What do you think?" Hind asked.

"I don't know. He was holding their testicles in his fists. But I have no idea how they could have killed him while he was killing them."

Ed put the cigarette that he never lit between his lips.

"Not twice anyway," Jim said. "You ever hear of somebody dying twice? Anyplace but a Bond movie."

Hind shook her head. "Report says that you brought the Black body back to Hattiesburg with you."

"The people in Money couldn't seem to keep up with him," Ed said.

"So, you think somebody took his body?"

"Dead people don't walk," Jim said.

"Except for Jesus," Safer said.

"Yeah, him, I guess," Jim said. "Anyway, the body is downstairs with the medical examiner, if you'd care to join us."

"Let's go," Hind said.

The Medical Examiner was a fifty-year-old British woman named Helvetica Quip. She had come to Mississippi with her Mississippian husband, who turned out to be a clumsy pyramid-scheme con artist. Ferris New, the husband, had skedaddled out of the state in the middle of the night before his arraignment. Helvetica Quip claimed no ill feelings toward the man and refused to play the victim, but said only that she was relieved that she had not taken the man's last name. "Helvetica New," she would say, "sounds like the name of a font. If I'm going to be named after a font, it's going to be Oriya Sangam or something with some exotic flare."

"Talk to us, Helvetica," Jim said as they entered the examination lab.

"Guess what? The DNA turned up nothing because your sample was no good," she said.

"How is that possible?" Ed said. "I did it by the book."

"You didn't do it wrong," Helvetica said. "But there's no blood in this guy. He's full of a mixture of formaldehyde, glutaraldehyde, methanol, and some solvents I didn't bother to identify."

Jim, Ed, and Hind looked at her.

"Embalming fluid. This man was embalmed."

They stood silently while this sank in.

"Okay, but are you saying there is no DNA to be had?" Jim said.

"I didn't say that," Helvetica said. "I had plenty of tissue to work with. And I got a hit. This man was in the database. He was arrested for carjacking and kidnapping twelve years ago in Illinois."

"That doesn't make any sense," Ed said.

"It gets better," Helvetica said. "He died in prison. The Big Muddy River Correctional Center, to be precise. How is unclear. But he was severely beaten about the face and head." She paused. "And it gets better. Mr. Hemphill's body—that was his name, Robert Hemphill— was, as we say, donated to science."

"Donated to science?" Hind said.

"You know, medical school, some lab somewhere. I don't know. That's where I lose him. He was picked up by Ace Cadaver Supply of Chicago. That's all."

"So, it's not the body of Emmett Till?" Ed asked.

They all looked at him.

"Somebody had to ask," he said.

"It's not Emmett Till," Quip said.

42

The Doctor Reverend Cad Fondle was sitting in his living room with his wife, Fancel. Fancel was a big woman, big enough that she hardly ever moved from her corduroy recliner, which was stuck in recline. There was a half a meat lover's pizza and two beers on the foldout tray between her recliner and her husband's. They were watching television, switching back and forth between Fox News and professional wrestling.

"They's right," Fancel said. "That Obamacare don't work worth a hill of puppy shit. We done bought in, causin' we had to, and I ain't lost nary a pound."

Fondle took long pull on his beer. "Well, the country's done with that experiment. Smart-ass uppity sumbitch. You know he thinks he's better'n us."

"That Hannity is cute," Fancel said. "If I could get my hand anywhere near my vajayjay, I'd rub me one out just watchin' him."

"You can't reach it, so shut up."

"How did the cross burning go the other night?" Fancel asked.

"It's called a lightin', a cross lightin'. It ain't right to burn a symbol of our Lawd Jesus H. Christ. I would think you knowed that by now."

Fancel sighed. "What's the *H* for?"

"What?"

"The *H* in Jesus H. Christ, what's it for?" She picked some pepperoni from a crease in her house dress.

Fondle paused to regard her with his head cocked. "Why, it stands for, um, heaven, that's right."

"Jesus Heaven Christ? That don't make good sense."

"What would make sense to you?" Fondle asked.

"I don't know," she said. "Herschel, maybe."

"Why?"

"It's a nice name and it's a name. Heaven ain't no name."

"It's the name of a place, so it's a name. In fact, the place is named after our Lord," Fondle said, his eyes narrowed.

"Why ain't the place just called Jesus or Jesusburg?"

"Shut up and eat."

"Tell me about that boy," Fancel said. "That Black boy what keeps showin' up dead. How come he done that?"

"Could be he weren't dead. Hell, I don't know."

"You know what they be sayin'," she said.

"What's that?"

"That he's the ghost of that boy Robert Bryant and J. W. kilt all them years back. They say he come back to get revenge. I guess he got it."

"Hush yo mouth, woman. Ain't no such thing true."

"How you explain it then?" Fancel pointed a fat finger at him. "And don't you tell me to shut up. You got stuff coming to you."

Fondle wanted to, started to tell her to shut up, but didn't. Instead he grabbed his New Reader's Bible from under his La-Z-Boy and opened it. He held it open there in his lap while he pointed at the wrestlers on the television screen. "Big Bob Burgess is goin' kill that little nigger."

43

Everyone in the Bluegum was Black except for the one waiter who came to Gertrude and Damon's table. He was lean, tall, and wore a blue T-shirt that said Rescued by Jesus on the front. There were a few patrons, well-dressed young Black men and women. They did not look up or in any way regard the entrance of Gertrude and Damon. At a window in the back a cook slapped a bell, and a muscular man collected the plates.

"Hey, Gertrude," the waiter said.

"Hi, Chester," Gertrude said. "Chester Hobnobber, this is Damon Thruff. Damon, Chester."

"Hey, man, how you doing?" Chester said.

"Very well, thank you. And you?" Damon asked.

"Good, man, good." Chester looked to Gertrude. "So, what brings you down here? Got tired of the big city?"

"Big city?" Damon asked.

"He's being funny," Gertrude said. "He's talking about Money. It is not a city. It's a shithole where people have put some buildings."

"What do you want to drink?" Chester asked.

"Bring me a Kool-Aid," Gertrude said. "You should try it," she said to Damon. "It's great."

"I don't like the sound of that," Damon said. "But, okay."

"Be right back." Chester walked away.

"What's with the shirt?" Damon asked. "Jesus?"

"We're in Mississippi, Damon."

"How do you know him?" Damon asked.

"I know everybody in here," she said. "This is a small world. What's that Disney song? 'It's a small world after all,'" she sang.

Damon looked about the room and saw that everyone was looking at them. They were not so much smiling as nodding in a friendly way. It was then that he realized that there were more people present that he had previously noted.

"What going on here?" Damon asked.

"Nothing, just a restaurant. A restaurant with friendly people. Don't you like restaurants with friendly people?"

"It strikes me that you are being cryptic. What are you trying to tell me? Are you trying to tell me something?"

"And just why would I be trying to tell you something?" She cocked her head like a puppy.

"See, that's cryptic," Damon said.

Gertrude laughed. "In due time, my brother."

44

"Hold still, Charlene," Daisy Milam said. "This here is a big one. I mean a big one. How you let them get like this?"

Charlene Bryant lay on her belly in front of the television. "You think that Nicole Kidman got any on her back? Look at her there. She looks so perfect, so tall, so White. And married to that singer."

"She is tall," Daisy said. "Triple J, you get down off that china cabinet right now. I swear he gonna break every dish in that thing. Hold still, I say."

"Hot Mama Yeller," Lulabelle said, "when Aunt Daisy is done squishin' yo pimples, can we go home?"

"No, baby, we gonna eat pizza here."

"Awwww," the child said.

"It will be fun, Lulabelle. We got us a meat lover's on the way with extra sausage," Daisy said. "Come over here and look at this big one."

Lulabelle stepped close. "Yuck."

"It's comin'," Daisy said.

"Ewwwww," the child said.

"There she goes!"

"Ouch!" Charlene screamed.

"That's gross," Lulabelle cried.

"It's all over the place," Daisy said. "Lulabelle, go get me a bunch of paper towels and wet one of 'em."

"Daisy," Charlene said, "did you ever get all that blood cleaned up? 'Cause I sure didn't. That grout's gonna be pink forever."

"It's in the cracks," Daisy said. "I found something when I was cleaning up though."

"Was it a little cross?"

"Why yes it was. How did you know?" Daisy asked.

"I found one too. And I know Wheat ain't had no little cross."

"You think that nigger left them crosses for us to find? You think maybe he was a Christian man?"

"Niggers usually is. I wonder why he left them crosses. You got yourn?" Charlene asked.

"Got it right here," Daisy said. "I put it on a chain round my neck."

"Looks just exactly like mine. I keep it in my little pocket here in my jeans. They's pretty little crosses."

Daisy nodded.

"Makes me feel good to rub mine through my jeans."

"Here are the paper towels," Lulabelle said.

"Took you long enough," Charlene said.

"Now, let me clean up all this pus. That pizza gonna be here any minute."

"Mama, Triple J is playing in the back room," one of Daisy's children reported, breathless.

"Lord, have mercy," Daisy said. "That boy ain't got sense enough to piss out of a boot with the directions wrote on the heel. Lulabelle, come over here and wipe that shit off your mama's back."

"Okay, Aunt Daisy. Hold still, Hot Mama Yeller," the girl said.

45

Ed Morgan sat in the back of the black Cadillac Escalade. Herberta Hind drove, and Jim Davis sat in the passenger seat. They were cruising along the highway toward Money, past shacks sitting off the ground on squat brick pillars, past spent cornfields and sadlooking, rib-bare cows.

Jim rubbed his hand across the black dash. "Don't you think this vehicle is a bit of a cliché?"

"I like it," Ed said from the back. "I'm comfortable."

"We use these because they are cliché," Hind said. "We're the FBI. We are walking clichés."

"Do you like the agency?" Jim asked.

Hind tilted her head and looked at him. "I hate every last motherfucker there, White, Black, and Asian."

"Don't mince words," Ed said.

"So, why stay?" Jim asked.

"Why are you in the, what do you call it, the MBI? That's funny."

"This is Mississippi," Ed said. "Somebody Black had better watch these White folks down here. Because for a lot of these crazy folks, it's still nineteen fifty."

"Shit, eighteen fifty," Jim said.

"Not just here," Hind said.

Another couple of miles slipped by.

"Do you really think going to Money is going help this investigation?" Ed asked.

"Not really, but that's how we investigate, isn't it?" she said.

Jim grunted an agreement.

"Anyway, it's worth seeing this place, these people," Ed said. "I also think that we're not done. For a minute I thought we were dealing with the ghost of Emmett Till. How crazy is that?"

"Maybe we are dealing with a ghost," Hind said.

Jim gave her a sidelong glance. "Whatchu talking about, Willis?"

"Unless you think that the folks in Money are suffering shared hallucinations, that they really did have a dead guy disappear and reappear at another murder scene. And it doesn't get better when we find out that body has been dead for years. The ghost theory is looking pretty good."

"Either way it's fucked up," Jim said.

"Are you men from Mississippi?"

"Biloxi," Ed said.

"New Orleans," from Jim. "My mother was from Hattiesburg. You? Where are you from, Special Agent Hind?"

"Washington, DC," she said. "Sixteenth and T, to be precise. Poor little Black girl grows up to be an FBI agent. Classic American story."

"Why did you become a cop?" Jim asked.

"Why did you?" Hind asked.

Jim and Ed together, "So Whitey wouldn't be the only one in the room with a gun."

Hind fist-bumped Jim.

Hind adjusted her mirror. "Well, look here," she said.

Ed glanced behind them. "A Mississippi Straight Pooper," he said. "And, of course, he's lighting us up."

"Wanna have some fun?" Hind asked.

"Don't get us shot, Special Agent Hind," Ed said. "Remember this is the sovereign state of Mississippi."

Hind pulled over onto the shoulder.

Jim sang, "*I wish I was a Mississippi trooper, that is what I truly long to be / cause if I was a Mississippi trooper, I could shoot them niggers legally.*"

"Catchy," Hind said. "Are you kidding me?" She was looking into the mirror.

The tall trooper approaching them wore a wide-brimmed hat and mirrored glasses. He had plenty of swagger in his gait. His hand found and rested on his sidearm as he arrived at Hind's window.

She pressed the button to lower it. "Officer, do we's gots us a problem?" she said, her voice high and thin.

The trooper leaned over to observe Jim, seemed a little surprised to find the big man, Ed, in the back.

"Where y'all goin'?" he asked.

"We is on our way to Money, Mississippi," Hind said. "We gots some business in Money. Was I speeding, officer?"

"You were going two miles over the speed limit. Now that could be very dangerous, What with the road conditions."

"These really are bad roads," Jim said. "You are indeed right about that, Officer Pecker."

The trooper touched his name tag. "That's Officer Peck," he said.

"Well, of course it is," Jim said. "Officer Peck. How could I make such a silly mistake? Must be my eyes."

The trooper was confused by the tone of it all. He studied Jim and Ed again. "Nice suits," he said. "You boys from 'round here?"

"Where's here?" Jim asked.

"The state of Mississippi, boy." The trooper was tightly wound and quite apparently displeased.

"Oh, Mississippi," Jim said. "That would be a no."

"License and registration."

"But, Mr. Officer Peck, sir, this here is a rental car, and they ain't give me no registration," Hind said.

"Okay, y'all some funny darkies. Well, out of the car, both hands on the window here." He pointed at Jim. "You put your hands on that dash." To Ed, he said, "Hands on the headrest in front of you."

"Mind if I put my badge away first?" Ed asked.

"What?" the trooper said.

"I need to put mine away too," Hind said.

"Ditto," from Jim.

The three held up their badges for the man to see.

The trooper sighed, looking at each of their faces in turn. "Fuck all of y'all. I ought just shoot y'all."

"Might have to shoot you back," Hind said.

Officer Peck stood stiff for a few seconds. "Go on. Y'all enjoy Money, now. Stupid sumbitches."

"Thank you, Officer Peck," Hind said. "I'll attempt to comply with the rules of the highway."

As they drove away, leaving Peck standing alone on the dusty road, Ed said, "I thought he might actually shoot us."

"Thought crossed my mind too," Jim said.

"History is a motherfucker," Hind said.

46

Reverend Doctor Fondle forced air through his pursed lips, making them buzz like a trumpet player's. He stuttered out a long string of b's, his hand stretching an imaginary thread away from his mouth in one continuous motion. He la-la'ed up and down the scale, his eyes fluttering and showing whites. There were twelve Bible students, as he called them, two men and ten women, Good Christians, in his makeshift house of the Lord that was his garage. He was in his bedroom, loosening his lips, his tongue, his thoughts, his spirit. He was about to deliver the word of the Lawd God Jesus unto his children, to lay bare his sinner's soul and so theirs, to show them the path, the way, the true path to glory and salvation. He stared at his face in the mirror and tried to summon the fire of Jesus Lawd God Almighty. He imagined his eyes as flames and they were flames. He imagined his voice a siren and it was a siren. He imagined he saw the face of a Black man behind him in the mirror and there was one. Before he could say Lawdy, before he could say Jessssssssussss, before he could say nigger, a length of barbed wire was wrapped twice around his thick, froglike neck. His arteries punctured on either side, he sprayed blood like a garden hose against the far wall. His mouth opened to form a scream, but not even breath escaped. His eyes rolled toward his receding hairline, showed white again; his arms stiffened, and his hands reached away from him like a scarecrow's. He was turned to face his unmade bed and there on the sheets with the yellow flowers was the body of a dead Black man. Through his mind flashed the image of a Black man, so many years ago, falling onto the sidewalk in front of some city building, falling dead from gunshot to his head. He then recognized the Brookhaven, Mississippi, courthouse, the standing, painted red clock on the grounds, his slope-shouldered father standing over the broken, dead man's body. He was a boy, sitting there in his father's half-ton Ford pickup. He watched as his father spat tobacco-tinged spittle on the lifeless man. Back in his room, in his present, he felt his trousers settle around his ankles, the barbed wire being pulled taut to keep him on his feet. He saw the glint of a large, curved blade. That was the last thing Reverend Doctor Fondle saw in this world. The last sensation was not pain, but the feeling of a sound, the wet, almost clean parting of skin and fat and muscle. His last thought, if he was capable of one, might have been that those other brown people were onto something with that notion of karma. Whatever, there was no time to ask his Lawd God Jesus Almighty for forgiveness.

47

The only person in the Money Police Department building was Hattie, the receptionist/dispatcher. She was visibly shaken, even whiter than she had been minutes earlier. Her big hair looked fragile, and her eyes were red from near crying. Still, she managed to be surprised to find Ed, Jim, and now Special Agent Herberta Hind standing in front of her.

"Where is everybody?" Ed asked.

"Oh, it's awful, just awful," Hattie said.

"What is just awful?" Hind asked.

Hattie cut her a sour look. "I don't know you. I know these here boys because they was here before, but I don't know you."

"I'm FBI Special Agent Herberta Hind."

"Lord have mercy, they's coming out of the woodwork."

"Will you tell us just what is so awful?" Jim asked.

"It's the Reverend Doctor Fondle," Hattie said.

"The coroner?" Ed asked.

"Yes, he's dead. Somebody kilt him in his bedroom while he was dressin' to go to meetin'. That's all I know."

"Is the sheriff there now?" Ed asked.

Hattie nodded.

"Give us the address, Hattie."

"The sheriff ain't said he want you out there," Hattie said.

"Why don't I just shoot you?" Hind said. "How about that?"

Hattie gave them the address.

48

"Was that good food or what?" Gertrude asked.

"I know you didn't take me there for the cuisine," Damon said. "So, please finish filling me in."

"Later," she said. "Get in the car."

"Why am I scared?" Damon asked.

"What?"

"I'm scared and I don't really know why. But you do, I think. Know why I'm scared, I mean."

"Get in the car."

Damon did. Gertrude started the car and proceeded to pull on to the highway. "Let me ask you a question," she said.

Damon looked at her.

"Have you ever been called a nigger?"

"No, as a matter of fact. You?"

"Not personally," she said.

"What's that mean, 'not personally'?"

Gertrude attended to the road, seeming to make a point of not looking at her friend. "Every time anybody gets called a nigger, I get called a nigger."

"What is that? A bumper sticker slogan?"

"Yeah, you like it? I've got more. How about this one: Once you go Black, you die. Or, Dead is the new Black."

"I wish you would just tell me what's going on," Damon said.

"I want you to meet someone."

49

It was not uncommon for snow to fall so early in Duluth, Minnesota, but the intense weather was unexpected, starting midmorning and becoming immediately heavy. It caught the road crews shorthanded. Parents struggled to find ways to collect their children from early dismissal. The storm promised to be a big one. Taggert Muldoon didn't have to worry about any of that. He'd just filled his refrigerator with new food, and it was his wife's week with the kids. If it was hard on her to get them home, then fuck her. He actually said that out loud to no one. Next week when the snow was gone, he would take his daughter for the twentieth time to Judy Garland's house, where the actress had been born. There was not much else to do. When he was by himself he liked to go look at the big ships. He wondered if the lake was going to freeze around the edges. He'd been recently laid off from the meatpacking plant and needed things to see. Those fucking Hispanics had come and scooped up the jobs. The plants would hire them, fire them before they had to give them any benefits, and then bring in a new batch. *Fucking greaser wetbacks*, he thought. They should all be run out of town, out of the country, just like his grandfather had helped get the niggers out of town back in the good days of 1920.

"Muldoon?" A man's voice called to him. He was startled

because he had been alone in the house. At least, he believed he was alone.

"Who's that?" he said.

Liam Murphy had been a detective on the Duluth police force for nearly ten years. Five before that he'd walked then driven a beat in the small city. In all that time, as detective and beat cop, the most gruesome thing he had ever seen was the shooting of a snow leopard that had escaped its enclosure at the Lake Superior Zoo. The cops that cornered the animal panicked and fired some one hundred bullets at the cat, hitting it three times. The poor animal had seemed mostly confused by the noise.

But here he was in a typical and depressing Duluth duplex staring down at two bodies. That of one Taggert Muldoon, dead from an apparent beating or from bleeding out, his testicles having been removed and now held in the hand of the second victim, an unidentified Black male. Muldoon's neck had been slashed by what must have been a large blade, his head nearly severed from his body. The concave linoleum floor of the kitchen was a lake of blood, strangely only the blood of the White man. A television was switched on. The Vikings pregame show was on.

"I didn't even know it was Thursday," Murphy said.

"Well, what do you think, Murph? Run it for me," said Detective Wesley Snipes, no relation and White, sipping coffee from a Starbucks cup.

"Where'd you get that?" Murphy asked.

"News crew outside. Channel Eight. They've got a whole table set up. Want me to grab you one?"

"No, thanks. I don't like Starbucks anyway. I can't seem

to reconstruct it." He stepped around the pool of blood. "It appears as if there was a struggle, but look at that guy." He pointed to the Black man. "He can't weigh more than a buck forty, and Muldoon here must go two fifty or sixty."

"So, maybe he was a tough little guy," Wesley said. "You know, maybe he had a punch like George Foreman or something."

"And they just managed to kill each other," Murphy said, but it was more a question. He knelt beside the Black man's body.

"It could happen. Double knockout. Kapow."

"While he's slicing off big man's nuts."

"Well, there's that."

"And there is no blood coming out of this guy. His face looks like it was not even touched. But he's dead."

"He is that," Wesley said.

"Tell Ernie I want pictures from every angle. And look around. I want to know how that guy"—he pointed to the Black man— "got in here. I want to if Muldoon knew him, was dating him, was screwing his girlfriend, was doing his taxes."

"What about the testicles?" Snipes asked.

"What about them?"

"I don't think they were sliced off," Wesley said.

"You don't?"

"Naw, I think they were snatched off. Like some kind of martial arts shit. You know how they can rip a man's throat out?"

"You watch too many movies," Murphy said.

"Maybe, but that man's testicles are in that man's hand. That's not quite normal. And that don't look like a slice. It looks like a rip."

"I can't argue with that," Murphy said.

"Muldoon has an ex-wife and two kids," Snipes said. "I already sent somebody from family services over to break the news."

"We'd better go talk to the ex," Murphy said.

"That's all we ever do," Wesley said. "Talk to exes."

"Yep. And do you know why?"

"Because the ex is always guilty."

"Guilty of something, anyway."

50

Carbon County Deputy Sheriff Rake Kearney was having lunch at the new Burger King restaurant on the business route of Interstate 80. He didn't like the burger because it didn't taste like beef. It might have been meat, but it wasn't beef. He liked beef, and if he could have made a living working with beef instead of the Carbon County Sheriff's Department, he certainly would have. He grew up wanting to be a cowboy, a real cowboy, not the town variety, not a rodeo guy. Sure, he wore a gun on his hip, but that was movie cowboying; he longed for the cowboying of his father and grandfather. There was no land that his family still owned on which to raise beef, and so he had no cattle of his own. Truth be told, he was clumsy in the saddle and no good with a rope. He finally wasn't cut out to be a cowboy.

A call came in over the radio he wore on his belt. There was a body on the access road that ran parallel to the freeway, not far from his present location. He always wanted to laugh whenever the dispatcher or another deputy asked for his twenty, instead of simply asking where he was. He threw more than half his sandwich and fries into the trash and got into the Ford Explorer that was his patrol vehicle.

A couple of motorists, as the sheriff liked to call them, were standing by the roadside. They appeared to be stealing furtive peeks at whatever lay between the freeway and the access road. Rake got out of his rig and walked toward them. He was met by a very excited young man with long hair.

"Dude, you're not going to believe this," the man said. "I stopped to take a leak by the road and I saw them. Scared the shit out of me."

"Them?" Rake asked.

"Yeah, man, there're two of them. And it ain't pretty. I mean it's really fucking ugly, man."

Lying in the alfalfa, sweet corn, and clover were, in fact, two bodies. One man was twisted, tangled up in the barbed wire fence that ran parallel to the interstate. His throat was cut, his head tilted to the side in an impossible angle. He was dressed in the striped uniform of the old territorial prison, the top of which was red and brown with what appeared to be blood. The prison issue pants were pulled to his ankles. There was a mess of grass, twigs, blood, and hair between the man's legs. Some yards away lay another man, slight in build, ashen, and quite obviously dead. Something bloody sat loosely in his open left hand. Flies were everywhere, but not yet the stench of death.

"Ain't that something," the young man who had met Douglas said. "Man, ain't that something."

Douglas spoke into his radio. "Dispatch, this is seventeen. I'm going to need a supervisor on-site pronto. We got us a serious crime scene here. I think I've got an escaped prisoner dead over here. His head is damn near cut off. White male, shaved head, maybe six feet. And another White male, slight build, light-colored hair, regular street clothes, and sneakers."

"There's no report of an escape from the prison," the man on the radio said. "Or the jail."

"All I know is this guy is wearing stripes, like the old territorial prison clothes, and prison shoes." Douglas turned his attention to the people starting to creep up behind him into the scene. "Everybody move back. Please move back. Don't leave, but move back." He looked at the long-haired man. "Were you the first person to stop?"

"No, dude."

"Who was the first person to stop here?" Douglas asked the crowd.

A Hispanic woman and her young son stepped forward.

"Why did you stop here, ma'am?"

"My son said he thought he saw a soccer ball in the grass, so I stopped," she said. "He ran to get it and came back screaming."

"That's when I pulled up," an older White man said. "The boy was crying and I went to look, and then I called 911."

"Did you see anybody else here?" Douglas asked. "See any cars leaving the area when you stopped?"

The woman and the man shook their heads no.

The sheriff arrived on the scene. He walked quickly through and around the area, then stood next to Douglas.

"What do you think, Chief ?" Douglas asked.

"Gruesome," the sheriff said. "Turns out there was an escape from the prison. Nobody missed him until they just did a headcount. Name is Aaron Henderson."

"That him?" Douglas asked.

"You got me."

The criminalists arrived and the sheriff instructed them to start processing the scene. The temperature had dropped considerably since Douglas's arrival, and snow had begun to fall. The wind picked up.

"What's that in his hand?" the sheriff called to one of his men.

"Sheriff, that would be testicles," the man said.

"What?"

"Testicles. And I suspect that they belong to him." He pointed to the dead man in prison clothes. "I say that because that guy is missing his."

51

Jim Davis and Ed Morgan walked into the house of the Reverend Doctor Fondle, followed by Herberta Hind. The deputies, apparently used to the presence of Jim and Ed, fairly ignored them, but did notice Hind.

"And who is this little lady here?" Sheriff Jetty asked.

"I'm FBI Special Agent Herberta Hind."

"Lord have mercy," Jetty said. "Another *special* somebody. What's next? Somebody special from the CIA, the NSA, NASA?"

"Very funny," Hind said. "I take it you're Sheriff Jetty."

"I am."

"Is this scene related to our other crimes?" she asked.

"*Our* crimes?" Jetty asked. "This here is a Leflore County situation."

Dill and Digby carried a covered body past them and out the door. Brady and Jethro followed with a second.

"A second body?" Ed said.

"Is this like the other two?" Jim asked.

Jetty dropped his head. "Damnit, yes. Fondle was strangled with barbed wire, and there was a ni—a dead Black man in the room with him. So, what do you have to say about that? You fancy-asses have your work cut out for you, because I don't know what the fuck is going on."

Jim cleared his throat. "I hate to ask, but is the Black man the same man you found at the other scenes?"

"No, he is not," the sheriff said. "He's a brand-new Negro gentleman that none of us recognize."

"We're taking the bodies," Hind said.

"What say?" Jetty asked.

She spoke to Jim and Ed. "Arrange to have these bodies taken to your medical examiner down in Hattiesburg. In fact, I want all the bodies down there."

"Wait a second," Jetty said, "what about the families?"

"Just the bodies," she said.

"Oh, an FBI comedian. I mean, what about the funerals? Folks want to give their kin a Christian burial in these parts."

"You don't need a body for a funeral," Hind said. "They can bury them when we're done with them."

"Sheriff, did Fondle have all of his parts?" Ed asked.

"What?"

"Were his balls cut off ?" Jim asked.

As if it pained him to say it, Jetty mumbled a quiet, "Yes." Then in a clear and loud voice, "His nuts were in the Black man's hand. You just wanted to hear me say that, didn't you?"

"Yeah, sort of," Jim said.

"I want to inspect the scene, and I want see both bodies," Hind said.

"What good is that gonna do?" Jetty asked.

"Perhaps you're not acquainted with the idea of an investigation," she said. "But we observe and actively look for evidence."

The sheriff said nothing.

"You can see the Black man. We know who the victim is."

"I'm going to see them both. And isn't the Black man a victim?" Hind was considerably shorter than Jetty, but was looking him in the eye.

"I don't see why you need to seen a man's mutilated body," Jetty said. "A good Christian man."

"Don't worry, I can take it," she said. "And he won't mind."

"He's got a wife and family."

"I won't touch his testicles, if that's what's concerning you."

"Jesus Christ," Jetty muttered.

"I'll get my evidence kit," Ed said.

"Do you know who the Black man is?" Jim asked.

"Hell no," Jetty said. "Nobody's seen him before either. We ain't had a chance to run his prints yet. We got strange Black men coming out of the woodwork."

"Well, don't bother," Hind said. "We'll take care of that."

"I'm sure you will," the sheriff said.

"Sheriff, do you have a problem with me taking over this case?" Hind asked.

Jetty removed his hat and raked his thinning hair back over his sweaty head. "As a matter of fact, I do. Murder is a local matter. We can handle our own business. We don't need no carpetbaggers comin' down here telling us what to do."

"Suck it up, Jetty. I'm here. You investigate your murder. We'll figure out what's going on."

52

Mama Z was painting her front porch when Gertrude arrived with Damon. "Hello, great-granddaughter," she said.

"Mama Z, this is my friend, Damon."

"Very pleased to make your acquaintance," Damon said.

Mama Z laughed. "Make your acquaintance? What century are you from, young brother? I'm happy to meet you too."

"What do I call you?" Damon asked.

"You call me Mama Z, just like everybody else."

"Damon writes books," Gertrude said.

"He does, does he? Maybe we can find you something to write about."

"I don't understand," Damon said.

"What do you know about lynching?" Mama Z asked.

"Some. I wrote a book about racial violence."

"I know," the old woman said. "I have a copy in the house. It's very…"—she searched for the word—"scholastic."

"I think you're saying that like it's a bad thing."

Mama Z shrugged.

Damon looked at Gertrude, as if for clarification, only to see her shrug as well. "Scholastic," he repeated.

"Don't take it the wrong way," Gertrude said.

"Your book is very interesting," Mama Z said, "because you were able to construct three hundred and seven pages on such a topic without an ounce of outrage."

Damon was visibly bothered by this. "One hopes that dispassionate, scientific work will generate proper outrage."

"Nicely said, nicely said," Mama Z said. "Wouldn't you say that was nicely said, great-granddaughter?"

"I would," Gertrude agreed.

"There are a lot of strange things happening in Leflore County, Damon," Mama Z said. "Other places too. Not only Mississippi. Supernatural things."

"Really now?" Damon smiled at Gertrude.

Gertrude nodded.

"Do you like the color?" Mama Z asked. She stepped away from the railing of her porch.

"It's black," Damon said.

"I know what color it is," the old woman said. "I asked you if you like it."

"It will be difficult to see in the dark," Damon said.

"That's very true, my boy, very true. I want you to remember that."

"What are you talking about?" he asked.

"Gertrude, take Damon inside to the library and show him the records."

"Come on," Gertrude said. "There's something inside that you have to see. Do you want some tea?"

"No tea. I just want to catch up here and understand. Supernatural? What's supernatural? What kind of bullshit is that? What are the records? Why is she acting so creepy? Who paints a porch black?" Damon followed Gertrude through the front room. He looked at the shelves. "She has a lot of books."

Gertrude led him into the library and gestured for him to regard the array of filing cabinets.

"What am I looking at?" Damon asked.

"These are the records," she said. "There is a file here for nearly every person lynched in this country since 1913."

Damon was gobsmacked. He looked from wall to wall. "That old woman compiled all of this?" He stepped forward and ran a hand along a cabinet.

"Open it. Read."

"Why 1913?"

"Mama Z was born in 1913. Shortly after her birth her father was lynched. He was a voting rights activist. His is the first dossier."

"How many are there?" Damon asked.

"I don't know."

"How did she do all of this?"

"She's not like the rest of us," Gertrude said.

53

"Is this guy's name really McDonald McDonald?" Orange County Lieutenant Detective Hal Chi said. He stood in the wide foyer of a massive home in Huntington Beach. Criminalists walked and crawled past him. Uniformed cops stood at every door.

"Yeah, that's his name," his partner, Daryl Ho, said. He looked at his notes. "No relation to the restaurant."

"Pretty well off, though," Hal said.

"Somebody said he's old money."

"Doesn't look like old money. Look at this place. Looks like a Restoration Hardware catalogue."

"Pottery Barn," Daryl said.

"Anyway, so money bags bought it," Hal said.

"Oh, you gotta see this." Daryl closed his notebook. "Scene's upstairs. They've been processing the rest of the house, but haven't touched that room yet. Except for some pictures. M. E. was in there, of course."

"Let's see it."

Hal followed Daryl up the sweeping spiral staircase. They didn't pause outside the door but stepped right in.

"Holly fuck," Hal said. He walked across the room and leaned over the body of a White male, midsixties, receding hairline, pajama clad and throat slit. "God, that's fucking deep. Katana?"

"Good call," Daryl said. "It's under the window."

"Who found him?"

"Housekeeper. He lives alone. Can you believe it? House this big. She found him and ran downstairs to call 911. Uniforms came and they found homeowner here and—" Daryl directed Hal's attention across the room.

Hal turned around to see another body. "*Nǐ hǎo*," he said. Without leaning over, he could observe the face of a dead Asian man, perhaps forty years old. "What are you doing here, *bèndàn*?"

"Look in his hand," Daryl said.

"What's that? Man, look at the blood."

"Those would be testicles. And they're not his."

Hal turned back to look at the White man. He saw that the man's pajama pants were open and covered in blood. "I thought that was blood from his throat."

"Some of it probably is, but homeboy here ripped his cojones off. At least that's what it looks like."

"Little fella did it with a big sword," Hal said. "But who killed *him*?"

"M. E. has gotta figure that out. I'm just a regular dude with a badge, a pistol, and handcuffs."

"No identification on the Asian?"

Daryl shook his head.

"I've seen enough," Hal said. "Call them in here and get this place processed." He looked at the scene. "I can't play it out. You?"

Daryl shook his head. "Nope."

54

The first dead Black man was still secure in his stainless steel drawer in Hattiesburg, and the second was on his way. FBI Special Agent Herberta Hind and MBI Special Detectives Ed Morgan and Jim Davis sat in what had become a familiar booth to the two men. Gertrude delivered three glasses of ice water to them and said hello.

"Gertrude, this is Herberta Hind," Jim said. "She's from the FBI."

"Fat Boys Incorporated?" Gertrude joked. "Federal Bureau of Intimidation?" She collected herself. "Sorry. Pleased to meet you."

Hind smiled, as much as she ever smiled. "Nice to meet you too, kid. Your name tag says Dixie."

"That's my stage name."

"I see."

"Do people call you Herberta or Berta?" Gertrude asked.

Hind studied the young woman for a long second. "My family called me Herbie."

The four were silent for a while.

"I'll get your coffee," Gertrude said and walked away.

"So, what do we do now?" Jim asked.

"I think we follow the body," Ed said. "Is there a chain of possession of this cadaver that was used by the killer?"

"I think that's right. Believe it or not, my office isn't allotting any more manpower, pardon the expression, to our investigation. Personally, I am not surprised. However, I have asked that your agency loan you to me. And they said yes."

"Well okay, boss," Jim said. "So, my question remains: What's next, Special Agent Hind?"

"Herbie," she said.

"Really?" Jim asked.

"I can take it if you can," she said. "Jim, I'd like you to, as Ed said, follow the body. And check out that murder in Chicago where the guy's balls were ripped off. So you're going to have to fly out tomorrow."

Gertrude came back with the coffee. "So sorry about the wait. I had to make a new pot."

"Gertrude," Ed said, "do you think you might introduce Special Agent Hind to Mama Z?"

Gertrude hesitated a beat, then said, "Of course."

"We should order," Hind said. "I'll have the chili."

"Do you like chili?" Gertrude asked. "You might want the chicken sandwich."

"Three chicken sandwiches," Jim said.

"Coming right up." Gertrude left.

Hind watched her walk away. "Pretty girl. Do you trust her?"

"It hadn't occurred to us not to," Jim said. "You don't?"

"I don't trust many people." Herbie Hind arranged her silverware and put her paper napkin in her lap. "Ed, I want you to find out more about the White men who died here in Money."

Ed nodded.

"I'm going to go back to Hattiesburg and go over the evidence and talk to the M. E."

55

Damon Thruff sat at the library table in the middle of the room full of gray file cabinets, a closed red folder on the surface in front of him. Mama Z leaned against the doorjamb and observed him.

"Aren't you going to open it?" the old woman said.

"Eventually," Damon said. He looked around. "I can't believe all of this. How did you do it?"

Mama Z shrugged.

"All of them?"

"I wouldn't say all. Many of them."

"This one is from 1913," he said or asked.

"It is," Mama Z said. "My father."

"Your father was lynched?"

"The year I was born. His name was Julius Lynch. I kid you not. He was hanged and shot three miles south of Hattiesburg. My mother died of scarlet fever three months later. I was raised by my uncle, John Lynch. But none of this is about me."

56

Julius Randolph Lynch
DOB: 19 August 1859
Place of Birth: Tacony Plantation, Concordia Parish, Louisiana
Mother: Catherine White, mixed-race, slave
Father: Patrick Lynch, White, overseer
Date of Lynching: 21 December 1913
Place of Lynching: South of Hattiesburg, MS, off Highway 49

Item 1
Forrest County Sheriff's Department Police Report
Case #: 1221191381a
Date: December 21, 1913
Reporting Officer: Deputy Sheriff Donald Sessions
Prepared by: Sheriff Larry Bolton
Incident: The body of a light-skinned Negro male was found 3.5 miles south of Hattiesburg in a stand of sycamore trees. The individual was found bound at the ankles and wrists with some kind of coated wire. The individual was found suspended from the large branch of an oak tree by a light brown rope tied in a loop around his neck. The individual was pronounced dead at the scene by the coroner. The cause

of death was determined to be a self-inflicted knife wound to the neck. The body was first discovered by a Negro sharecropper named Chancey Boatwright. He reported the body to Sheriff's Deputy Donald Sessions, who was parked about a mile away at a filling station. Boatwright was brought to the station house to give his statement, then released.

Statement of Chancey Boatwright (taken by Sheriff Bolton):
I was taking a shortcut from my house to Mr. Sims's general store. I ain't sure what time it were. I ain't got no watch, but it was early. The ground was still dew wet. My boot toes was dark. I wanted to be there when Mr. Sims open up. First I didn't know just what I was seeing up in dat tree, cause the sun was behind it. I thought it was maybe a kite or somebody's laundry or something. Anyways, when I got close up I seen it was a man, and Lawd have mercy it scared me to death. That poor man looked like he ain't had no blood left in him, nary a drop. I prayed to Jesus and I then I run up to the filling station to tell the man there to call the police. But that deputy, Sessions, was there, and I told him what I seen. The deputy put me in the back of his car and drove me to where the dead man was. I stood there while he looked around.

Statement of Sheriff's Deputy Donald Sessions:
At 9:30 a.m. I was checking the air in my tires at the filling station on Highway 49. A nigger I knowed from before by the name of Chancey come running into the station, all excited, panting like a dog. He said he'd found a lynched man. I instructed the man to calm down. He then got into

my squad car and showed me where he seen the body. I recognized the body as the Negro man named Julius Lynch. I radioed the sheriff and the sheriff called the coroner. I looked all around the area and couldn't find no sign of nobody else. I searched the area while I waited for the sheriff and found what looked like a man's wallet and a pair of what looked like a man's eyeglasses. The wallet didn't have no ID or money.

Notes: The body of Julius Lynch was claimed by his brother, John Lynch. The body was picked up by the Pierce Funeral Parlor. No one was interviewed. No suspects were identified. No one was arrested. No one was charged. No one cared.

57

Helvetica Quip nursed a cup of chamomile tea while she sat at the stainless steel desk in the autopsy room in the basement of MBI headquarters in Hattiesburg. Special Agent Herberta Hind drank Coke from a can and held a slender, unlit cigarette between the fingers of her other hand.

"One seldom sees a cigarette these days," Helvetica said.

"I hold them, but don't smoke them. Not anymore. My father smoked cigars," Hind said. "He was a janitor at the White House."

"You mean 1600 Pennsylvania Avenue?"

"Yes."

"That must have been interesting."

"You might think so. Especially because he was there during the Nixon administration. But he claimed it wasn't all that interesting. He said Kissinger was polite, believe it or not. John Dean was nervous."

"Wow. Nixon."

"My father worked nights. He said Nixon was always in the Oval Office. He often had to clean around him as he slept at his desk." Hind finished her soda and tossed the empty can in the nearby wastebasket. "He said that Nixon saw him more than a thousand times and never said hello."

"Racist?" Helvetica asked.

"Drunk. Oblivious. Who knows?"

"I didn't know my father."

"He left when you were a kid?" Hind asked.

"No, he lived in the house my entire life, but I never knew him. He was an anesthesiologist, and you would have thought he simply put himself to sleep every day. I can't even remember the sound of his voice. I think he put me to sleep, and that's how I ended up marrying someone as remote as he was. Want to hear something funny?"

Hind nodded.

"I fell in love with my husband's Southern accent. Can you believe that? A Mississippi accent."

Hind laughed. "Well, Doctor Quip, I'm sure he fell in love with your exotic British accent."

"My accent doesn't seem to impress people down here."

Hind considered this for a while. "My father hated that I ended up working for the Bureau."

"Why was that?"

"He didn't trust White people."

"Yet he worked at the White House," Helvetica said.

"Even he liked the irony."

The computer behind Helvetica dinged. "It seems we have a hit, ladies and gentlemen." She opened a screen and studied it. "The DNA of our second cadaver belongs to a Mr. Gerald Mister. Good name. It seems Mister Mister did a couple of years in Cook County Jail. Released quite a while ago. Died last year. Get this: His body was taken to Acme Cadaver Supply of Chicago. Same as our other body."

"I guess that's our next move."

"Just what is going on, Special Agent Hind?"

"I don't know, Dr. Quip. I don't know."

"I sent Davis to Chicago."

58

It was extremely cold in Chicago, at least for Jim Davis. Jim was from New Orleans, and his body reminded him of this fact when the Chicago wind slapped him around. He thought he'd dressed properly, putting a wool overcoat over his wool suit coat, but he was wrong. Jim drove his rental car to the Brighton Park precinct station and walked into the overheated building.

He stepped up to the desk officer. "I'd like to speak with Detective Sergeant Daniel Moon."

"And who the hell are you?" the fat cop asked.

"Special Detective Jim Davis of the Mississippi Bureau of Investigation," he said. He hated the way that sounded.

"Oh really?" the man said.

"I'm part of an interstate task force working with the FBI. Officer, may I have your name?"

The man retreated into his body and reached for the phone. "I'll call Detective Moon. Have a seat over there."

Jim sat in a chair against the wall next to a woman in handcuffs. He nodded a hello to her.

"I'm being booked for prostitution," she said.

"Sorry to hear that," Jim said. "Are they tough on that up here?"

"If you walk the streets," she said. "They don't care if

you work the internet and go to hotels and such."

"Is that right?"

"Oh yeah. Unless the guy at the hotel spots you and don't like you. That's what happened to me."

"Sorry to hear that." Jim peeled off his overcoat.

"Son of a bitch," she said. "All because I would give him no cut."

"Is that customary?" Jim asked.

The woman stared at Jim for a second and grew grim.

"You know what, fuck you," she said.

Jim nodded, let his head rest on the wall behind him.

"Who are you to judge me?" the woman said.

Without opening his eyes, Jim said, "Listen, sugar, I'm from New Orleans, Louisiana. Down there you can sell pussy to your heart's content as long as you don't roll somebody. So be cool."

"Agent Davis," a man said.

Jim opened his eyes to find a tall Asian man standing next to him. "I'm Moon. Come on back."

Jim sat in the chair in front of Moon's desk. Moon sat on the edge of his desk. "So, you're interested in the Milam murder."

"You observed the scene," Jim more said than asked.

"It was the worst thing I've ever seen."

"Was there barbed wire?" Jim asked.

"There was," Moon said.

Jim pulled a folded manila envelope from his overcoat pocket. "Was the scene similar to these?"

Moon studied the pictures and then stared back at Jim.

"What the fuck is this? What's going on?"

"Your scene look like these?"

Moon looked back at the pictures. "Pretty much exactly. Except there was only one body."

"Was there any sign that another body had been there?" Jim asked.

"What do you mean?"

"Did you find anything strange?" Jim caught himself. "Besides the obvious. Anything that bothers you?"

"The criminalist did find some dark fibers that we can't account for. There was no sign of a struggle, but the killer must have shed them. Lab said they were rotten."

"Would you mind showing me the scene?"

Moon looked at Jim and then again at the photographs. "Yeah, I'll drive you over there."

"Thanks, Detective."

"This is all pretty ugly, you know?" Moon said.

"Yes, I know."

"You want to tell me what's going on?"

"I wish I knew."

59

Ed Morgan was less clear on his assignment than was his partner. He was charged with learning as much about the four White victims as possible. The initial problem, as Ed saw it, was that the three men and one woman were so unremarkable that there was little to uncover about them. They were simple in the strictest sense, and not in a good way. It came as no surprise that in a town of such size that they would all know each other. In fact, Carolyn Bryant, Wheat Bryant, and the Milam they called Junior Junior were related by blood. The coroner, Fondle, was the odd piece. And so Ed decided to start with him. He went to the man's house, knocked. Fancel Fondle called for him to enter. He found her filling a recliner in the living room.

"I apologize for disturbing you in this time of grief, ma'am, but I'm investigating the death of your husband," Ed said.

"You ain't no gawddamn deputy," she said.

"No, ma'am, I'm not. I'm from the Mississippi Bureau of Investigation, down in Hattiesburg. I've been assigned to the case."

"From Hattiesburg?" She appeared momentarily impressed by that fact.

"Yes, ma'am." Ed decided to go with it. "Your husband

being a government official, the Bureau has taken extra-special interest in the circumstances of his sad and untimely demise."

"Fuck you," she said.

"Excuse me, ma'am?"

"I may be fat and White, but I ain't stupid."

"I apologize, Mrs. Fondle."

"So, they sent *you*."

"I'm a special detective, ma'am."

"Well, sit yo ass down."

The only other chair in the room was another recliner, not quite matching, a vinyl one, beside hers. It made an embarrassing noise as Ed sat on it. "Sorry," he said.

"Everybody makes that sound when they sit there," she said. "You know, you could stand to lose a little weight yo own self."

"Yes, ma'am. I apologize if I ask some of the same questions you've already answered," Ed said.

"Oh, that's awright," she said. She was younger than her husband, perhaps forty, but who could tell through the weight and rough life? She was slightly cockeyed. "You're actually nice," she said, "for a Negro. You sound educated. Are you educated?"

"Yes, ma'am. Tell me, do you know of anyone who would have wanted to hurt your husband?"

Fancel Fondle laughed softly. "Probably a whole mess of folks wanted him hurt, but not dead. He weren't well liked."

"I see."

"He thought being coroner made him somethin' special, and people around here didn't take to that. He weren't no real doctor, you know that?" She took an unwrapped mint from a bowl on the table by the arm of her chair and put it in her mouth. "But they called him doctor anyway."

"Was he a reverend?" Ed asked.

"I suppose you could say that. I don't know what makes somebuddy a preacher. He didn't go to no school for it. He did preach. He weren't no damn good at it. Always got the scriptures all wrong."

"Maybe he was good at comforting people," Ed said, because his mother always taught him to find something good and to say something nice.

"I wouldn't say that," Fancel Fondle said. "He was kinda an oaf. I think that's the word. He always said the wrong thing."

"Anybody hate him?"

"Nobody in particular, but plenty of 'em in general," she said, shaking her head. "He sho hated enough folks."

"Who did he hate?"

"He hated colored people," she said. "Sorry."

Ed shrugged.

"Lots of folks 'round here hate coloreds. He was just one of them."

"It doesn't sound like you liked your husband very much. Just why did you marry the man?"

"This is Money, Mississippi, Mister Detective. Leflore County, Mississippi. My husband weren't much to look at or talk to, but he had him a steady job. I didn't finish high school, I cain't sing a lick, and I don't look good with my clothes off. I was just tryin' to have a life. Mine."

He was sorry he'd asked the question, realized it was one he shouldn't have asked. "Give me a couple of names of people he hated."

"He hated Red Jetty," she said. "Oh, Red wouldn't have knowed it. Cad never hated him to his face. He was kinda scared of Red."

"Why did he hate him?" Ed asked.

"Because of Red's daddy."

"Red's daddy?"

Fancel Fondle studied Ed for a long moment. "Red Jetty's daddy quit the Klan way back when Cad's daddy, Philbert, was Grand Kleagle. Cad's daddy just hated that, called him a traitor and all sorts of unsavory names. Anyway, a bunch of folks walked out of the Klan with him. That's what really upset him, that he took a mess of folks with him. Some of that hate got passed."

"Why did Jetty's father walk out?" Ed asked.

"I don't know. Something about a killin'." She paused to regard Ed again. "I'm sorry to talk about this with you."

"It's okay, ma'am."

"Something about a ni—Black man gettin' kilt." She loaded a couple more pieces of candy into her mouth. "This is why I'm fat."

"Are you saying that your husband's father killed a man?"

"I don't know. Maybe. Yes."

"Do you think a lot of people knew he killed a man?" Ed asked.

"It was one of them secrets what everybody knows." She paused, pushed the candy bowl away from her. "Exceptin' for my cleaning woman, Sadie, you the first colored person ever been in this here house."

"Is that right?"

"You're nice."

"Was your husband a member of the Ku Klux Klan, Mrs. Fondle?"

She didn't answer.

"Can't hurt him now," Ed said.

"Yes." The woman looked ashamed.

"I'd better be going, ma'am. Thank you so much for your time."

"Cad wasn't real nice to anybody, colored or White," she said.

"Yes, ma'am."

"I don't guess that makes too much of a difference to you."

She shook her head.

"No, ma'am."

60

Damon Thruff read dossier after dossier, name after name. At first he was terribly careful to return a file precisely back into its place before selecting the next one. The first twenty or so were sequential, but now he was taking them willy-nilly from any drawer from any cabinet. And no longer was he bothering to return them, but rather many remained on the table, open to the air and light. What was most unsettling was that they all read so much alike, not something that one wouldn't expect, but the reality of it was nonetheless stunning. They were like zebras, he thought—not one had stripes just like any other, but who could tell one zebra from another? He found it all depressing, not that lynching could be anything but. However, the crime, the practice, the religion of it, was becoming more pernicious as he realized that the similarity of their deaths had caused these men and women to be at once erased and coalesced like one piece, like one body. They were all number and no number at all, many and one, a symptom, a sign.

Mama Z came into the room and set down a plastic tray with black tea and little cookies.

Damon looked at the woman and then at the dim light outside the window. "Is it dusk already?" he asked.

"Dawn," the old woman said.

"I've been at this all night?"

She hummed an affirmation.

"You did all of this?" Damon asked.

Mama Z poured the tea.

"Yes."

"It's incredible," he said.

"I have chronicled the work of the devil."

"The devil?"

"I don't believe in a god, Mr. Thruff. You can't sit here in this room, touch all of these folders, read all of these pages, and believe in a god. I do, however, and I'm certain you do too, believe in the devil."

"And hell?" Damon asked.

"And hell. This is hell, Mr. Thruff. Haven't you been watching? Babies are smarter than us. It seems they're always trying to kill themselves. That's why we have to watch them every second, so they don't swallow nickels or drink weed killer or eat Tylenol like candy. Then we get stupid and want to live."

"What's it like? Being over a hundred?"

"That's a stupid question," the old woman said.

"Sorry," Damon said.

"I didn't say it was a bad or unreasonable question."

There was a knock on the door.

"Probably Gertrude," Mama Z said.

Gertrude stood on the porch with Herberta Hind. Gertrude fumbled with her knock, at first too soft and then too hard. Hind made her nervous.

"This Mama Z," Hind said, "she's your grandmother?"

"Great-grandmother."

"I never had a great-grandmother. Well, of course I did, but I never met her. It's something, generations."

The door opened and they stepped into the house. Mama Z was not nervous. "And who have you brought with you?" she asked.

"Mama Z, this is Agent Hind from the FBI."

Hind shook the old woman's hand. "Special Agent Herberta Hind, from the Washington, DC, office."

"Oh my," Mama Z said, feigning being impressed. "Herberta Hind," she said the name to the air, as if looking for something. "I hope your parents didn't give you the nickname Herbie." She laughed.

Hind laughed politely. She showed no embarrassment but was markedly impressed by the quickness of the woman.

"Special Agent Hind is investigating those murders," Gertrude said.

"Is she now? I didn't know the FBI investigated murders," Mama Z said. "I thought such things were matters for local authorities."

"There might be some civil rights violations involved," Hind said.

"Whose civil rights?"

"I don't know yet."

"I ask because you have to have civil rights in order for the them to be violated." Mama Z let that hang in the air. "I'm sorry. Forgive my manners. We can sit in here. Gertie, be a dear and make us some tea and bring some cookies. Make sure the cat doesn't come in here and bother us."

Gertrude nodded.

"I actually like cats," Hind said.

"This one sheds like crazy," Mama Z said. "Your suit

would be a mess before you could say, 'Mississippi goddamn.'" She didn't quite sing the words.

"What is your last name, Mama Z?" Hind asked.

"Everybody just calls me Mama Z."

"But for my notes."

"Lynch. My name is Adelaide Lynch." To Gertrude, "Go get that tea, baby."

Gertrude left.

"Where does the Z come in?"

"I don't quite remember," the old woman said. "It's easier to spell than Omega." Mama Z looked Hind in the eye.

"How old are you?"

"One hundred and five."

"You look great. Moving around like this. Do you live alone?"

"Yes."

"That's amazing. What's your secret?"

"Venom."

"What?" Hind asked.

"It's what I call my nightly tea," Mama Z said, then, conspiratorially, she added, "I mix it with bourbon."

"I see."

They sat silently for a moment.

"I'm told you know about almost everything that goes on in these parts," Hind said. "I guess that comes with a century of life."

"I know a little."

"Do you know about the body of the Black man that turned up at three different murder scenes?"

"You are direct, aren't you?"

"There's really no other way to ask that," Hind said.

"I heard about it. Confusing. Confounding? Would that be the correct word? It all sounds kind of magical, doesn't it?" Mama Z opened the wooden box on the table and pulled out a cigar. "Would you like one?"

"No, thank you." Hind stared at the cigar and the woman.

"I know it's eccentric," the old woman said. "I've had one a day for the last seventy-five years. They might just be the secret of my longevity. Along with the bourbon. Who knows? Have you ever smoked one?"

"No, I've never thought to try."

"They're frightfully expensive, but worth it, I think. These are Cuban. I probably shouldn't tell you that."

Hind waved off her concern.

"I wouldn't want to put you in a compromising position," Mama Z said.

"What can you tell me about the Bryants?"

"Well, you know Carolyn Bryant was the woman who accused Emmett Till of saying things to her."

"Things she later recanted, I read," Hind said.

"You can't unfire a gun."

Hind nodded.

"What that woman did to that child might not be forgivable even by one of them Christians or their god."

"You're not a Christian?" Hind said as a question.

"Not forgiving enough. You?"

Gertrude brought out a tray with tea and crackers.

"Thank you," Mama Z said. "You can leave us to talk now. Okay, my dear, sweet great-grandbaby."

Gertrude left.

"I was asking after your religion," Mama Z said as she

poured the tea. "Are you a Christian?"

"I might be. I haven't decided," Hind said. "I'll make up my mind when I'm as wise as you."

"No one has ever called me ancient in a nicer way." Mama Z smiled.

"Did we get off on the wrong foot or something?" Hind asked.

"I don't think so. Why?"

"There seems to be a tension here, between us. Like you perhaps don't trust me. Do you trust me?"

Mama Z said nothing.

"Why not?" Hind asked.

"You're from the FBI."

"I'm also a Black woman," Hind said.

"So you see my problem."

"But I take it you don't have a problem with Agents Morgan and Jones."

"They're not FBI."

Hind sighed. "No, but they're MBI. It's all just letters, right?"

Mama Z looked at Hind for a couple of seconds, then called back into the house. "More hot water!"

"Is there reason for you to fear the FBI?"

"Is that rhetorical?"

"I suppose it is."

"My father was lynched."

"I'm sorry," Hind said.

"Is that an official apology from the United States government?"

"From a Black woman."

"Again," Mama Z said, "you see my problem. That's

194

practically nothing. I've heard nothing, and it sounds just like that."

"Don't you think there should be some of us in places like the FBI, CIA, Congress?" Hind said.

"No."

"Why not?"

"Bad company. I don't keep bad company."

61

The apartment house was nondescript insofar as it looked exactly like every other house on the block, a block that looked exactly like every other block in the neighborhood. Inside, the only distinguishing feature of apartment 3, upstairs to the right in the front of the building, was the yellow police tape stretched across the door and the red 8.5" x 11" green notice stapled to it. Moon let Davis step into the apartment first. Jim looked first at the light coming through the open blinds of the bay window on the street side, then around the room, recalling the crime scene photos.

"The body was over there, on the floor in front of the sofa," Moon said, pointing with an open hand.

Jim nodded.

"It was gruesome all right, but the weird thing was just how clean everything appeared to be. I mean, there's dust here now, but not so much then. And he'd been dead for over a week when he was discovered."

Jim nodded. He studied the dried black blood on the throw rug and wood floor. "Why did it take so long to find him?"

"Nobody liked him, I guess. As for the stench, everybody thought a rat had died in the walls somewhere."

"That makes sense," Jim said. "Your gut tell you anything?"

Moon shook his head. "It was just ugly. The way that barbed wire—and it was nasty, old, and rusty barbed wire—was wrapped around his neck, it cut almost all the way through. You know what kind of force that would take?"

"I take it you do?"

"The guys in the crime lab say that two men pulling on either side couldn't do it. What do you think of that?"

"I'm trying not to." Jim stepped over and looked in the refrigerator. "Three cheap beers and a bottle of mustard."

"The same as found."

"Gourmet."

"What's your gut tell you?" Moon asked.

"Not a damn thing."

"Where you going now?"

"Believe it or not, a place called the Acme Cadaver Company of Chicago. Want to come along? Actually, I'd like you to come. Your badge will be more impressive than my Mississippi shield."

"Yeah," Moon said. "I'm there."

62

Ed Morgan stood outside the home of the coroner's assistant, Dill. He knew him only as Dill. The man lived with his mother, whom everyone referred to always with her first and last names, Mavis Dill. The yard of the house was overgrown, shabby, and in need of water. There were several concrete benches in front of the house, more that seemed necessary or useful, one broken into a V. The midseventies Buick Riviera sat in the drive, close to the garage door, the right rear tire flat for some time. The trunk and rear bumper were covered with stickers: If Guns are Outlawed then Only Outlaws Will Have Guns; There Would Be No First Amendment if there was No Second Amendment; Defend America, Vote Republican; His Pain, Your Gain; When the Trumpet Sounds, I'm Outta Here; WHTE AM Radio; TRUMP for Precedent; My Other Car is Also a Buick. Behind the Riviera was a rusted-out midseventies Datsun B210.

Ed knocked.

Dill came to the door. He did not appear surprised to see the detective. "Which one are you?"

"The Black one," Ed said.

Dill let out a snorting laugh. He stepped back to allow Ed to enter. "I heard y'all was funny," he said.

They sat in what Dill called the front room, both on the sofa. Ed was beginning to get used to sitting beside the person he was interviewing. "Is your mother here? Seems everybody talks about her."

"Yeah, they do. She's asleep. Mavis Dill." He said her name and let it hang in the air.

"Why is she so well known?"

"I guess because she seems to know everybody's business. Whether it's her business or not. She's the town gossip."

"And everybody calls you just Dill. Do you have a first name?"

Dill nodded, sheepishly. "It's Pick. My middle name is Leon."

"Pick L. Dill? Okay, I see."

Dill chuckled slightly. "School was tough."

"I'll bet." Ed looked out the window. "Tell me about your boss."

"He's dead."

"Before that."

"Before that I wished he was dead. But I didn't kill him. He was a piece of human shit, but I didn't kill him." Dill was unblinking.

"What didn't you like about him?" Ed asked.

"There was nothing to like about him. He was an uneducated, faux-religious, bigoted fool who fell into the office of coroner and nested there. He assigned causes of death on a whim, never based on science. He was a criminal."

"Tell me."

"Well, he's dead now, it's not like you can arrest him, right?"

"I might try," Ed said.

Dill laughed.

"Between you and me, I don't even care who killed him.

I just want to figure this mess out. It's sort of my job."

"You want some coffee? All I got is instant." Dill was fidgety now.

"No coffee, thanks. Something wrong?" Ed asked.

"No."

"Give me an example of one of Fondle's crimes."

"Here's the thing." Dill leaned forward. "I'm worried about implicating myself. I mean, I did do what he told me to do. I didn't want to lose my job."

Ed offered what he hoped was a reassuring smile. "Like I said, you could have killed Fondle yourself and I wouldn't care. I'm just trying to figure out what's going on. Disappearing bodies is a new thing."

"You got that right." Dill took a long, deep breath. "About four years ago, a deputy called in to report a dead body in back of the old icehouse. It's all abandoned now. Somebody tried to turn it into a dance hall some time back, but this is Money, Mississippi. No dancin'."

"No?"

"You know why Baptists don't fuck standin' up?" Dill asked.

"Tell me."

"They're afraid somebody might think they're dancin'." Ed nodded.

"Anyway, this Black man was dead in a dumpster, been shot in the back of his head. Thirty-eight or maybe a forty-five. Big hole." Dill put his hand on the nape of his neck to show. "The deputy, he's gone now, Jetty fired him, I think. He seemed real nervouslike. He talked to Fondle for a long time. And do you know what Fondle did?"

Ed shook his head.

"He typed *suicide* on the cause of death line. Just like that! Who shoots himself in the back of the head in a dumpster?"

"What was this deputy's name?" Ed asked.

"I should have said something at the time. But who would I have said it to?"

"The deputy's name?"

"Mustard or Ketchum? I remember it reminded me of a condiment. Mayo, that was it. Mayo. Don't remember his first name. If I ever knew it."

"He still around?"

"Gone for a long time."

"The victim, what was his name?"

"Garth Johnson. I remember because I thought, *Garth, that sounds like a White name*, even though I know there ain't such things as White and Black names, but you know what I mean."

"I guess."

"Like if a White guy had the name LaMarcus, you'd remember that, right?"

"I guess I would. Who identified the body?"

"We all knew him. He worked at the gas station. Lived in the Bottom, of course."

"Did he have any family? Anybody come in to officially identify him?"

Dill shook his head. "If he had family, I didn't know about them."

Ed loosened his tie. He was angry.

"I'm sure that wasn't the only time Fondle did something like that."

"Other than you, who do you think might have wanted to kill Fondle?"

"Everybody, I guess."

"How did he stay in office?" Ed asked.

"It's hard to lose if you're the only name on the ballot."

"Do you know anyone who would have wanted Wheat Bryant or Junior Junior Milam dead?"

"They weren't no prizes, but no."

"Thank you, Mr. Dill."

"You know I only came back to this shithole town to take care of my mother."

Ed nodded.

63

Gertrude left before Special Agent Hind and Mama Z concluded their meeting. She drove Mama Z's pickup because she had left her car in town to ride with the FBI woman. She drove south to the Bluegum. Though it was closed, she pressed a code into the keypad on the front door and entered. She walked through the dining room, then the kitchen, and then into a large well-lit room. Bright sun shone through an array of skylights. The walls were stark white, windowless, and the floor was covered with mats or varying thicknesses and colors. On the mats some twenty men and women dressed in black gis practiced martial arts. Two women sparred with long spears, heads swiveling wildly as they dodged the pointed weapons. Three hooded men practiced kicking ropecovered posts. Another man practiced disappearing. Gertrude knew this only because she had witnessed one of them fade into the shadows another day. Chester broke brick after brick with his forehead off in a far corner. Gertrude inhaled the sweat-filled air, smiled.

"Who let the White girl in?" a small woman asked.

"All right now," Gertrude said. "Are we looking sharp?"

"Sharper than frog's hair."

A tall man walked over to Gertrude. He scratched his beard and said, "If it isn't Dixie and Pixie."

The shorter woman said, "You know I can kick your ass."

"I wish she was joking," the man said to Gertrude. "So, are we making a splash out there?"

"Yes."

64

Damon Thruff wrote with a number 3 pencil sharpened with his Phi Beta Kappa penknife again and again. He scratched out names on a yellow legal pad. He scratched and scratched:

Bill Gilmer
Shedrick Thompson
Ed Lang
John Henry James
Charles Wright
Henry Scott
Arthur Young
George Dorsey
Mae Dorsey
Dorothy Malcom
Eugene Hamilton
Paul Booker
James Jordan
W. W. Watt
Lemuel Walters
George Holden
Will Wilkins

John Ruffin
Henry Ruffin
Eliza Woods
Anderson Gauss
Huie Conorly
Dago Pete
Laura Nelson
William Fambro
Isadore Banks
unknown male
Tony Champion
Michael Kelly
Andrew Ford
Henry Hinson
unknown male
Charles Willis
William Rawls
Alfred Daniels
Manny Price
Robert Scruggs
Jumbo Clark
Jack Long
Henry White
unknown male
Rev. Josh Baskins
Bert Dennis
Andrew McHenry
Stella Young
Abraham Wilson
George Buddington
Albert Martin

unknown male
unknown female
Richard Puryear
John Campbell
John Taylor
Ernest Green
Charles Lang
Ed Johnson
Andrew Clark
Alma Major
Maggie House
Nevlin Porter
Johnson Spencer
James Clark
Levi Harrington
Jack Minho
Elbert Williams
Will Brown
Wyatt Outlaw
John Stephens
Perry McChristian
Felix Williams
unknown male
Bartley James
John Campbell
Eugene Williams
Robert Robinson
Bob Ashley
Cleo Wright
Lemuel Walters
Benny Richards

Lloyd Clay
Henry Prince
Jim Waters
Frank Livingston
William Miller
Berry Washington
James Chaney
James Jordon
George Armwood
Sydney Randolph
George Taylor
James Carter
Emmett Divers
Smiles Estes
Dick Lundy
Jennie Steers
unknown male
16 adult men
John Peterson
Frank Morris
James Byrd Jr.
Albert Young
James Reeb
Frazier Baker
James Scott
Joseph Smith
Francis McIntosh
George White
Zachariah Walker
Tom Moss
unknown male

unknown male
Calvin McDowell
Elias Clayton
Elmer Jackson
Isaac McGhie
Will Stewart
John Holmes
Thurmond Thomas
Elijah Lovejoy
Amos Miller
Jim Taylor
Elwood Higginbotham
Wade Thomas
Nelson Patton
David Jones
Ephraim Grizzard
Samuel Smith
11 adult men
Angelo Albano
Ficarotta Villarosa
Lorenzo Saladino
Arena Salvatore
Giuseppe Venturella
Francesco DiFatta
Giuseppe DiFatta
Giovanni Cerami
Rosario Fiducia
Sanford Lewis
unknown male
Miles Phifer
Will Temple

Robert Crosby
John Heath
Matthew Williams
David Walker
David Walker's wife
David Walker's 4 children
George Grant
Raymond Gunn
Henry Lowry
Sam Hose
Jan Hartfield
Bunk Richardson
Lee Heflin
Mrs. Wise
Dave Tillis
George Hughes
William Shorter
Joseph Dye
Orion Anderson
H. Bromley
Allie Thompson
Charles Craven

"Well, the fuzz is gone," Mama Z said as she entered the records room. She observed the open dossiers and Thruff's disheveled appearance.

Damon looked up.

"The FBI lady," Mama Z said. She studied Damon's red eyes and then the pages in front of him again. "What are you doing?"

"I'm writing their names by hand."

Damon sharpened his pencil over a sheet of white paper.

Mama Z pulled the pad toward her and looked at the list. "Why are you doing this?" she asked.

"When I write the names they become real, not just statistics. When I write the names they become real again. It's almost like they get a few more seconds here. Do you know what I mean? I would never be able to make up this many names. The names have to be real. They have to be real. Don't they?"

Mama Z put her hand against the side of Damon face.

"Why pencil?"

"When I'm done, I'm going to erase every name, set them free."

"Carry on, child," the old woman said.

Benjamin Thompson
John Parker
Joseph McCoy
Magruder Fletcher
Adam
Abraham Smith
Joe Coe
Emmett Till
Anthony Crawford
Leo Jew Foo
Leo Tim Kwong
Hung Qwan Chuen
Tom He Yew
Charles Wright
Claude Neal
Dick Rowland

Mar Tse Choy
Leo Lung Siang
Yip Ah Marn
Leo Lung Hor
Leo Ah Tsun
Leans Ding
Eli Persons
Fred Rochelle
Henry Smith
Jim McIlherron
Yuen Chin Sing
Hsu Ah Tseng
Chun Quan Sing
Jesse Washington
John Carter
July Perry
Leo Frank
Mary Turner
Rueben Stacey
Sam Carter
Slab Pitts
Thomas Shipp
Willie Earle
Will James Howard
Ah Wang
Dr. Chee Long Teng
Chang Wan
Ah Long
Matthew Shepard
Wan Foo
Day Kee

Ah Waa
Ho Hing
Lo Hey
An Won
Wing Chee
Wong Chin
Charles Mack Parker
unknown male
Michael Donald
Johnny Burrows
Ah Cut
Wa Sin Quai
2 adult men
unknown male
unknown female
James Byrd
Jimmy Actchison
Willie McCoy
Emantic Fitzgerald Bradford Jr.
D'ettrick Griffin
Jemel Roberson
DeAndre Ballard
Botham Shem Jean
Antwon Rose Jr.
Robert Lawrence White
Anthony Lamar Smith
Ramarley Graham
Manuel Loggins Jr.
Wendell Allen
Trayvon Martin
Kendrec McDade

Larry Jackson Jr.
Jonathan Ferrell
Jordan Baker
Victor White III
Dontre Hamilton
Eric Garner
John Crawford III
Michael Brown
Ezell Ford
Dante Parker
Kajieme Powell
Laquan McDonald
Akai Gurley
Tamir Rice
Rumain Brisbon
Jerame Reid
Charly Keunang
Tony Robinson
Walter Scott
Freddie Gray
Brendon Glenn
Samuel DuBose
Christian Taylor
Jamar Clark
Mario Woods
Quintonio LaGrier
Gregory Gunn
Leo Sun Tsung
Leo Kow Boot
Yii See Yen
Leo Dye Bah

Choo Bah Quot
Sai Bun Ning
Leo Lung Hong
Leo Chih Ming
Liang Tsun Bong
Husband Ah Cheong
Lor Han Lung
Ho Ah Nii
Leo Tse Wing
Akiel Denkins
Alton Sterling
Philando Castile
Terrence Sterling
Terence Crutcher
Keith Scott
Alfred Olango
Jordan Edwards
Stephon Clark
Danny Ray Thomas
DeJuan Guillory
Patrick Harmon
Jonathan Hart
Maurice Granton

65

The Acme Cadaver Company of Chicago was located just north of Midway Airport, a pancake of a building tucked in between a car rental place and a sad-looking grocery market. A lone woman sat at the lone desk marked Reception in the very large and bare front hall. The woman, well past being young but short of middle age, heavily tattooed and a bit weathered, half-smiled at them. Her short bob of blonde hair hovered above her text-riddled neck. Despite the cold air she wore a thin white tank top. She didn't appear surprised to see them, but neither did she seem much like a receptionist. Jim stood in front of her desk and looked around at the empty walls.

The woman stared at him.

"No 'May I help you?' or 'Welcome to Acme Cadaver Company'?" Jim said.

"Welcome to Acme Cadaver Supply of Chicago. You kill 'em, we chill 'em. May I help you?"

"We'd like to speak to someone in records or accounting."

"You stab 'em, we slab 'em."

"I'm Special Detective Davis, and this is Detective Moon." Jim did not want to say Mississippi.

"You slay 'em, we lay 'em."

"Okay, I apologize," Jim said.

"Ma'am, we would like to speak to the manager," Moon said.

"So would I," she said. "I come here every morning, sit at this desk, read three romance novels, and then I go home. My check is waiting on the desk for me every other Friday."

"No one ever comes out here?" Moon asked.

"As far as I know they're all dead back there. And I ain't going back there to find out. You understand."

The men nodded.

"How do we get back there?" Jim asked.

The woman pointed to a far door. "I'm assuming that's the door to the back. It *is* the only door. You're welcome to try it."

"Thank you," Jim said.

Their steps weren't so loud against the linoleum tiles, but they echoed crazily. Jim looked back to see that the woman had returned to her book. "Did you read the tattoo on her neck?" Jim asked.

"I couldn't make it out."

"*Break here in case of emergency.*"

"You're shittin' me."

"Plain as fucking day."

"I don't even get it," Moon said.

"What's to get? She be crazy."

Jim tried the knob, but the door was locked. He gave a good cop knock and listened. Nothing. He knocked harder, an urgent police knock. It echoed worse than their footsteps.

Finally the door cracked open an inch. A short man peered at them through the small space. "What do you want?" He had an accent, perhaps Hispanic.

"We'd like to talk to the manager," Jim said.

"Did you knock on this door? Nobody ever knocks on this door. I've worked here fifteen years and nobody ever knocked on this door." The man appeared shaken.

"Well, we just did," Moon said. "Now, let us in and take us to the manager before I shoot you."

The door swung open fully.

The warehouse was freezing. Not much could have prepared Jimmy Moon for what they saw. The lights were bright enough to be slightly blinding, even though they hadn't come into the room from the dark. It was like a cleaner's facility, except instead of shirts, blouses, and jackets, corpses, women and men, slid by on suspended rails. Farther away, through the center of the room, naked cadavers glided along, head to toe, on a conveyer belt. The music of the Jackson Five blared. A-B-C. One two three. Chicago Bears and Bulls banners hung from the ceiling some twenty feet above them. Jim looked at Moon, tossed him a sidelong glance. The detective scratched his chin and shrugged. The music changed to Marvin Gaye. What was going on?

"What's your name?" Jim asked the small man.

"Ditka."

"Like Mike Ditka?" Moon asked.

"No relation," the man said.

"So, why the Spanish accent?"

"It's fun."

"Where's the manager?" Moon asked.

Ditka pointed beyond the conveyer to an office at the top of a set of stairs.

"What do you do here?" Jim asked.

Ditka did not appear to want to answer.

"Mr. Ditka?"

"Okay, I'm a nipple scrubber." When the detectives looked at him, he said, "You can't send these bodies out to medical schools all dirty."

"That's all you do, wash nipples?" Moon asked.

"First of all, I scrub nipples. I also wash, not scrub, wash the genitalia."

"You're a ball washer?" Jim asked.

"Like I said, the office is up there."

The rickety stairs were slightly more unnerving than the stroll through the parade of corpses. Jim, naturally a bit afraid of heights, tried not to look down as the structure swayed and rattled. The inside of the office was plastered, walls and ceiling, with centerfold pictures of naked women. The only person inside was a tall, old, androgynous-looking person wearing powder-blue coveralls, who turned to face them as they entered. In contrast to the rest of the floor, this room was overheated.

"Who are you and what do you want?"

"I'm Special Detective Davis, and this is Detective Moon."

"So?"

"What is your name, sir?"

"Chris Toms. I'm the manager of this facility. I've been working here since it opened in seventy-five." Chris Toms smiled. "Nineteen seventy-five."

"Thanks for clearing that up."

"I am also the owner."

Jim looked down at the floor below and thought he saw a man kick a skull. He looked again and realized he was seeing two men playing soccer with a head. "What the fuck? Moon, look."

Moon did. Both men turned to Toms.

"Hey, the guy's dead," Toms said.

"Where's the rest of him?" Moon asked.

"I don't know. Pittsburgh, maybe. Some of him, anyway. We send complete cadavers and body parts all over the country. That's our business."

"How does this business work, exactly?" Jim asked.

"People die every day—you know that, right? And a lot of them don't have nobody. Nobody claims them, so we do. We clean them up and send them to labs and schools all over. In a way, we're saving lives."

"Okay, I get that," Jim said. "Since nobody seems to care about them, do you keep less than close tabs on your, your wares?"

"Wares?" Toms felt the word in his mouth. "I like that."

"Do you keep good records? If I told you that one of your bodies was missing, say a Gerald Mister, would you have any record of where that body was sent and when?"

"First of all, they ain't my bodies."

"Okay," Jim said.

"Like I said, these folks are all dead."

Moon leaned forward to stare down at the floor. "Are they playing catch with an eyeball?"

"Hey, again, they're dead. Ain't nobody cared about them when they was alive, and sure as hell nobody cares about them now that they're—" Toms paused for effect. "Dead. Except apparently for you two."

"Don't you find that a bit sacrilegious?" Jim asked.

"They're dead! Dead. Dead. Dead. Sacrilegious? Ain't no souls down there, just arms and legs, hands, heads and elbows, tongues, testicles and nipples, ears and eyeballs.

You need an eyeball, we ship you a fucking eyeball. It don't come with a nameplate or a testimonial. You just get an eyeball."

"Do you have any records at all?"

"I know where to pick up dead bodies. I know how to store dead bodies. I know how to pack dead bodies, and I know who to send dead bodies to. I know how to pay my live people, and I know how to pay my goddamn taxes. Tell me what you want, cause nobody here is breaking the law."

"Have you ever had any shipments disappear?" Jim asked. "Either on the way to you or on the way to a destination."

Toms looked out the window. "You know, they're considered hazardous waste. I'm not required to keep track of their identities, but I need to account for each and every one of them. Thing is, nobody checks up on us. No one ever has. There ain't no office for that. There ain't no state cadaver control."

"What are you trying to say, Mis—" Jim caught himself, not knowing whether Mister or Ms. "Sir?"

"You won't make trouble for me?"

"No, sir."

"We had a truck go missing about two months ago. We found the cab, but not the trailer."

"In the trailer?" Moon asked.

"Twenty-one cadavers."

"Where did they find the truck?" Jim asked.

"South of St. Louis."

"The driver?" Jim had his notepad out. "Where is he?"

"Nobody knows. He had a funny name. Charles Hobbit or someshit." Toms went to his files and dug around, pulled out a folder. "Here he is. Chester Hobsinger. I was close. Don't know what happened to him. Weird dude."

"How so?" Moon asked.

"I don't know. Seemed suspicious. Took the job and drove off in my truck. Last time I saw him. Here's a photocopy of his license."

"I can take this copy?" Jim asked.

"I don't need it. Weird dude. Guys on the floor called him Wegro."

Jim cocked his head.

"You know, a White dude who wants to be Black."

66

Daryl Ho hung up the phone and looked across the desks at his partner.

"Something?" Chi asked.

"Sort of. Remember our dead Asian?"

Chi stared at him.

"M. E. lost him."

"What do you mean?"

"Tech put him in a drawer and then the drawer was empty," Ho said. "They looked in all the drawers. *Gē men* be gone."

"Well, let's go look at the empty box," Chi said.

When Chi and Ho arrived at the medical examiner's building news crews were already there. They stretched out cables, fussed with camera's, did sound checks, but mostly drank coffee and yawned.

"Is it true that OCPD has lost a body?" a woman asked Ho, shoving a microphone at him.

"OCPD didn't lose anything or anybody." Then, thinking better of speaking at all, he said, "No comment."

"Does this involve the MacDonald murder?"

"No comment."

Chi managed to slide around the woman and rejoin Ho.

"How did everybody find out so fast?"

"This is Southern California," a woman on camera said. "Beats a freeway car chase, right?"

Chi reached back and dragged Ho by the arm away from the woman with the microphone.

Once inside they wondered why they had bothered making the trip. The drawer was now filled with someone else, and the staff were busy cutting up other folks. A morgue was no place for a crime scene.

Chen asked to see the surveillance camera playback, but the guy at the desk just laughed. "This is the fucking morgue, buddy," he said. "What are we going to surveil? Ghosts?"

Ho's phone buzzed. "This is Ho."

"Detective Ho, I'm Special Agent Herberta Hind of the FBI."

67

Daniel Moon fell in behind the wheel of the department-issue Ford Taurus and looked over at Jim. "What now?"

"Well, I've got Mr. Hobsinger's address right here."

Moon cranked the engine. "What is it?"

The address was on the South Side. The two men made some small talk about being cops and hating being cops and not knowing anything but being cops but then fell into normal silence. They parked and stood in front of the building. It sat on a corner in a neighborhood that had begun to gentrify. Jim Davis hated that word because it seemed to suggest that something better was coming, or at least that something bad was leaving.

"Is there an apartment number on that license?" Moon asked.

"No."

"I think this is just a house."

They stepped onto the porch. Moon knocked and rang the bell. Davis tried to look through the windows and past the curtains.

"Nobody's home," Moon said.

"Or he's dead in there," Jim said. "He's been missing. Tied to a murder case. I'd call that probable cause."

"I don't know. What if he's in there banging his old lady?"

Jim kicked open the door.

"What the fuck?" Moon sad.

"MBI!" Jim shouted as they walked in. "That's some crazy shit to yell out. MBI! Fucking ridiculous."

"The air is stale. There's nobody here," Moon said. "But we're in here now, so let's look around."

They checked the rooms and found no one. Moon scanned a bookcase. Jim pushed around the papers on a desk.

"This guy has a lot of books. Lots of history. Books on trains. Here are some judo and karate books." He picked up a big martial arts picture book. "With my name you'd think I'd know some of this shit."

"I didn't say that," Jim said.

"Check this out." Moon lifted a sheathed sword from its display stand. He pulled the blade out a few inches and whistled.

"Is that a real sword?" Jim asked.

"It's a real katana."

Jim walked back to the desk, which was beneath a large window that overlooked the backyard, where fallen branches had collected on the dead lawn. He poked through the papers. Grocery store receipts, bills. He grunted.

"Find something?" Moon asked.

"A map of Mississippi."

"Fuck me."

"And get this: one place is circled—the town of Money."

"What's that written in the corner up there?" Moon pointed.

Jim studied the scrawl.

68

Ho put the phone to his chest and turned to Chi. "Fed on the phone." Back to his ear, "What can I do for you, Special Agent?"

"I see on the news here that you have lost a body," Hind said.

"A body was lost, anyway," he said, a bit defensively.

"We lost a body here in Mississippi also. We got it back, but it was lost. Twice, in fact, lost."

"Okay. You're telling me this because?"

"The body we found was next to another body."

"Go on."

"Was there any mutilation at your scene?" she asked.

"Only if you count severed testicles."

"Did your lab people manage to collect any DNA?"

"I don't know."

"All right. I'm going to have the M. E. here in Mississippi I'm working with contact your lab. Oh, and Detective Ho, know that body will resurface. You will see your body again. Call me when it does."

"What are you trying to tell me?" Ho asked.

"Call me when it does."

"Yes, ma'am."

"You have my number now. Herberta Hind."

"Yes, ma'am."

Ho put the phone in his pocket.

"What was that all about?"

"You got me. Some crazy woman says she's FBI. She kinda creeped me out. Said our body will be back. Like that: 'You'll see your body again.'"

69

Ed Morgan felt cramped in the Bureau car on his way to Hattiesburg. After his interviews he knew little more than he did before, except that he now knew he hated the White people of Mississippi. *Hate* was actually too strong a word, he told himself. As much as his profession had led him to believe there was no god, he had been raised to be a good Christian. So no, he didn't hate them. But he was actively and intensely indifferent. Then again, he caught himself. Even in Money, Mississippi, not all of the White people were the same. He laughed. But enough of them were the same.

He parked in the MBI garage and walked up the five flights of stairs to the office he shared with Jim and now also with Herberta Hind. Hind hastily put out her cigarette when he entered.

"Sorry," she said, fanning the smoke.

"I don't mind. Ever since I quit I kind of like the smell," he said.

"I still smoke when I'm nervous," Hind said. She pulled down a slat of the blinds for a better look out the window.

Ed sat behind his desk. "What's got you so nervous?"

Hind looked at him for a couple of seconds and said, "Mama Z. Mama Z makes me nervous."

"Oh yeah?"

"There's something going on. I get that she doesn't trust me because I'm FBI. Hell, I don't trust FBI agents. But there's something else. It was like she was trying to tell me something. Or was expecting me to know something."

"She's over a hundred years old," Ed said.

"So?"

"She's seen a lot. It might be hard for folks like us to read her. There are a lot of wrinkles there."

Hind considered this.

"Think about it. She's got sixty years on us. Her father was lynched. She lives in Money, Mississippi."

"Yeah, okay." Hind absently put another cigarette in her mouth, then pulled it out and looked at Ed.

"Go ahead. I won't tell. In fact, let me have one."

Hind tossed him the pack, then the lighter. Ed lit up.

"That old lady is up to something. I can feel it. Hell, I know it."

"Whatever it is, she's not running around killing these racist peckerwoods, and that's our job, strange as it sounds. To catch the killer of killers."

"That's our job," she repeated. "Have you heard from Jim?"

"Just a text. Said he'd call later."

"Let's call him now."

Jim was sitting in O'Hare, at a bar, when his phone buzzed. He answered.

"Hey, Jimmy," Ed said.

"Partner."

"I'm here too," Hind said.

"Are you smoking?" Jim asked.

Ed instinctively put the cigarette behind his back. "No. Why?"

"You guys sound like you're smoking."

Hind mouthed the word *spooky*.

"Have you two turned up anything?" Jim asked.

"Not much," Ed said.

"No," from Hind.

"Well aside from discovering that there is such a place as a cadaver factory, I have a name for us. One Chester Hobsinger was driving a truck that was hijacked a few months ago. The truck turned up, but the trailer full of dead folks did not."

"Hobsinger?" Hind asked.

"Missing. I went to his house. It's a nice place. I found a map of Mississippi there. Can you believe that? If you can, then you won't believe this: the town of Money was circled with a marker."

Ed whistled.

"Anything else?" Hind asked.

"The words *blue gun* were scribbled on the map. I think it's *blue gun*. It could be *glue gun* for all I know. Anyway, I have a photocopy of his driver's license."

"Send me a picture of it and I'll run it through the system," Hind said. "Anything else?"

"That's pretty much it."

70

"It's fucking Sunday and we're driving on the fucking Sixty to fucking Corona. It's not even in fucking Orange County. Hell, it's not even in fucking LA County."

"How many times you gonna say *fucking*?" Ho asked his partner. "It's Riverside County."

"Fucking Riverside County."

"Captain says we need to see a scene, we go see a scene."

"A fucking scene. Tell me, why are we cops? We're competent guys. I'm good looking. We could be doing anything, making money. Hell, we would even make good criminals."

"You wouldn't last a day as a criminal," Ho said.

"Why's that?"

"You're not smart enough."

"Yeah, but you have to admit I'm good looking."

Ho parked the car on packed red ground in front of a tavern. There were three Riverside County Sheriff's rigs parked and two Corona city police cars. There was a saddled horse tied to a hitching post just outside the wooden deck.

"Where the hell are we?" Chi asked.

They showed their identification to the wall of a Corona cop at the door and walked into the bar. All the lights were turned on. There were a couple of boxes of doughnuts on a table just inside.

Chi grabbed a fritter. Ho looked at him. "What? I like fritters. You don't see them every day. I'm hungry."

"You won't be for long," a deputy sheriff said. "You the guys from Orange County?"

"Ho."

"Chi."

"Minh. Riverside Sheriff's Department." The woman shook their hands. "Can you spell grisly?"

"What you got?" Ho asked.

She led the way through the bar and into the office, where she stepped aside so they could see.

Chi took a bite of fritter. "Oh, this is some fucked-up shit."

The body of a White man hung from a rafter, his face twisted, his tongue out, his crotch and thighs covered in blood.

"Somebody chopped off his nuts," Minh said.

"It doesn't sound so pretty when you say it," Chi said.

"Might have been this guy." Minh pulled back a sheet to reveal the body of a dead Asian man. He clutched something bloody in his fist.

"We've seen him before," Ho said.

"What the hell?" Chi said.

"That's why we're here," Ho said to Chi. "That's the same guy, right?"

Chi nodded. "I'm pretty sure."

"She said this would happen," Ho said.

"What?" Chi asked.

"That FBI agent. She said we would see him again."

"What the fuck is going on?" Chi walked around the

body, studied the testicles in the man's hand. "It's the same fucking dude."

"I need to make a call," Ho said and stepped away.

"What is it?" Deputy Minh asked. "You know this man?"

"You might say that," Chi said. "He was at a murder scene we processed two days ago."

"And now somebody's killed him," she said.

"No, not exactly. He was dead then too." He looked at her and then at the hanging man. "Dead Asian was at another murder, dead like I said, holding another dead man's testicles in his hand. His body disappeared from the M. E.'s lab."

"And he's here?"

"Tell me about this guy." He nodded toward the hanging man. Minh looked at her notepad.

"His name is Jesse Mendel. He's part owner of this place and manages it. His partner is in the hospital."

Chi questioned her with his eyes.

"Unrelated. He's in there for some kind of surgery." Minh went on. "The two bodies were discovered by Becky Wilmer. She tends bar here. They open at ten. She got here late, ten twenty. She's sitting outside in my rig. Pretty shaken up."

"I can imagine. Did she claim to know the Asian man?"

"Said she never saw him before."

"Mendel married?" Chi asked.

"Divorced. I think there was something between this guy and the bartender. Just saying."

"You think she had anything to do with this?"

Minh shook her head. "How's that fritter?"

"Kind of losing interest in it."

71

Ho to Hind: "What the hell is going on?"

72

Damon Thruff sat in a folding director's chair on the wooden deck behind Mama Z's house. Mama Z sat beside him in a bentwood rocker. Damon took a deep breath and stared off into the trees.

Mama Z snipped the ends of two cigars and handed one to Damon. Damon held it between his fingers and stared at it.

"You don't have to smoke it," the old woman said. "If you simply hold it I'll feel like I'm not smoking alone."

"Okay." Damon fumbled with the cigar, put it between his lips, took it out, and looked at the label. "Are these Cubans?"

"They are."

"Mama Z, may I ask you a question?"

"Of course."

"Why am I here?"

"Gertrude wanted you here. She trusts you. She says you're smart."

"All right, but that doesn't answer the question."

"She thinks you can chronicle this, have it make sense for everyone else." She blew smoke away from the man.

"Chronicle what?"

"You'll find out." She pulled on her cigar and made it

glow. "In good time, my young brother. We all figuring this out as we go."

"I wish I had some idea what you're talking about."

They sat in silence for a couple of minutes. "The records, that's really something. I don't think I'll ever be the same. Writing down all those names. It was too much."

"No, it wasn't. It isn't. Too much is coming."

"There must be six thousand dossiers in there. How did you do that? The amount of work."

"Seven thousand and six," Mama Z said. "And it wasn't work. Every one of them has a name."

"There are many unknown males. Those were hard to write down just like the names." Damon closed his eyes tight for a second.

"Unknown Male is a name," the old woman said. "In a way, it's more of a name than any of the others. A little more than life was taken from them."

"In all of those files I read, not one person had to pay. Not one."

"One would like to think that payment is rendered on judgment day."

"You don't believe that."

"Even if I believed there was a god I wouldn't believe that. Less than 1 percent of lynchers were ever convicted of a crime. Only a fraction of those ever served a sentence. Teddy Roosevelt claimed the main cause of lynching was Black men raping White women. You know what? That didn't happen."

"Why do you think White people are so afraid of that?"

"Who knows. Sexual inadequacy, maybe. An amplification of their own desire to rape, which they did."

Mama Z puffed out smoke. "But I think rape was just an excuse."

"You think Whites are just afraid of Black men?"

"I think it's sport."

73

Sheriff Red Jetty sat in a booth in the back of the Dinah. He was tracing the yellow lines in the red Formica tabletop when he glanced up to see two of his deputies approaching. He dipped two cold fries into his puddle of ketchup and ate them. The men fell into the booth seat across from him.

"What now?" Jetty asked. "Your head cold, Brady?"

Braden Brady removed his hat.

"Everybody's talkin' about how that nigger detective been all over town talkin' to folks," Delroy Digby said. "Interviewin' them like."

"He's doin' his job," Jetty said. "More than I can say about some folks."

"What's eatin' you, Sheriff ?" Braden asked.

"I don't know." The sheriff signaled to Dixie with his mug to bring more coffee. "I just feel something in the air. I don't know what."

"Like what?" Digby asked.

"I just said I don't know."

"I heard a rumor that that detective put the moves on Reverend Fondle's old lady," Digby said.

"Shut up, Digby," Jetty said.

"My daddy told me that in the old days, a rumor like that would be enough to string a darkie up," Brady said.

Dixie poured the sheriff another cup of coffee.

"Hey, Dixie," Digby said.

"Deputy." Dixie nodded. "You boys want anything?"

"Just coffee for me," Digby said.

"Chili," Braden said. "And a Diet Coke."

"Comin' up."

When Dixie was away, Jetty said, "Your pappy didn't have sense enough to pour piss out of a boot with the directions wrote on the heel."

"Don't you—"

"Hush up, Brady. You hate that man 'cause he beat yo ass with a razor strap."

Brady said nothing.

"Still, are we just lettin' them niggers take over?" Braden looked back at Dixie. "I heard tell that Dixie has got a drop in her."

"We all got a drop in us, you stupid peckerwood. And take over what? Money, Mississippi? Who the fuck wants Money, Mississippi? Who the fuck wants Missi-fuckin'-ssippi?"

"Lordy, Sheriff, what's wrong?"

"You haven't heard?" Jetty asked.

"Heard what?" from Digby.

"In the dog-shit town of Hernando, Mississippi, maybe the only place anyone would want be in less Money, they found six dead White people and one dead old Black man."

"I ain't heard," Brady said.

"Six dead White men with their fuckin' balls cut off."

"What the fuck?" Brady said.

"All strangled. In a fuckin' locked room."

"Did the nigger kill all of them?" Brady asked.

"Hell, man, I don't know. And then I guess he killed himself. What I do know is that the world has become six gallons of shit in a one-gallon bucket. I don't understand fuck, and I don't like it." Jetty looked at his deputies and shook his head like he was disappointed.

"What?" Brady asked.

Jetty stood, grabbed his hat. "See you back at the station."

Gertrude was on the phone by the register. She put her hand over the mouthpiece and nodded a goodbye to the sheriff as he left.

He nodded back at her. "See you, Dixie."

When he was out the door, she stole a glance back at the deputies and then spoke into the phone. "Something's wrong. I just overheard Jetty talking. Something happened in Hernando. I don't know what. But find out and get back to me and Mama Z."

74

In Hattiesburg, Helvetica Quip, Herberta Hind, Ed Morgan, and Jim Davis sat at a table in the commissary of the MBI. All the other tables were empty. It was after six, and very few people ever dined there anyway. There were three or four barbecue joints just steps away in any direction. The four compared notes and drank coffee from a machine because they dared not eat the food there.

"You've been smoking," Jim said to Ed.

Ed glanced at Hind. "Have not."

Jim looked at the two of them. "Terrible liars," he said, shaking his head. He looked at Helvetica.

"Terrible liars," she repeated.

"What makes you think I've been smoking?" Ed asked.

Jim's phone buzzed. He pulled it from his jacket pocket and looked at it. "The Captain," he said. He stepped away from the table and answered.

"You smell like smoke," Helvetica said. "Nobody smokes anymore, so it's easy to smell it now. You should wear coveralls when you light up. Of course the odor will still get in your hair. I suppose you could wear a shower cap." She looked at them in turn. "Is a cigarette worth a set of overalls and a shower cap?"

Hind and Ed thought about it, then they nodded together. "Yes, yes, pretty much," they said.

"You could, of course, hang one of those cabbie Christmas tree deodorizers around your necks."

"Might do that next time," Hind said.

Jim came back to the table. "Let's go."

"Where?" Ed asked.

"You too, Herberta. We're going to Hernando. Seven dead men. Just like our other crime scene."

"Where the hell is Hernando?" Hind asked.

"Just outside Memphis," Jim said. "It's a goddamn four-hour drive. Grab your go bags and let's hit the road."

"Am I invited?" Helvetica asked.

"Up to you," Jim said. "Want to be out in the field for a while?"

"I might spot something," she said.

"We can use all the help we can get," Ed said. He let his shoulders sag. "I need to call my future ex-wife."

"Want me to talk to her?" Jim asked.

"I'm sure that will make it better."

75

The Bluegum restaurant didn't look like much, but it was lit up in the night and bustling when Jim parked the state-issue sedan on the gravel parking lot. Ed's chair was pushed back so that Quip was sitting knees to chest.

"Why are we stopping here?" Ed asked.

"Because it's here," Jim said. "Helvetica is being squished back there and we're all hungry. Am I right?"

"You're right," Hind said.

They fell out of the car, walked into the restaurant, and were seated by a young woman with a large Afro in a booth against the far wall. Recorded acoustic blues played from speakers in the corners of the ceiling. Blind Blake. Mississippi Fred Mcdowell. Robert Johnson. All of the clientele was Black; most were thirty or younger. There was a stage near the double doors to the kitchen, empty save for one microphone stand and an old amplifier.

"Quite the joint," Hind said.

"I feel suddenly old," Ed said.

"Handsome crowd." Quip opened the menu. "Barbecue chicken and quinoa. You don't see that every day. Jicama slaw, jambalaya, jalapeño poppers, and jerk chicken. That's a lot of j's."

"No jive," Jim said. "Sorry, couldn't help it."

The woman who sat them returned for their drink orders. Quip ordered a white wine and watched as the others asked for coffee.

"So I'm the lush," Quip said when the waitress was gone. "You going to tell me you're on duty, right?"

"No, I just like coffee," Ed said. Ed saw Jim become interested in something across the room. "What is it?"

Jim nodded toward the door.

They all looked over. "Isn't that Gertrude?" Hind said.

"It is," Ed said.

Gertrude was greeted by a couple of the waiters. There was a lot of hugging and smiling, nothing unusual for friends greeting each other, but then, after some words, she marched, with a deliberate gait, perhaps urgency, to the double doors of the kitchen. Even that wouldn't have seemed odd, but at the doors she turned to survey the room, suspiciously.

Jim looked at Ed.

"What?" Ed asked.

"Something's strange," Jim said. "I've got a funny feeling."

"That's hunger you're experiencing," Ed said. "I want me some of them jalapeño poppers."

Jim pulled out his phone.

"What are you doing?" Hind asked.

Jim held up a finger to pause the others. He entered Gertrude's number and waited through three rings.

Gertrude answered. "Hello, Special Agent," she said, playfully. "What can I do for you?"

"We're on our way to a crime scene. Where are you?"

"I'm here at Mama Z's," she said.

"How is she?"

"She's the steadiest person I've ever met, one-o-five and still cranking. Is that why you're calling?"

"I wanted to know if Mama Z can be available to talk with us later in the week. We want to know more of the history of Money. Is she there?"

"She's actually asleep right now. I'll find out tomorrow and get back to you. Will that work?"

"Yes. Thanks, Gertrude."

Jim put his phone away. "She's in Money with Mama Z."

"I see," Ed said.

The room became suddenly silent as everyone's attention turned toward the stage. A tall woman with a striking Mohawk plugged a microphone into the amplifier, causing a second of loud feedback, then stood erect and placed the mic onto the stand. She faced everyone and stood silently for nearly half a minute. Then she sang, her voice deep like a man's, the amplifier full of reverb:

> *Southern trees bear strange fruit*
> *Blood on the leaves and blood at the root*
> *Black bodies swinging in the Southern breeze*
> *Strange fruit hanging from the poplar trees*
>
> *Pastoral scene of the gallant South*
> *The bulging eyes and the twisted mouth*
> *Scent of magnolias, sweet and fresh*
> *Then the sudden smell of burning flesh*
>
> *Here is fruit for the crows to pluck*
> *For the rain to gather, for the wind to suck*

For the sun to rot, for the trees to drop
Here is a strange and bitter crop

The woman did not hold that final note, that final *crop*, but let it fall as if spoken. Even the reverb offered no echo. Yet the word hung there in the air of the room. Again, a chirp of feedback as she knelt by the amplifier to switch it off.

"Wow," Hind said.

"Indeed," said Quip. Her British accent seemed to offer the appropriate sentiment.

Ed looked at Jim. "There's something going on."

The restaurant erupted with applause and cheers. The whole effect of it was as moving as the song had been.

Jim nodded to his partner in agreement.

"What is it?" Hind asked.

"I don't know what's happening," Jim said. "But something's going on in the state of Mississippi."

"*Virtute et armis*," Ed said.

Quip looked at him.

"Motto of the state of Mississippi," Ed said. "'By valor and arms.' Nice, isn't it?"

76

Sheriff Red Jetty sat in his basement, a wide and deep single room lined with Ole Miss pennants and banners. A Confederate flag was draped against the back wall. Jetty sifted through photographs in a box. He had laid out several on the table in from of him, three black-and-white and two color pictures that had faded almost entirely away.

Jetty's wife came down the stairs and stood behind him. "What are you looking for, honeybunch?" Agnes asked.

"I don't know."

"Who's this one of ?" She pointed to one of the black-and-white pictures. "Is that your father?"

Jetty said nothing.

"Red? Is that a nigger beside him? He's light, but I can tell."

"No, the nigger is my father."

"What?" She looked at the picture, held it to the light, looked at her husband's face. "Jesus, I can see it. Red, is you black?"

"I always wondered why my daddy hated niggers so much, why he hated me. I been lookin' at these pictures my whole life, and I just now see it."

"Lawdy have mercy," she said. "Your pappy is a nigger. That make you a—" She stopped.

"Go ahead and say it," Jetty said.

"That makes you an n-word, Red," she said, as if she'd found a new conscience about her language.

"Yes, it does."

"Who is he? Where is he?"

"My daddy kilt him. Lynched him."

"Yer daddy kilt yer pappy?"

"Yeah."

"What about yer mama?" she asked.

"My mama was scared of my daddy until the day he died."

"You think she loved yer pappy?"

"A White woman cain't love a nigger," he said. He looked at his wife. "You know what I mean."

77

The scene in Hernando was worse merely because there was so much more blood, so much more barbed wire, so many more displaced genitalia. The body of the Black man had a different appearance from the corpse of Mister Gerald Mister, from the crime scenes in Money. Ed and Jim identified themselves to the Hernando sheriff, a Black man named Kwame Wallace. Hind walked the outer edge of the huge room in the Masonic Hall of Hernando. One look at the blood and Helvetica Quip had to excuse herself.

"So, what do we have here?" Jim asked.

"I'll start with the White males," Sheriff Wallace said. He was a tall man with voice similar to Sidney Poitier's. He pointed. "One James Cooke, forty-three, a local house framer, one kid, no wife. One James Killen, twenty-three, called Jimbo, worked in the Best Buy up in Memphis, married, nine kids, nine. Lawrence White, thirtyfour, known as Larry Dub, played the national anthem on the harmonica once at a Grizzlies game, divorced, no kids. Joseph Robert Patterson, fifty-one, known as Joey Bobby, sold used cars, widowed, suspected briefly in the death of said wife, grown daughter turns tricks in Memphis. And Reginald Dimp, fifty-nine, nickname Dimp, a foreman at the landfill, long history of DUI arrests, married to an eighteen-year-old just out of high school, two kids."

"Very colorful," Jim said.

"We try," Wallace said.

"COD?"

"Take your pick." He pointed to each White man in turn. "Strangled by rope, nearly decapitated by barbed wire, stabbed, shot, and set on fire."

"And him?" Ed pointed to the dead Black man.

"All of the above, maybe. He appears to be a Black male and he's covered with dirt. That's about all we know. Well, that and he's got a bunch of testicles in his hands."

"There's a lot of that going around," Jim said.

"I heard about that down in Money. That your case?"

"Yeah."

"Who's she?" Wallace said, nodding toward Hind.

"FBI."

"Oh yeah?"

"She's okay," Ed said.

"You can see that this is just a clusterfuck," Wallace said. "You men act like this ain't nothing new."

"Wish we could say it was," Ed said.

"The Black guy looks so dead," Wallace said.

"What do you mean?" Jim asked.

"Well, these White men look pretty dead, but at least they look like they were once alive. But this man—" He paused, knelt beside the Black body. "He looks like he's never been alive. The White guys, terror on their faces. You can see their fear. Brother man here looks, well, almost happy." He stood and shook his head. "What am I saying?"

"No, we get you," Jim said.

"I'm not just talking crazy?" Wallace said.

"I wish you were," Ed said. He pulled out a pack of

cigarettes and put one in his mouth. He caught Jim's eye. "Shut up."

"Sheriff, do you have any idea what these men were doing here tonight?" Ed asked.

"The manager of the building says there were no planned events or meetings. He's the one who found this mess. I suppose you'd like to talk to him." Before they could answer, Wallace said, "Well, you can't. This sight was way too much for the old dude. After he dialed 911 he clutched his chest and proceeded to have a heart attack."

"Is he okay?" Ed asked.

Wallace shrugged. "He's eightysomething and he had a coronary. He might die, he might not. Regardless, he can't tell us a damn thing."

"That's a bit cold," Jim said.

"That ancient cracker is old-school racist. Even without the heart attack you wouldn't get anything coherent out of him."

Hind walked over to them. She introduced herself to the sheriff. "These detectives have pretty much filled you in?" she said.

"Pretty much, I guess," Wallace said.

"What do you think?" Jim asked. "All you imagined?"

"This is by far the worst one," Ed said.

"Minnesota, Wyoming, and California," Hind said.

"What about them?" Jim asked.

"Crimes just like this. Two murders in California." Hind pulled her jacket closed. "It's cold in here."

"Five states?" Jim said.

"The unidentified body in California—ready for this?— was an Asian, and his body disappeared only to show up at another murder scene."

"What the fuck are you people talking about?" Sheriff Wallace asked. "Somebody fill me in."

"Come on, Sheriff," Ed said. "Let's take a walk."

"There goes his evening," Jim said. "So, what do you think, seeing one of these up close and personal?"

"It's a beaut," Hind said.

"Are you feds required to take a course in sarcastic understatement at Quantico?"

"No, it's an elective." Hind scanned the room again. "It just doesn't add up. I can't even begin to play it out."

"T-I-M."

"What?"

"This is Mississippi. Welcome."

78

Mama Z stood in her front yard, the paper-white moon making the dense woods around her home just slightly less than pitch black. The headlights of a couple of vehicles brushed over her on the way to park in front of the railroad ties that marked the edge of her yard. She stepped between the car and the pickup and spoke to the young people in them.

"I think you had better take your cars around back of the barn."

"Yes, ma'am," the driver of the car said.

As they disappeared around the house another car arrived. It was Gertrude. Gertrude put down her window. "You want me to park around back too?"

"No, you're okay here," Mama Z said. "The fuzz know your car."

Inside the house, three women and two men joined Mama Z, Gertrude, and a weary-eyed Damon Thruff. They sat in the front room with a fire in place and two pots of tea.

"I just love saying that there is tea on the coffee table," Mama Z said. "Why don't you children tell me what the problem is."

"We figured everything was over after the Bryant

woman," a woman with a Mohawk said. "But then that coroner . . . what was his name?"

"Fondle," Gertrude said.

"Yeah, Fondle. Then he turned up dead. What was up with that? I mean, is it one of us?"

"First of all, you have to stay calm," Mama Z said.

"That's easy to say," a short man said. He was poking around in the fire with an iron. "Gertrude told us that the FBI was here."

"Of course they were here," the old woman said. "They're investigating a crime, a crime of history. They need to know about this place, so of course they would come to me."

"I guess so," the Mohawk said. "But Mama Z, I'm scared. We're all scared. Either somebody knows about us, is watching us, or something even worse is going on."

"Like what?" another woman asked.

"And it wasn't one of us," the man at the fire said.

"Now it's worse," this from a man who just then stepped into the room.

"What are you talking about?" Gertrude asked.

"Turn on CNN," he said.

Gertrude grabbed the remote from the table and clicked on the old, fat television that sat on an unused stereo console.

"Hernando," the man said. "They just found five dead White men in a room with a dead Black man."

They turned their attention to the screen. There was an ad for car insurance playing.

"The news said that the men were mutilated."

"What the fuck?" another of the women said. "The news didn't say how or who was mutilated."

The Breaking News banner flashed. The woman on

camera was from a local station in Memphis, excited to be on national television. "In the small town of Hernando, Mississippi, a suburb of Memphis, a gruesome discovery this evening. The bodies of six men have been found murdered—*horribly mutilated* were the words used by Hernando Sheriff Kwame Wallace. One criminalist, who prefers to remain unnamed, told me that this has all the signs of a ritualistic killing. There is some speculation that maybe the men belonged to a cult of some kind. Five of the victims are White and they have been identified, though no names have been released. The sixth victim is a Black male, I am told, of indiscriminate age, and he remains unidentified."

In the background, talking to a uniformed man, was FBI Special Agent Herberta Hind. Gertrude spotted her and then she also saw Special Detective Jim Davis. "Well, the FBI and the MBI are there," she said. "Probably the CIA and TSA as well."

"Who's the FBI?" Mohawk asked.

"The tall woman talking to the uniform," Gertrude said.

"She was in the Bluegum tonight," Mohawk said.

"Yep," the short man said. "Sitting in a booth with those two men and a White woman. Brigette waited on them."

"Fuck," Gertrude said. "I wonder if that's why Davis called me."

"Called you?" Mama Z asked.

"Yeah, out of the blue, said he was looking to meet up with you, Mama Z. I had just walked through the restaurant and into the kitchen."

"So what?" Mama Z said. "So you were in a restaurant?"

"I lied to him. I told him I was here with you."

"Shit," from the short man.

"People lie all the time," Mama Z said. "It's not a crime. They know nothing. And as for these other crimes—if you weren't there, then there's no trace of you there."

"What do we do?" Mohawk asked.

"You don't panic, that's the first thing," the old woman said. "If you all take off into the wind you'll attract attention. Just be cool."

Finally Damon, who had disappeared into the sofa, shook his head, as if coming out of a trance. "What in the world are you people talking about? Traces of you at crime scenes? My god, what are you doing? Gertrude?"

Gertrude walked over to Damon and put her hand on his shoulder. "My brother, we need to have a little talk."

79

The rain came suddenly, and then there was a tornado watch that turned into a warning, and any thought of driving back to Hattiesburg was promptly dropped. The detectives and the doctor drove into Memphis and checked in to the Peabody Hotel. Ed looked around the lobby and whistled.

"Federal government's dime," Hind said. "There's got to be some perk for everybody hating you."

Hind took care of business at the desk.

Helvetica Quip was still shaken by her truncated glimpse of the murder scene. "Are you okay?" Jim asked.

"I've never been in the field," she said. "I'm just a lab rat. I'm used to viewing the bodies as evidence on a metal table. But those people were dead in the real world, blood all over a floor that people walk on."

"It bothers me that I'm used to it," Jim told her.

"How do you get used to something like that?"

"Sort of used to it."

"Two rooms left," Hind said. "Shall we flip to see who bunks with whom?"

"I can't believe I'm sharing another room with you," Jim said to Ed as he switched on the television. "*SportsCenter*?"

"Sure."

"Porn?"

"Puts me to sleep."

"I never understand it anyway," Jim said. "The faces they make. I thought fucking was supposed to feel good."

"I wouldn't know. I'm married with a kid and I have this job." Ed picked up the ice bucket. "Do we need ice?"

"Not me," Jim said.

"I guess I don't either. Just seems like if you have an ice bucket you ought to put some ice in it." He put down the bucket and sat on his bed.

"Why do you think Gertrude lied to me about where she was tonight?" Jim asked.

"Who knows? Maybe she simply didn't want to explain where she really was. Sometimes people don't feel like talking and they just say whatever."

"Maybe."

"What did you think about what that sheriff said?" Ed asked. "About the Black dude seeming more dead that the others?"

"I understood what he meant, and then again, I didn't. The guy's clothes looked really old."

"He was covered with dirt," Ed said. "But you're right, his clothes seemed out of date or something."

"You want to walk over to Beale Street?"

Ed looked out the window, stood, and walked over to look down at the street. "Out in that weather? How come tornadoes never take out big buildings?"

"It's just rain," Jim said. "We can leave our neckties here and go hear some blues."

"For a little while."

"It's Beale Street, man."

"It's still Tennessee."

80

Damon was shaking. He was sitting on the bed in Mama Z's guest room. There was a crazy quilt folded at the foot of the bed that was mostly purple. He didn't like purple. "What the fuck is going on?" he asked.

Gertrude was standing across the room, leaning on the closed door as if blocking his escape.

"Are you guys murdering people?" Damon asked.

"*Murder* is a strong word. I don't know if it applies. Do soldiers murder when they shoot an attacking enemy?"

"They do," Damon offered without hesitation. "That's precisely what soldiers do."

"We're simply offering a little retributive justice."

"So, why am I here?" Damon asked.

"You're the smartest person I know," Gertrude said. "You're here to chronicle this thing. You're here to make sense of it. You're here to figure out a way for all of this to make noise and yet keep all of it secret."

"That makes no sense whatsoever."

"Mama Z told me you were writing down the names."

"What's that got to do with anything?"

"How did it feel?" Gertrude asked.

"Horrible."

"And?" she asked.

"What?"

"What else did it make you feel?"

"Free," he said. "In a weird way, free."

"Alive," Gertrude said.

"I guess."

"Well, those people are dead. Their names are alive, but they are dead. They don't get to say their names anymore. Do you understand? They don't get to hear their names."

"What does murdering people have to do with names?"

"Nothing," she said. "And everything."

Damon stared at her. "Well, the smartest person you know can't figure out what the fuck you're talking about."

Gertrude sat on the bed beside him. "Maybe I'm not making any sense. That's possible. But we've got a different problem now."

"What's that?"

"We killed only those related to the murderers of Emmett Till. And his accuser."

"How many is that?" Damon asked.

"Three."

"Only three. Well, congratulations. What restraint you people have shown. Who's next? The grandchildren?"

"I admit it's really messy, but what about justice? And don't say it's in God's hands."

"I don't believe in a god," Damon said.

"Precisely," Gertrude said. "There has to be some way to have these deaths be symbolic. Don't you see?"

"Mama Z, that old lady, one-hundred-and-five-year-old Mama Z, she's the mastermind behind all of this? Is that what you're telling me? That's what you're expecting me to believe?"

"Yes. She's seen it all. She's seen enough."

"You're crazy. You're all crazy. This is what I think: I think that none of you killed anybody. I think you're all delusional, suffering from some kind of mass hysteria. Maybe it's even viral. You're infected, that's what it is."

"Stop." Gertrude put her hand on his leg.

"What? Is that hand on my leg supposed to calm me down? Is it supposed to make me realize that you all are, in fact, actual killers and at the same time make me relax?"

"Stop," she repeated.

"So, when you called me down here about the same body showing up at these murder scenes, you already knew what was going on?" he stated as a question. "You lied to me and now, if all of this is true, I'm implicated in this crime. I'm an accessory after the fact of murder."

"I know this is a lot. But this is a war. One that's been going on for four hundred years, and now we're fighting back."

Damon looked at Gertrude for a long, hard moment. "You believe all of this."

"I believe it because it's true."

"That's very nice rhetoric, but it doesn't change the fact that you lied to me. Why did you want me here? Why am I here?"

"Somebody's got to tell this story," Gertrude said.

"Bullshit."

"Damon."

Damon lay back on the bed and closed his eyes. "Close the door on your way out. I need to process this."

81

"Jesus H. Christ on a crutch in a cornfield," Harlan Fester said. He was still wearing his work clothes from the paper mill. "Somethin' is afoot, y'all, and it ain't good." Harlan was addressing other members of the Whites for Social Justice Committee online. Their virtual meeting had started some ten minutes earlier. Now that they were done with the Pledge of Allegiance and prayer, Harlan had initiated the night's business. "As you know, I am vigilant in my coverage of the internets. I follow all the newspapers and monitor all the police blotters and feeds. Nothing happens in the country without me knowing about it, and I'm tellin' y'all, somethin' is afoot."

"What you done learned spying on the web, Brother Harlan?" Pete Rupter said, his face on the left upper corner of Fester's screen.

"Somebody or bodies is killin' White people," Harlan said. "Our kind of White people."

"People gets kilt every day," Morris Lee Morris said. He was sitting on the deck of his house in Temecula, California. It was still light outside for him. He was doing something in front of him.

"What you doin', Morris?" Rupter asked.

"I'm cleanin' my pistols," Morris said. "We got to be ready."

"Never was more true words spoke," Fester said. "I got

me a new Smith and Wesson thirty-eight, five-shot."

"Pussy gun," Morris said. "This here is a Desert Eagle, fiftycaliber."

"Shit, that ain't shit," Rupter said. "By the time you get off a second round, niggers will have put twenty caps in yo ass. From one of them, what do you call 'em, MAC-10s."

"Bullshit," Morris said.

"Stop fightin'," Fester said. "We got bigger fish to fry. Seems like some suicidal niggers is out there killin' Whites."

"What do mean by 'suicidal'?" Morris asked.

"I mean these niggers been killin' us and then they up and kill themselves. At least that's what some cops is sayin'."

Rupter whistled.

"We got to get the membership together and get prepared. That race war I been tellin' y'all about is here, I fear," Morris said.

Rupter laughed.

"What you laughin' at, Rupter?" Morris barked. "And why you cover yer mouth with yer hand like some kinda Korean girl?"

Rupter took offense. "You know I'm sensitive about my missing teeth. And what you know about Korean girls?"

"I fought in Korea," Morris said.

"Fuck you, Morris," Fester said. "You was too young to go to Vietnam. And you was too old for the Gulf War."

"Shut up."

"I'll shut up," Fester said, sarcastically.

"But what were you laughin' at?" Morris kept on it.

"You rhymed," Rupter said.

"What?"

"You said the war is here, I fear. You rhymed. I thought it was kinda funny. Sorry."

"Jesus Christ," Morris said.

"Shut up, both of y'all," Fester said. "You act like children."

"Fuck you, Harlan."

"Hey, sorry I laughed," Rupter said. "What we gonna do?"

"We have to get everybody together," Morris repeated.

"You make it sound like we got numbers," Rupter said. "Far as I can see, we got us and two other people. Where's this war taking place? My boy's got Little League this week."

"Yeah," Fester said. "We is scattered all over the country. The very thing that makes the FBI afraid of us is our weakness."

"Amen to that," Morris said.

"Aw, shit, I forgot to tell you the worst of it," Fester said.

"What's that?" Morris asked.

"The White men had their balls cut off."

"What the freegone fuck you say?" Rupter said. "You mean their testiculars?"

"That's exactly what I mean."

"Talk about burying the lede," Rupter said.

"What kind of animal would do that?" Morris said.

"They sure it was niggers that done it?" Rupter asked.

"I don't know," said Fester. "At one of the places the nigger was holding the White man's nuts in his hand."

"Lawd-a-mercy," Morris said. "We'd best clean every goddamn gun we got. This thing sounds for real. If it's true, what will we do?"

Rupter laughed.

"Jesus, Pete."

"Sorry, but rhymin' is funny. You know there ain't no rhyme for *orange*? You'd think there would be, but there ain't."

82

Thunder sounded in the distance. Beale Street was not overly crowded but was littered and dirty as if it was. The bad weather didn't help. Ed and Jim walked without their ties or their weapons. This made them happy and somewhat nervous. They weren't policemen in Tennessee, just a couple of Black men. They didn't want to end up the subjects of a *60 Minutes* segment with Mike Wallace shaking his big White head. Electric blues spilled out of every bar they passed.

"What makes the blues sound so . . ." Ed searched for the word.

"Nasty?" Jim offered.

"Yeah."

"Because it's nasty," Jim said. "You know, that good nasty. What did Louis Armstrong say? Oh yeah: the blues is when a woman tells you she's got another mule in her stall."

"That would be the blues, all right. What do you think those ballless White boys were singing at the end?"

"I don't know. What goes around comes around?"

Ed nodded.

"You ever been to Graceland?" Jim asked.

"No."

"I was there once."

The rain started to fall again. Ed looked up at the sky.

"You think a tornado is coming? I've lived my entire life in Louisiana and Mississippi and I've never seen a tornado."

"I saw one when I was a kid. At least I think I saw one. I was asleep in the back of my family's station wagon. I woke up and thought I saw the storm and fell back asleep. I used to wake up in the back of that car and see lots of shit."

"Do you think ghosts are showing up to kill rednecks all of a sudden?" Ed asked.

"No," Jim said. "I wish, but no."

A small man ran from an alley, chased by a heavy woman dressed only in an orange thong. The man wore one shoe and held the other in his hand. His other hand held his pants closed and up. Still, he managed to put distance between himself and the woman.

"It's going to take a while to unsee that," Jim said.

"It's strange we didn't feel that way at any of these crime scenes. What do you think that means?" Ed asked.

Jim shrugged. "Let's find some blues."

They walked into a tavern called the Mississippi Goddamn. The bar was long and had vintage scrolled woodwork at the corners. They sat at it and ordered a couple of whiskeys from the old woman pouring and mixing drinks.

"Where are your guns, boys?" the woman asked. When they just stared at her, she said, "You're cops, right?"

"We're that obvious?" Jim asked.

"As clear as you're Black," she said.

"That makes me sad," Ed said.

"Things is what things is, baby. Ain't no shame in it," she said.

"Yeah, but you don't walk into the dentist's office and get recognized as a bartender," Jim said.

"True dat," she said. "I'm glad y'all is cops. Don't want them all to be lily white."

"We're not Memphis cops," Jim said.

"Oh I know, honey. I know."

The sound of a guitar came from the tiny stage across the room. A gray-bearded man sat alone and started to play. His guitar playing was simple, his voice was gravelly, and neither Ed nor Jim could understand a word he was singing. His blues were slow and seemingly heartfelt, perhaps because of the minor key. He played slide with a bone on his little finger.

Jim leaned toward the bartender when she came back their way. "What's he singing?"

"Hell if I know. He sings in here every night. I don't know his name, where he comes from, nothing. I sure as hell don't know what he saying."

They listened. "It doesn't matter what he's saying," Ed said.

"What?" Jim asked.

"It doesn't matter what he's saying."

"How long should we sit here?" Jim asked.

"I don't know. All night?"

"Sounds right."

83

Charlene stood in her backyard next to the empty pool and watched her next-to-youngest toddler try to pedal his lime-green Big Wheel through the overgrown, yet brown grass. Lulabelle rubbed more rouge on her cheeks and yanked at her mother's leg.

"Hot Mama Yeller, did I put it on right?" the girl asked.

"Lawd-a-mercy, child, don't bother me now. I'm thinkin'."

"What you thinkin' on, Hot Mama Yeller?"

"I'm thinkin' grown things you wouldn't understand. Like how I'm gonna pay the rent on this here house with your daddy all dead. And when is Pete Built gonna call me on the CB radio?"

"Who is Pete Built?"

"Never you mind." Charlene lit a cigarette and took a long pull on it. "Let me ask you something."

"What?"

"You hear any noises last night?"

"Yeah," Lulabelle said.

"I mean strange noises, not just yer brother tootin' gas."

"No, I heard me some strange noises. At first I thought I was dreamin', but then I seen I was awake, and I still heard 'em."

"What was they like?"

Lulabelle closed her eyes and tried to recall. "One noise was like a chain being dragged. Then I thought I heard a scream. Then I heard me some laughin'."

"Like men laughin'?"

"Yessum." The child looked up at her mother. "Is that what you heard too, Hot Mama Yeller?"

Charlene ignored her question. "Lulabelle, you look a fright. Your rouge ain't even, and your lipstick don't match your eye shadow. Have mercy."

"Is that what you heard too?" the child repeated.

"Go over there and push your brother's Big Wheel out of that mud. I gotta go in the house and make a call."

Lulabelle walked to her brother, muttering. "I cain't even get my makeup on because of this dang fool baby."

Inside the house, Charlene picked up the handset of the CB radio. She set it to channel 19. "This here that Hot Mama Yeller. I'm lookin' for that Pete Built. Y'all out there?"

A scratchy voice replied. "I sho is girl. You got that Pete Built. Come back."

"Switchin', baby." Charlene changed the channel to the one she and Pete Built shared to speak somewhat privately.

"Where you at?" Pete Built said.

"You know I'm at home," she laughed. "Where else would I be? Question is, where you at?"

"Got out early this mornin', and now I'm just about forty miles south of Money on that Highway Five Eighteen. Wait a second. What's that? There's somethin' on that road up ahead there. Looks like a couple of people is laying on the shoulder. Another one in the weeds there. Somethin' looks wrong. I'm pullin' over now to see what's goin' on'."

"What is it, baby?" Charlene asked. She turned the squelch up to get rid of the static.

"There's a nigger walkin' over."

Charlene listened. "What he want? Be careful, Pete Built. What's that nigger want?"

"Hang on, Yeller. What's goin' on out there, boy? What's that on yo hands? What you doin', boy? Oh, my sweet-smellin' Jesus! What the fuck? Jesus! Lawd-a-mercy!"

"Pete Built!" Charlene shouted. "Can you hear me? Let go of the button, baby. Pete Built! What's happening, baby?"

"Jesus Lawd!" Static.

"Baby? Pete Built? Honeybunch?" Charlene let the handset drop.

Lulabelle came in through the kitchen door. "That baby can push his own damn trike. What's wrong, Hot Mama Yeller?"

"Get the hell outside!"

Charlene picked up the phone and dialed 911.

84

The scene on anything-but-scenic Highway 518 caused the rough and seasoned Mississippi state trooper to do a double take. He even removed his mirrored sunglasses and pushed up the brim of his big hat to get a clearer look. There were five dead bodies in all; four were White and one was Black. The Whites were covered and soaked with blood; the Black man was covered with dirt, his hands bloody. The first troopers on the scene had effectively blocked off traffic in either direction and had detained the couple of drivers who had stopped to check out what had happened. A willowy White woman leaned against the hood of her BMW and cried into her hands. A large Black man paced in front of his Chevy three-quarter-ton pickup and kept an anxious eye on the state troopers.

"Goddamn," the old trooper said. "This is a shitload of blood."

"Pretty messy," another trooper said.

"You got ID on any of these folks?"

"All of them had identification on them," the young trooper said. "Exceptin' the nig—" He glanced over his shoulder at the Black man by the truck. "Weren't no ID on the Black man."

"And it definitely ain't no robbery," the other young one

said. "That one and that one had lots of money in their wallets, damn near six hundred bucks. Nothing at all in the Black's pockets."

"It kinda looks like their nuts have been cut off," a young one said. "What?"

"They're scattered all around here."

"What are?"

"Their nuts. Testicles. All of them got their pants pulled down some. Except for the—the Black man. I tell you it's sick, like some Charles Manson shit, or somethin' cultlike."

The older trooper looked at the victims again. "They been shot?"

"Could be. All I know is there is a lot of blood. No casings around. No weapons. No nothing. Exceptin' them testicles."

"I hope you idiots didn't touch anything."

"Are you kiddin'? I ain't about touching nobody's balls. Hell, I feel funny touchin' my own."

"You touched their wallets."

"Oh, yeah. Sorry about that."

85

Ed described the scene on the highway as it had been described to him and Jim by the captain. Special Agent Hind sat across the table and rubbed her temples as she listened. They were seated in the back of the Capriccio Grille in the Peabody.

Dr. Quip put down her fork and pushed away her plate of scrambled eggs, pancakes, sausages, and bacon. "I'm no longer hungry."

"Sorry," Ed said. "Work."

"There is something really strange going on," Jim said. "I realize that's really obvious, but I mean something really, really strange."

"Just south of Money," Ed said. "That's where it happened."

"The whole works," Jim said. "Severed testicles and everything. Solitary Black victim with challenged fashion sense. See what I mean? Everything the same all over the place. Chicago. Mississippi. California."

They sat quietly for a moment.

"I guess we will miss the ducks," Quip said.

"What's that?" Hind asked.

"I read that real ducks live in the penthouse here. They

walk them out at eleven to the fountain. They ride down in the elevator just like people. I was hoping to see them."

"Maybe next time," Jim said.

"Mama Z," Hind said.

"What about her?" Jim asked.

"There's something going on there," she said. "She's connected to something. I can just feel it."

"Like what?" Jim asked. "She's a hundred years old. Over a hundred years old."

"I know, I know."

"I think Herbie's right," Ed said. "Something's not right. Okay, I will admit that the Black Power scarf is a bit much."

"I'll say it again," Jim said. "The woman is a hundred years old. She's old and she's cagey and she's a bit of a smart-ass, but hell, she's earned it. And that thing she wears—just being red, black, and green doesn't make it a Black Power scarf."

Ed stared at Jim and raised his brows.

"Okay, it's a Black Power scarf. So what?"

"There's more," Hind said.

"What?" asked Quip. "She's too smart?"

"I've never heard of that as a problem," Jim said.

"It's not a problem," Hind said. "It's an observation."

"Did you see the records?" Ed asked.

"The what?"

"The room with all the files," Jim said.

"No, what are you talking about?"

Ed put his napkin on the table and leaned slightly back. "That old woman has, in her house, cabinets full of dossiers of nearly every lynching victim in United States history."

"She didn't mention this to me."

"I'm surprised," Jim said. "She seemed proud of it. *Proud* is not right word. It was obviously a lot of work."

"Well, we'd better get rolling," Ed said. "There's not going to be anything left of that scene on the highway, but we need to see the bodies."

"Before the locals lose them," Jim said. "Him."

"Sorry about the ducks, Doc."

"There will be more ducks," Quip said. "A sentence I never imagined myself saying."

"Nonetheless true," Jim said.

Ed drove. He did not deliver them directly to the freeway that led out of Memphis. Instead he took a circuitous route through the rundown city. "Sorry about taking the long way," he said. "It's just that every time I'm in Memphis I have to drive by one place, not to get out, but just to pause and look."

"Graceland?" Hind said and chuckled.

"I've been there, but no," Ed said. "Here we are. The Lorraine Motel. There on that corner of that balcony. I was ten. That's why I'm a cop."

"It's a museum now," Jim said.

"And it shouldn't be," Ed said.

"Why not?" Quip asked.

"It's just a motel. That's what it is. That's all it is," Ed said. "People should rent out that very room and sleep in that very bed and step through that very door and stand on that balcony and realize what happened there. People should know, understand that not all Thursdays are the same."

"Come on, Ed, let's go," Jim said.

86

Delroy Digby and Braden Brady stood looking at the flat tire on Brady's patrol car, scratching each other's heads. At first they scratched their own heads, but that told them nothing. But as soon as Brady scratched Digby's head, Digby said, "Maybe we had oughta change that tire."

Digby struggled with the lug wrench, but it would not budge. "Brady, we got any WD-40?" he asked.

"I'll look in the trunk," Brady said. He paused on his way to the rear of the car and pointed. "What the fuckity fuck is that?"

"What?"

"Coming down this here road."

Digby abandoned the lug nuts, put down the wrench, and stood to look. "Shit. What the fuck?"

"That's what I'm saying. What the hell is that?" Brady said.

Moving toward them, as an undulating mass, though there was no synchronization to their jerky movements, was a mob of Black men. The sky, which had been bright and clear, was now darkened by green-tinged clouds. A wind pressed into the chests of the two deputies.

Digby and Brady stepped back, dropping their hands to their holstered pistols. Brady, then Digby drew their weapons.

The mob was perhaps thirty or forty strong. Old and young. Some walked spryly. Some nearly dragged themselves along. Moving like that they resembled an ungainly tangle of octopi. A light rain began to fall. The mob made a collective noise, chanted a syllable.

"What they saying, Brady?"

"Lawd if I know." Brady lifted his pistol and shouted, "Y'all boys just stay right there now! Y'all hear me?"

"Rise," the mob barked, breathy and raspy, and not all together. It was like Tuvan throat singing.

"What you boys want?" Digby yelled.

Brady reached into the patrol car and grabbed the radio. "Hattie, this here is Brady. I'm thinking we need some backup out here."

Hattie's staticky voice said, "Hold on, Sheriff's right here."

87

"What's going on, Brady?" Red Jetty asked. He stood at front desk of the station. Hattie watched him. Ed, Jim, Hind, and Quip had just entered the building.

"Oh Lawd, Lawd, Jesus Christ!" Brady's voice scratched through the four-inch speaker on the desk.

"What's going on?" Jim asked.

Jetty raised his hand. "Brady?"

"Oh, Lawd Jesus!" Shots were fired.

"Brady?"

"Watch out, Delroy!"

Shots fired.

"Brady!" Jetty shouted into the handset. "What's goin' on? Where are you?"

"Sheriff," Brady cried, "they's got Delroy!"

"Who?" Jetty asked.

"They's everywhere!"

"Brady! Brady!"

Silence.

"What the hell was that?" Ed asked.

"Hell if I know," the sheriff said. "Hattie, what was their last location?"

Hattie was shaking in her chair, near tears. "What happened to them boys?" she asked, tugging at Jetty's sleeve.

"Where were they, Hattie?"

"They was out on Nickelback Road, I think. I don't know whereabouts on it. Delroy said he thought they had a flat tire. What's happening, Red?"

"I don't know, Hattie." Jetty looked at the others. "Y'all want to ride out there with me?" His manner was different. He was asking for help.

"Yeah," Jim said.

Ed turned to Quip. "Why don't you stay here with this woman," he said.

Quip nodded.

Ed, Jim, and Hind followed the sheriff out to his rig, where Ed sat in the passenger seat. Hind checked her .38 revolver and slammed the cylinder shut. Jetty looked in the rearview mirror at Jim and Hind and said, "Thank you."

Hind nodded.

The sheriff drove them out of town toward Small Change, and then up an incline. At the top they looked down and could see the deputies' car.

"I don't see them," Ed said as they approached.

"There," Hind said. She pointed. In the trees.

Hanging in the trees were the bodies of Digby and Brady, their legs crazy with blood, their pants down around their ankles, their boots stopping the clothing from falling off. Jetty nearly drove into the ravine stopping the car.

"Oh Lord!" he cried.

Jim, Ed, and Hind kept some distance. Ed looked at Jim and shook his head.

"This is no good," Jim said. "This is no good at all."

Jetty was pacing wildly, shaking his head. He had his

pistol drawn for no reason.

"Look at all these tracks," Hind said. "It's like an army marched through here. Everything is trampled."

"Shoes and bare feet," Jim said, taking a knee and touching the surface dirt lightly with his fingers.

Ed walked over to Jetty and looked at the bodies. Brady had been hung with a length of chain, Digby with a thin blue nylon cord, much like a clothesline.

"I'm sorry, Sheriff," the big man said.

"Will you help me cut them down?"

"Shouldn't we process the scene first?"

Jetty shot him a look.

"Okay, Sheriff."

Hind turned to see Ed open his knife and approach the base of the tree. "No, no," she said, but stopped when Ed waved her off. She looked over at the highly agitated Jetty. She nodded that she understood.

"Hurry, get them down," Jetty said.

Ed cut through the cord, and the sheriff caught Brady's bloody body and guided it to the blood-matted leaves.

Ed pointed. "The chain is tied up there to the branch."

Jim looked up. "How the hell did anyone get up there?"

Jetty raised his sidearm and emptied his clip shooting at the chain. He missed. Bark rained down. He popped in another clip and fired three more rounds. The chain snapped and Brady crashed unceremoniously onto the ground. Brady's body didn't fall flat but landed on his knees, his rounded back and slumped shoulders giving him the appearance of a man in prayer.

While Jetty stood and stared at his friends' bodies, the others spread out and observed the area. Ed called his captain and gave a report, asked for a team of criminalists to be dispatched.

Hind whistled for their attention. "Gentlemen, I need you over here."

Jim and Ed quickly covered the thirty meters between them. Hind stepped back as they arrived. The three stood shoulder to shoulder and looked at the ground. Before them lay the bodies of two disfigured Black men. Clad in old clothes, dirt encrusted, and dead, they resembled the other Black corpses they had recently encountered. In their hands was a bloody something.

"Are those . . ." Hind started a question.

"I'm pretty sure they are," Jim said.

The sheriff came over and joined them, looked at what they had discovered in the high grass. "You gotta be fuckin' kiddin' me."

"I think we need a bigger boat," Jim said.

88

Today in Elaine, Arkansas, three men were brutally murdered in what is being called a racial killing. The victims were discovered in the basement of the Second Coming Baptist Church. A police spokesperson stated that they believe the victims killed each other, this because one of the men held severed parts of the mutilated men in his fist. Two of the men were White, one was Black. Authorities are at a loss to describe the crime and to offer possible motive. The White victims were members of the Baptist church and longtime friends, and it appears the Black victim was unknown to the community.

In Longview, Texas, four White men were found mutilated in the barn of a local farmer. The farm was owned by one of the victims. That man's name was Carl Winslow. He was discovered by his adult daughter, who claimed she saw a mob of Black men exit the barn and march away across a pasture. Miss Laurel Winslow said, "I seen maybe twenty of 'em come out of that there barn. They's ones that killed my pappy, fo sho. The was gloatin' over it, moanin' and walkin' all funny, like they was pimps." She paused to look into the camera, "Those negroes killed my pappy. And them other mens too."

Omaha, Nebraska.

Chicago, Illinois.

Bisbee, Arizona.

Tulsa, Oklahoma.

"They wasn't human, I tell you. The just marched through here. They was dirty and smelly and they was niggers all."

"They walked right by me. A couple of them looked me up and down, and I just know they was thinking about raping me, but I think all the screaming scared them off. I heard they killed eight good, Christian White men right there in the Walmart. I guess the guard got him one of them. That's what somebody said. I don't know about anybody else, but I'm scared to death."

"I ain't never seen nothing like it."

"I could tell them coloreds was angry. I looked at one of they faces and I thought I was gonna die, straight up. I seen the devil, all right. And he was Black as pitch. My wife told me that the death count is up to nine. At least them boys killed themselves a couple before they got kilt. You heard what them niggers did, didn't you? That's some shit."

This morning in Conway, South Carolina, a roving band of Black men rioted through the streets of the small downtown area. They killed six White males. It appears that the individuals were targeted. Several people, adult males included, who fell or were cornered by the mob were passed over, ignored, officials say. This is being called a race riot and a hate crime. Police who showed up at the scene fired shots into the mob, though it is unclear whether any of the rioters were struck. The six victims were local residents. Their killers were not recognized by any of the witnesses. Racial tensions are high, and a curfew is now in place.

The governor of South Carolina, Pinch Wheyface: We are deeply saddened by this morning's events, good citizens of South Carolina, and in grave peril. We understand, all of us, that the actions of a few members of any group are not and should not be an indictment of an entire group. That said, all of these killers are Black men who have no regard for human life. These unknown individuals are still at large, so for safety's sake, we are encouraging the good White people of South Carolina to be wary of any Black individuals, especially those unknown to them. I am calling in SLED and the National Guard to assist local law enforcement. Questions?

RUPA O'BRIEN, CNN: Governor, was the attack orchestrated, and if so, were there one or more individuals leading the group?

GOVERNOR: I'll hand this over to Sheriff Pellucid.

SHERIFF CHALK PELLUCID: We has interviewed the numerous eye witnesses to this morning's attack, and we is still in the process of processing that information. All I can tell you for certain is that the gang that done this was about thirty Negro men, and that six good White residents of Conway is dead.

BUCK ROGERS, FOX NEWS: Sheriff, what do you have to say about the fact that your men fired over a hundred rounds at these rioters and not one was hit? Does that reflect poorly on your department's training?

PELLUCID: Who say ain't nobody was shot? Where are you from?

ROGERS: Fox News.

PELLUCID: No, I mean, where you from?

ROGERS: I was born in Pennsylvania.

PELLUCID: Damn Yankee.

GOVERNOR: We're hoping to have the public contact us with information that will lead to the apprehension of the darkskinned individuals involved.

ROGERS: What do you mean 'damn Yankee'?

GOVERNOR: Any other questions?

NANCY HIPPS, STATE NEWSPAPER: There are some reports that the assailants used barbed wire and ropes to kill the victims. And also that several of the victims were mutilated. What can you say about that?

PELLUCID: Ummm, we're still processing the crime scene. It's quite extensive. From one side of downtown to the other. It's a mess. We're pleased to see that the Governor has sent us help from the State Law Enforcement Agency.

SOMEONE OFF TO THE SIDE: Division.

PELLUCID: Division. SLED. The D is for division.

89

Ed and Jim sat with FBI Special Agent Hind in her FBI rental Cadillac Escalade outside the Bluegum. It was six in the morning. Jim held a photocopy of Chester Hobsinger's driver's license.

"Do you really think all of these murders are connected?" Ed asked.

"How can they not be?" Hind said.

"I know, but how? It's so fucking crazy. Is this what they mean when the say the shit is hitting the fan?" Ed leaned forward between his partners and pointed with an open hand. "Check him out."

The three watched a long-limbed White man get out of a Kia SUV and walk toward the door of the restaurant.

"Well, it looks like him to me," Jim said. "And I'm not saying that because they all look alike." He glanced at the photocopy of the license. "Would you say he's about six three?"

"About that," Ed said.

The man knocked with a loose hand and was let in to the restaurant by someone they could not see.

"Let's go," Hind said.

Ed opened his rear door and put out a foot. "I hope this guy isn't a runner. I just hate it when they run."

"Crazy, isn't it?" Hind said. "All this wild shit is happening all over the country and our lead is a White guy."

"So we'd better not shoot him," Jim said.

"I say we shoot him in the leg before he has a chance to run," Ed said. When Hind and Jim looked at him, he said, "It's early in the morning and I don't feel like chasing anybody. I'm just saying."

"Don't shoot him," Hind said.

"I won't shoot him. If he runs, I might."

They walked to the door. "Shall I knock?" Jim asked Hind.

"Let's start with a knock."

Jim knocked.

The Mohawked woman who had sung onstage was surprised to find them at the door. "We're not open yet." She gave a glance back into the room.

"That's okay," Jim said. "We're not here to eat. We're looking for this man." Jim showed her the image on the license.

"I've never seen him before," the woman said.

"Why do they always say that?" Ed asked, under his breath. He shook his head. "There's going be some running, I just know it."

"Strange," Jim said. "We just saw him come in here. You lying like that gives us probable cause to enter." He stepped inside, caused the woman to step back. Hind followed. Ed did not. "The man's name is Chester Hobsinger." Jim looked around the empty dining room. Chairs were still on the tables. A mop stood in a bucket in the middle of the floor.

"What do you say we go into the back?" Hind said to the woman. The young woman turned and led the way toward the kitchen. She was nervous, walked with her arms unmoving by her sides; her fingers seeming to reach without reaching. Jim noticed this and had a bad feeling. When she put her hand out to push open the swinging door, Jim stopped her.

"Thank you," he said. "We'll take it from here."

She stepped away.

In the kitchen Jim and Hind found three people manning the stove and butcher-block table. Two Black men and a Black woman paused to observe the visitors.

"It's okay, go on with what you're doing," Hind said.

The three looked to Mohawk for help. She nodded and they carried on with their cutting and cooking.

Jim looked at the next door and started toward it. "What's back here?" he asked. The Mohawk said nothing. Jim opened the door and they stepped into the bright, cavernous dojo. The ten or so people there stopped their exercising and sparring and turned to face Hind and Jim. Jim scanned the room and locked eyes with the sole White person, Hobsinger. Jim took a small step forward and the White man used his long legs to cover the distance between himself and the door in the far wall in seconds.

Jim and Hind ran across the uneven mats on the floor. No one in the room uttered a sound. Hobsinger bolted through the door and it slammed after him. Jim opened the door and he and Hind emerged into a brighter morning's light to find Ed holding Hobsinger facedown over the hood of a derelict pickup in high weeds.

"I told you he was going to run," Ed said. He got one cuff around the White man's left wrist.

Jim was out of breath. "I've got to exercise more."

Hind was barely winded. She stepped back to the door of the building, opened it, and peered back inside. "Jim," she said.

Jim joined her and looked back inside. The big room of mats was empty; everyone was gone. "What the hell?" he said.

Ed got the other cuff on Hobsinger and pushed him back inside behind Hind and Jim. They walked through the gym and into the now-deserted kitchen. Mohawk was gone too. Jim turned to face the White man, tilted his head, and looked into his eyes. "Chester Hobsinger?"

The man said nothing. "I know my rights," he said.

"I know your name, asshole. I've got your driver's license right here. Want to tell me why you ran?"

"I know my rights."

"Everybody knows their damn rights," Ed said. "Television."

Hind walked over and turned off a gas burner that had been left on under a pot. She looked at the food. "Grits."

"Sounds good," Ed said.

Ed pushed Hobsinger forward and they moved on through the kitchen to the dining room and found that empty as well.

"Where'd they go?" Hind asked.

The White man said nothing.

"I say we let him cool his heels in the Money jail," Jim said.

Ed laughed and looked at Hobsinger. "We'll let you spend some time with someone who doesn't know your rights. How about that?"

90

The snow was blowing in all directions. The eight people in the Grick of Bold Tavern in Rock Springs, Wyoming, were that pathetic kind of drunk that they were doomed to remember as being just like yesterday's sad kind of drunk. The owner and barkeep, Isaiah Washington, stood at the end of the bar and talked to his cousin, Kaleb Washington. They were drunk enough to watch but not comprehend the breaking news panic on CNN, but not drunk enough to disregard the gang of nearly thirty Chinese men that burst through the antique swinging barroom doors. Isaiah Washington quickly and instinctively grabbed the double-barreled twelve-gauge that had been his great-grandfather's from under the bar next to the good stuff. He was able to discharge both barrels, but to no obvious effect. He was unable to even break open the weapon to pull out the spent casings.

Slashing.

Burning.

91

Red Jetty did not place Chester Hobsinger in a cell. Instead he handcuffed the man's ankles to a rolling desk chair that was set atop a table in an otherwise empty office.

"You'll notice that your hands are free," Jetty said. "If you come off that table, even if you fall off that there table, I'm gonna shoot you someplace on your body. If I leave this room and I hear a thump, I'm gonna come in here shootin'. I'm gonna ask you once if you understand me. Do you understand me?"

Hobsinger nodded.

Jetty walked around the table while he spoke. "It appears you're somehow involved in the deaths of my deputies."

"I know nothing of your deputies."

"What kind of way you talk, boy? You know nothing of my deputies. Well, you know something. Your driver's license says you from Chicago, Illinois." Jetty pronounced the *s*.

Hobsinger was silent.

"Tell me what y'all doin' down here in Mississippi, Mr. Hopsettler."

"That's Hobsinger."

"Now that we know that's your name, we can keep this going."

Hobsinger was visibly upset with himself.

"You see, boy, I am a rube just like you thought, but I ain't as dumb as my home and my DNA would have you think. I'm a different kind of redneck. I'm the kind of redneck before and after he takes a shit."

"What?"

"I'm the kind of redneck that you don't want to dream about, because I ain't got no boundaries. No boundaries. I'm a redneck that doesn't pretend to believe in a god. I'm a redneck what knows he's a redneck."

"You're crazy."

"See, you ain't as stupid as you look."

Hobsinger followed the sheriff with his eyes.

"You don't like me behind you, do you? You gonna learn to love it at the county work farm. Them good ol' boys gonna love the way you talk. You ever seen a work farm, boy?" Jetty stopped directly behind the man. "Don't worry about dropping the soap. There ain't no soap. Hell, there's hardly any water on the farm. You want to tell me what's going on around here?"

Hobsinger collected himself. "I know my rights. Are you going to threaten to lynch me now? That's what you people do, isn't it?"

"Shut up."

92

Eight Wyoming Highway Patrol cars and four black cars from the Wyoming Department of Criminal Investigation filled the narrow street in front of the Grick of Bold Tavern. The Rock Springs police department ferried suited FBI agents from the helicopters that had landed on the high school football field. There were no witnesses to the actual crime. No one had seen the attackers entering or leaving the bar. All that was clear was that there were many assailants and that they had no respect for life. The eight White men, well known third and forth-generation Wyomingites, had been slashed and stabbed, mutilated, some of them burned. Plenty of physical evidence—hair, dirt, prints, blood—cluttered the scene, and a trail of it led out of the bar and into the rocky and littered field behind it. Local hunters tried to get their dogs to pick up the scent of whoever had done the killing, but the animals could not or would not.

An old Shoshone man came and stood next to two FBI agents.

They looked at him and he looked back at them. "

Can I help you, sir?" one agent said.

"You need to move on," the other said. "This is an active crime scene. You can't be here."

"They were Chinese," the Shoshone man said.

"What?"

"Your killers. They were Chinese."

The FBI men laughed. "Is that right?"

"Maybe you can tell us how many there were."

"Twenty-eight."

"You saw twenty-eight Chinese men run out of this building?"

"No. I was in the bar when they came in."

"Twenty-eight Chinese men came into this tavern, and you were in there just watching some murders?"

"Sort of."

"What is 'sort of'?"

"They came in just as I was headed to the can to take a piss. When I came out, weren't nothing but dead *wasi'chu*. No Chinese men."

"How long does it take you to pee?"

"A couple of minutes. I come back out and a couple of *wasi'chu* was on fire. That's when I realized something was wrong."

"Yeah, people on fire is a red flag."

"Yeah."

"A couple of minutes you were in there."

"Three, tops."

"Where you drinking, sir?"

"Hell, I was straight up drunk. But I know a Chinese man when I see one. And now I know what a man on fire looks like."

"What's a Chinese look like?" one wasi'chu asked.

"A lot like that fellow over there in them weeds."

93

The Cadillac rental was parked on the side of road just out of view of Mama Z's house. Hind, Jim, and Ed were out and walking the trees that lined the drive.

"Tell me again why we parked way back there," Ed said. "You don't really believe that old woman is involved in all this."

"That's exactly what I believe," Hind said.

"All I know is that Gertrude lied to me," Jim said. "I get nervous when people lie to me."

"So, we're sneaking up on a hundred-year-old woman?"

"Pretty much," Hind said.

The front yard was covered with crows. It was covered with birds because the ground was covered with crumbs and seeds.

"What do you make of that?" Jim asked.

"Crazy lady feeds birds," Hind said.

"It's an alarm," Ed said.

"What?" Hind asked.

"An alarm. Somebody approaches and the birds take off. Okay, now I'm wondering about Mama Z."

"Let's go," Jim said.

They stepped into the open and the crows erupted in noisy flight.

"It works," Ed said.

At the door, Hind knocked.

Mama Z answered. "My friends," she said. "Where's your car?"

"We felt like walking," Hind said.

"Of course you did, dear." Mama Z stepped back. "Come on in."

The three stepped into the house. And followed the old woman into the living room. A fire burned in the place.

"So, why do I have the pleasure of your company?"

"Two deputies were killed yesterday," Jim said.

"Just south of Money," Ed said.

"Oh my. That's terrible."

"Yes, it is," Hind said. "Do you know anything about these deaths?"

"Oh no."

"What about the deaths of the Bryants and the Milam man?" Jim asked.

"Only what I hear, and most of that was from you," Mama Z said.

"Where is Gertrude?" Jim asked.

"She's not here."

"Is there anyone else here?" Ed asked.

"I do have a visitor. A scholar is going through the records. His name is Damon Thruff. Would you like to meet him?"

"Yes, we would," said Hind.

"I'll be right back," Mama Z said. She stood, seeming suddenly her age, catching herself on the arm of the sofa. Then she stood completely and easily erect, smiled at Ed, and said, "Gotcha." She left the room.

"Is this where we roll our eyes and stuff ?" Ed said. "I'm

back to where I was before. This is just an old woman. She's a smart-ass, I'll give you that, but she's not involved in any murders."

"I didn't say all that," Hind said.

"Then what are you thinking?"

"Something's fishy, that's all I'm saying."

Jim nodded his agreement.

Mama Z returned, followed by the very nervous Thruff. She introduced them to him as her detective friends. "Detectives," she said. "Doesn't that sound exciting?"

"So, why are you down here, Mr. Thruff?" Jim asked.

"My friend Gertrude invited me. Gertrude Penstock."

"To see the records," Jim said.

"Actually, I'm not clear on why she asked me to come, but I have been going through the dossiers."

"What do you do?" Hind asked.

"I'm an assistant professor at the University of Chicago. I'm in the Ethnic Studies Department, which doesn't really make sense to me since I write on justice and biomechanics. I have a couple of PhDs. I'm fairly sure they just put me there to have me somewhere. I'm talking a lot."

"So, you're Dr. Thruff," Hind said.

"I guess. I prefer Professor, or Mister is good."

"How long have you known Gertrude?" Ed asked.

"Since college. Well, she was in college and I was in graduate school. At Cornell. That's where we met. At college."

"Are you nervous, Professor Thruff?" Hind asked.

"Me? Nervous. Yes. I'm always nervous. Ask anybody."

Hind looked at Jim and Ed and moved to the edge of her seat. "You've heard that there has been a rash of murders around here."

"No. I mean, yes. Yes, I've heard about it, but mostly I've been reading the files. You know?"

"Who told you about the killings?" Jim asked.

"Gertrude. Gertrude told me."

"Where is Gertrude?" Jim asked.

"I wouldn't know," Mama Z said. "She comes, she goes."

"May I use your bathroom, Mama Z?" Jim asked.

"It's not working. The toilet's broken."

"You have just the one? I'm pretty handy," Jim said. "Would you like me to take a look at it?"

"No, no. I can handle it," she said. "I just haven't gotten around to it."

"Was Gertrude over here visiting you three nights ago?" Jim asked. "Was that three nights ago?" He looked to Ed.

Ed nodded.

"No, she wasn't. Why do you ask?"

"I called her on the phone and she said she was here."

"Then I guess she was. I'm old and, you know, my memory isn't what it once was. I guess we can all say that, right?"

"Mr. Thruff, would you mind if I had a look at your identification?" Hind asked. "Your driver's license?"

"You don't have to show it to her," Mama Z said, looking Special Agent Hind in the eye.

"That's true," Hind said. "You don't."

"I don't mind." Thruff pulled his wallet from his back pocket, removed a card, and handed it over. "That's my faculty ID. I don't have a driver's license. My passport is in my luggage. Would you like me to get it?"

Hind studied Thruff for a few seconds. "That won't be necessary." She handed back the faculty card.

"We were about to have lunch," Mama Z said.

"Okay then," Jim said. "Mama Z, would you mind letting Special Agent Hind have a look at the records?"

"Maybe some other day," the old woman said.

Outside, walking back along the driveway to the Cadillac, the three detectives said nothing. Jim led the way, somehow more agitated, angrier than the other two. He stopped at the car and turned to them. "This is bad. There is something really wrong here," Jim said.

"That poor Thruff is caught up in it, but he's hardly killing people," Hind said.

"Maybe Mama Z is some kind of a witch, and she does some mumbo jumbo and turns Thruff into a killer," Ed said.

Jim leaned against the car and kicked at the gravel. "Listen to you. A few minutes ago you were telling us she's just a nice old lady. Now, you've got her as a fucking voodoo priestess or some shit."

"Yes, well."

Jim looked at Hind. "What do you want to do?"

"I want to see if that redneck sheriff got anything out of Knobfucker or whatever his name is. What do you think?"

"I need to find Gertrude."

94

FBI Supervisory Special Agent of the Southeast Regional Office Ajax Kinney disembarked from a commercial flight at Hesler-Noble Field just north of Hattiesburg. He was met by several other agents arriving from offices in Chicago, Dallas, and DC. The agent from Dallas was a man named Hickory Spit, a legend in the Bureau only because he was the oldest active agent in Justice Department history. Born in 1934, he was just shy of eighty-five. He was the only man currently in the FBI who had actually worked with J. Edgar Hoover. A Texan by birth, he was famous for leading the FBI efforts to discredit Martin Luther King, Jr., having once penned a letter to King suggesting that he commit suicide. He was there with the others, wearing his Stetson, cowboy boots, and pearl-handled sidearm, because he was the only member of the force who had actually witnessed a lynching. He was there also because it had been so ordered by the president of the United States, who considered him an American hero. Spit thought Hoover and Eisenhower were the same person, didn't like Kennedy's hair, hated Johnson's politics, loved Nixon, once claimed to have a bullet with Jimmy Carter's name on it, was suspicious of Reagan, didn't care for George H. W. Bush, unofficially investigated Clinton, considered George W. Bush an intellectual elite, near died of a stroke when Barack Obama was elected, and was in love with the current clown. He still had a badge and a gun but could barely wipe his own ass. He smelled of shit, Aqua Velva, and pimento cheese. He had one living relative, a son he had sexually abused and who now hated him from another country. Clint Eastwood had plans to make a biopic of his life and career.

The FBI set up a headquarters on the top two floors of the Hotel Indigo. And that's where they all sat, in conference room A, eating popcorn shrimp from Popeye's, doughnuts from Krispy Kreme, and hush puppies that the hotel restaurant claimed was their worldfamous specialty. While they waited for Special Agent Herberta Hind, they were assailed with theories from Hickory Spit.

"I'm tellin' y'all boys that this here what's happenin' in the good ol' US of A started back with that Kennedy. You know I was there at Dealey Plaza on that twenty-second day of November nineteen hundred and sixty-three. I heard the shots. There were eight of them if there was one. Most said they heard three. But some folks said they heard eight, and they was right. As you know, that Italian rifle of his had a six-round magazine, and so there had to be another damn shooter. Only three casings was found in the Depository, so where did them shots come from? I'll tell you where, and it weren't from behind no wall. They was on the third floor of the Dal-Tex Building. Black Panthers dressed up like custodians. You know a Negro janitor can go anywhere without being noticed. Them Panthers was secret then and ain't nobody knew about them, and they was mad because Kennedy was backing off of promises he made to them in exchange for delivering the Black vote. You know that's why he won, because of the Black vote. Nobody ever talks about that. Anyway, Oswald didn't fire a damn shot. The Russians was working with the Blacks, but Lee Harvey didn't know that. He just thought he was working for the Ruskies. They gave him blanks. Can you imagine his surprise when he didn't hit nothing? Anyway, them Panthers never went away. They came out with a public version in the late sixties, but they're still secret as shit, and they have started up this race war we all knew was comin'."

"How are they doing it, Hick?" someone asked. "Killing people and disappearing? How do you do that?"

Hickory Spit looked out the window. "Ninja training. The Japs had been teachin' them Panthers all along. You seen how many of them Panthers were toting around that *Art of War* book by that Sonny."

"That's Sun Tzu," another agent said.

"And it's Chinese," from another.

"You say that like there's a difference," Hickory Spit said. "They're ghosts, these niggers."

"Is that right?" Special Agent Hind said from the doorway.

Ajax Kinney put his face in his palm.

Hickory Spit shrank just a little.

Jim and Ed stood on either side of Hind.

"Why don't you tell me about these ghost niggers?" Hind asked. She stepped toward the old man at the head of the table.

"Who are you?" Hickory Spit asked.

"I'm Special Agent Herberta Hind," she said. "I'm the lead investigator down here. Who and what are you?"

"Special Agent H-h-h—Hickory Spit, from D-d-d-Dallas."

"Pleased to meet you," Hind said. "Now, sit and hush."

"The president wanted him here," Kinney said.

"Of course he did."

"What do you have to share with us, Special Agent Hind?" Kinney asked.

Hind looked at the faces of the White men and settled on a long look at the craggy skin of Hickory Spit. "We have nothing to report," she said. "The investigation is ongoing, and we haven't connected enough dots to form a theory."

"I understand that, but you're here to tell us about the dots," Kinney said.

"Yeah, what about them dots?" Hickory Spit said.

"Shut up," Hind said. She turned and walked out. Ed and Jim followed.

In the elevator, Jim said, "What do the kids say?"

"That was awesome," Ed said.

"Very funny," Hind said.

"What got into you?" Ed asked.

"I just looked at those pasty white faces and got mad. Hickory-fucking-Spit. Fuck all of them. They're huddled in a room waiting for us to give them permission to shoot at somebody. And you know what somebodies they want to shoot at."

They stepped into the elevator and faced the closing door.

"I couldn't find an address for Gertrude Penstock," Jim said. "The diner hired her as Dixie Foster and the address is fake, as is the social."

"So you think she's in the wind?" Hind said.

"Somehow I don't think that," Jim said.

"I would be," Ed said.

"I'm going back to Mama Z's," Jim said.

Hind nodded. "We'll go over and take a turn with Hobsinger."

Back in conference room A:

"I ever tell you youngsters about the lynching I saw back in forty-six? I was just eleven years old. My daddy woke me up and said come on, he wanted to show me somethin'. We got into his beat-up old Ford pickup and drove out past the oil fields. My daddy was a hotshot oil man, used to put out them fires. You seen that movie with John Wayne? Well, that movie was based on my daddy. He had red hair too. Looked just like his damn head was on fire. Anyway he drove us out there, and these fellers dragged this nigger out of this shack, and I tell you that boy was kickin' and screamin'. Them boys ain't got no kind of spine. He was saying he didn't do whatever they said he done, and so I asked my daddy what he had done, and he told me that that nigger said hello to a White girl in front of the drugstore. I couldn't believe it. In the very drugstore where that girl bought her feminine products. Of course I didn't know nothing about that stuff then, but I knew it was bad. What would be next? That's what my daddy wanted to know. He said Black boys would be runnin' all over creation saying howdy to White girls, and the next thing you know there would be all these half-and-half babies crawlin' all around and that would be the end of White people, sure as shit. We was out in the middle of that field, but weren't but one tree out there, and it was clear to everybody that no branch on that sucker was gonna hold up that Negro long enough to strangle him or get his neck broke or whatever else can kill you when you get hung.

But then this Black boy stood up straight and stopped fighting. He looked at every one of them men and he settled on Fabric Wilke, the leader of the group, and he said, clear as a bell, 'Y'all trash cain't hang me. I'm already hung. Ask your wife.' Fabric turned red as a beet and stepped up and gut-punched him with a rifle butt. That nigger barely bent over. 'You can ask you mama too.' Fabric was cryin' now and didn't nobody say a word. Then that boy looked at another man and another and another and said over and over, 'Ask your wife. Ask your mother. Ask your daughter.' I tell you, them boys went crazy and tried to stone the nigger to death. But if them rocks hurt, he never let on. Then the shootin' started, but since them men were standing in a circle, all they did was shoot each other. Finally, that Black boy dropped to his knees, blood spillin' from the corners of his mouth, and he said, 'I'm gonna die now, for a while. But I'll be back. We'll all be back.'"

The room was dead quiet. The White men were ashen.

"That's the war we got." And right then, right there, in conference room A on the fourth floor of the Hotel Indigo in Hattiesburg, Mississippi, Hickory Stonewall Spit appeared to suffer a stroke and fell silent.

Ajax Kinney did not move from his seat. "Is he dead?"

The Chicago agent reached over and looked for a pulse on the old man's neck. He nodded.

Kinney looked out the window. "Thank God."

95

The screaming was all anyone could hear. One could not even hear the alarm for the screaming. Secret Service agents ran with their Heckler & Koch MP5s and their FN P90 submachine guns shoulder slung and ready. They ran through the halls of the West Wing of the White House, some to the Oval Office and some to the Roosevelt Room. The alert had called every present agent to station. A couple still wore pointed party hats from a celebration in the Navy Restaurant. Reginald "Razorback" Reynolds, former senator from Alabama and not Arkansas, despite his nickname, was now the former Secretary of the Treasury, former because he lay dead on the rectangular table in the center of the Roosevelt Room. His midsection was a bloody mess.

The president cowered under the Resolute desk in the Oval Office. Secret Service filled the room, faced the doors and the windows while the vice president tried to talk the president out of hiding. "All the men with guns are in the room now," the vice president said. "No one can get in."

"Did you hear that screaming? That was the loudest screaming that anyone has ever heard. You wouldn't believe how loud that screaming was."

"Yes, sir, but it's safe to come out now."

"I'm stuck. Goddamnit, I'm stuck. My knees are all

pressed up against my stomach. Get somebody over here to help me, you whitehaired clown."

The vice president signaled for a couple of agents to come help. One man's P90 fell from his shoulder near the president's face. The president screamed. "Jesus Fucking Christ, man, what if that thing goes off ? It could happen. You never know. First, I find out that those assholes are moving forward with impeachment, and now this. What was all that screaming? I'm still stuck. Fuck, something's got my hair."

"It's gum, Mr. President," an agent said.

The president pointed a short finger at the vice president. "You've been sitting in my chair again. I'll get you. Goddamnit."

Another agent came and took a knee beside the president. "Sir, Secretary Reynolds is dead."

"So fucking what? Get me out of here. Somebody call my hairdresser. This gum is all over." He sniffed his fingers. "Juicy Fruit." He pointed at the vice president again. "It was you. Juicy Fucking Fruit." The men got him to his feet.

"Reynolds was murdered, Mr. President," the agent said. The president tried to get back down under the desk.

"We have the killer."

"Oh, good." The president straightened his clothes and tried to press down his hair. "Good. Get my royal helicopter. I need to go to Camp David."

"Sir, this is a crime scene. We all need to stay here for a while. We don't know if there are more assailants on the grounds."

"What?"

"Secretary Reynolds's testicles were severed from his body."

"Say what?"

"The murderer is a Black man, and he's also dead. Strangely, he seems to have been dead for some time."

"Balls cut off ? This is not good." The president counted the security team in the room with him. "Lock the doors."

"They're locked," the vice president said.

"Shut up, Mr. Juicy Fruit."

"Sir, the First Lady is secured."

"Who?"

"Your wife, sir."

"Oh, Melanie."

"Melania, sir."

"Yeah, right. How did the killer get in here? This place is supposed to be the most protected place on the planet. How, man, how?"

"We don't know, sir."

"Get me to the fucking bunker. I want my bunker. Where is the Secretary of Housing and whatever? He's Black. Did he kill what's-his-name?"

"No, sir. The man is as yet unidentified." The agent put his finger to his ear to listen on his earpiece. "The grounds are clear, sir."

"Call the army. Surround this goddamn place."

"Sir, the grounds are secure."

"I want my army here now!"

96

Pasty-faced White boys from Terre Haute, Greencastle, New Castle, and Muncie walked slue-footed up and down the streets of Indianapolis. They carried leftover M16A2 rifles that had never fired more than six rounds in any one day. They wore desert fatigues that more illuminated their presence than camouflaged them. They had no idea what they were looking for or what they were guarding. Public officials stayed pretty much off the street, as did many White people. Some shops were closed, some were in the process of installing buzzer entry systems. Black people stayed mostly indoors because of the White boys carrying rifles through the streets.

Newspapers and networks attempted to connect the incidents of violence across the country. Fox News called it "a race war, plain and simple." The death toll was twenty-five White people. The score was twenty-five to five. Clearly there was a Black and Asian conspiracy, the workings of which were secret, complex, and well organized. There were spies everywhere. No one was to be trusted. How could that Black man have gotten into the White House to kill Razorback Reynolds? There had to be inside help. The cooking and cleaning staffs of the White House were detained, held in a makeshift camp on the

White House grounds, in the middle of the eclipse.

In the Upper Peninsula of Michigan, on Drummond Island, several leaders of various White supremacy groups met to discuss the development of a strategy. They would be going to war, but where and how and with whom? They agreed, one and all, that they needed to strike first, immediately, and unexpectedly, but where and with what kind of weaponry would they strike?

Dempsey Hauser, the Supreme Commandant of the Midwest White Power Legion, took charge of the meeting, as it was at his fishing lodge where they had convened. "Men, we always thought we would strike the first blow in this war that we knew was coming. But clearly we was too late, too comfortable with our cable TV and our cellular telephones and all these other toys that the commies have infected us with. We never saw the niggers and the chinks and the slants all getting together. We can't lose our America to them. Are you with me?"

Woof. Woof. Woof.

"I know we got plenty of stores of weapons and ammo. That's because that's what we're good at, collecting guns and bullets and things that go boom. But we gotta have a plan if we're gonna win this thing. It appears that the enemy got one. They got a head start on us. The floor is open for suggestions about what we do next."

"My daddy said this day was comin'," said Kyle-Lindsey Beet from Tuscaloosa, Alabama. He was the High Grand Serpent of the Revived Brotherhood of White Protectors. "My pappy told me to apologize to you boys for not taking out more of them niggers when he had the chance."

"How is he?" someone asked.

"He's got the Alkhammer's now and don't know what a shoe is most of the time, but he got his moments. He can remember every game pre-nigger Bear Bryant Alabama football score, but he cain't wipe his own butt."

"He didn't do that before the Alzheimer's," from someone in the back of the room.

"Fuck you," Beet said.

"Okay, settle down," Hauser said.

Larry LaChemise stood up. "Yeah, we got us tons of guns and thousands of shells and even grenades, but we ain't got that many people. I say we hire an advertising company and try to build our numbers. Have an ad campaign. Some commercials on the Fox Network. On that Hannity."

"Sit down, Larry," Hauser said. "We don't have that kind of time. We've got to attack now!"

LaChemise looked at the floor. "I don't know about you boys, but I can only shoot two guns at a time."

"Larry's got a point there," a man in back said. "There's fifteen of us and we all got about ten men in our groups, so that makes, what, ninety men in all? Two guns a man makes that one hundred sixty guns, and that ain't a lot of firepower. There must be thousands of niggers out there."

"Millions, dummy," another said. "Where have you been?"

"Utah, asshole. Where the fuck you been?"

"Okay, settle down," Hauser said.

A rock smashed through the window behind Hauser. He ducked. Another, larger rock landed just feet from him.

"What the freegone fuck?" LaChemise said. The men scrambled toward the far Confederate flag–draped wall.

There was a brief silence. Hauser squeaked, "Steady, soldiers."

Before a single man among them could purse his skinny lips to whistle the first notes of that old American classic "Dixie," the meeting room was filled with dirt-encrusted, dead, doll-eyed, Black men.

97

While Jim drove north toward Money, Hind and Ed had Chester Hobsinger pulled from his holding cell and chained to a table in an interrogation room. They watched through the glass as the man fussed with his restraints, but he was clearly not seeking to free himself.

"I guess I'll play good cop," Ed said.

Hind looked at him.

"It makes sense, doesn't it?"

"Because it's ironic that a woman would be the bad cop?" Hind asked.

"No, because I'm a nice guy and you're, well, you know, kind of a hard-ass," Ed said. "No offense."

"Do you mean asshole?" Hind asked.

"You said it."

"I can't argue with you."

"Let's do it."

They walked out and into the room with Hobsinger. They sat across the table from him.

"They treating you okay, Mr. Hobsinger?" Ed asked. "Chester, can I call you Chester?"

"Sure."

"I'm Ed."

Hobsinger looked at Hind.

"Special Agent Hind," she said.

"Tell us about the truck, Chester," Ed said. "How long did you work for the Acme Cadaver Supply Company?"

Hobsinger said nothing.

"How did you and the truck end up missing? Were you hijacked? I hate it when that happens. You're driving along with a trailer full of dead people and somebody jumps out of the bushes and jacks your rig. Had you made runs for Acme before this job or was this your first?" Ed asked.

Nothing from Hobsinger.

Hind leaned forward and rested her elbows on the table. "Mr. Hobsinger, I want you to know that you're in a hill of shit. You're connected with murders that can possibly be construed as hate crimes; might even call it terrorism. Do you understand the ramifications of that? That means we can put you away for a long time while we figure out what to do with you."

Hobsinger looked at Ed.

Ed shrugged. "I don't want that. But you are connected to these murders. I'd like to understand so I can help you. We know that you cut off Milam's testicles."

"What?"

"We found your DNA on the man's balls," Ed said.

"That's impossible."

"We also know that it was you who cut off Bryant's fingers and put them in his mouth," Hind said.

"There were no fingers in his mouth."

"That's right, Mr. Hobsinger," Hind said.

"Fuck."

98

Jim received a call from Ed telling him that Chester Hobsinger had given up the location of a house where members of his group had holed up and where Gertrude was likely to be. He followed the directions, made numerous turns onto dirt back roads, and ended up parked in front of a large but rundown shotgun house typical of the region, set extra high on brick pillars. An unsafe-looking porch wrapped the front and north sides of the structure. He looked at the door. There was no sign of anyone. If they were correct, and these people were involved in the murders, then they were quite possibly dangerous. He unholstered his pistol, popped the clip free and gave it a check, tapped it on his knuckles, and reinserted it. He slowly pulled back the slide and chambered a round. It was just after noon and it was hot; he could feel the car becoming an oven. He left his jacket on the seat and walked toward the house.

He stepped over the cracked first porch step only to have the second squawk loudly and make certain that every creature in the vicinity knew he was there. He imagined the rooms of the house filled with corpses from the Acme Cadaver Supply of Chicago. He imagined them moving, dead limbs moving in space. He stood away from the doorway, pushed open the screen door slowly, only to have it announce his presence as well. There could be no surprise after the step and the screen, and so he turned the knob and pushed into the house. There were no cadavers, but there was Gertrude sitting in a Shaker chair in the middle of the room.

"Miss Penstock."

"Special Detective Davis."

Jim looked around the room and down the hall through to the back door. He listened but heard nothing. The room was comfortably furnished, well kept, clean. Sheets of thin fabric were draped overhead, hippie-style, softening the light of a bright bulb. "Anyone else here?"

"No. Everybody's in the wind."

Jim nodded. He grabbed the back of another Shaker chair from beside the sofa and set it in front of Gertrude. "Why don't I just sit here."

"Please."

He studied Gertrude's face. He knew that look all too well, had seen it many times before. She was trying to play cool while not. "So, Dixie, Gertrude, Caped Crusader, whatever your name is, were you a part of this from the beginning?"

"My name is Gertrude."

"Penstock?"

"Harvey."

"Are you related to Mama Z?"

"No."

"I wouldn't have suspected you at all if you hadn't lied to me," Jim said. "Lying always comes back to bite you."

"Suspected me of what?"

"Well, that's what we're here to figure out, isn't it? Why don't you tell me why your friends had a need to be in the wind, as you said?"

Gertrude said nothing, looked past Jim and out window. "Everybody talks about genocides around the world, but when the killing is slow and spread over a hundred years, no one notices. Where there are no mass graves, no one notices. American outrage is always for show. It has a shelf life. If that Griffin book had been *Lynched Like Me*, America might have looked up from dinner or baseball or whatever they do now. Twitter?"

"You've been sitting here rehearsing that speech?"

"Pretty much."

"Did you kill people?"

"Depends on what you mean when you say people."

"That's not up to me. Did you, were you involved in the killing of Wheat Bryant?" Jim looked at the pistol still in his hand, felt a moment of embarrassment, and put it away. "Were you present during his murder?"

"I was not."

"Were you involved in the planning of the murder? Let's change that. Were you present during the planning of the murder?"

"Let me just say this: People I know were involved in three killings, and that's it. Not that three is not a lot, but that's all. Three."

"And I'm supposed to believe that a hundred-year-old woman is the head of an assassination cult?"

Gertrude didn't reply.

"Tell me about Mama Z."

"What you know about her is true."

"The three murders—Wheat Bryant, Junior Junior Milam, and Carolyn Bryant."

Gertrude shook her head. "Not the old woman. All we did was put the corpse in her bedroom. That was a last-minute decision."

"So, number three?"

"The Milam in Chicago. That's it. We don't know what's going on everywhere else. I swear. I mean, the White House? Who can do something like that?" Gertrude held her own hand because she was shaking.

Jim's phone buzzed and he answered. "I'm at the house and there's no one here. Someone was here, but it's empty now. I'm going to look around. Call you back." He put the phone back into his pocket. "That was Ed. He's my partner and my best friend, and I just lied to him."

"Thank you."

"Don't thank me. Just don't bullshit me. Is Mama Z behind all of this?"

"Yes."

"The White guy, Hobsinger, how did he come to be involved?"

"He's Mama Z's great-grandson. His Black grandfather was killed by the KKK for being with his White grandmother."

"How many of you are there?" Jim asked.

"Sixteen, not counting Mama Z."

Jim stood and walked to the window, looked out at his car. "There's something else going on, that's for fucking sure."

"Are you going to let me go? Is that why you lied?"

"I want to talk to Mama Z. Is she in the wind too?"

"Oh no. Mama Z wouldn't run."

There was a loud click, the overhead light dimmed, and a hum and vibration filled the room. Jim questioned her with his eyes.

"That would be the freezer."

99

There weren't enough troops. Colfax, Louisiana. Omaha, Nebraska. Tulsa, Oklahoma. Chicago, Illinois. Thirty-five White casualties. Panic in the streets. Rosewood, Florida. A mob of dead-eyed Black men left behind six dead Whites. The governor of Florida asked the populace to remain calm. Shortly after, he was found dead in his office washroom. Detroit, Michigan. Springfield, Illinois. East St. Louis, Illinois. Black men marched through police stations, leaving dead in their wake. The army was called up, positioned around the White House and the Capitol. Longview, Texas. An entire town was left dead. Wounded Knee, South Dakota. The Lakota called them Ghost Dancers. The White people ran. Thirteen dead in the Black Hills. Elaine, Arkansas. There was blood everywhere. Rock Springs, Wyoming. A mob of twenty Chinese men showed no fear of law enforcement and marched through Rock Springs, headed for Rawlins and Laramie. In New York City, a fat policeman shot a young Black man in Central Park, only to find dirt-encrusted Black men waiting for him at his patrol car.

100

It was a walk-in freezer made by GE. Gertrude removed the locking pin from the heavy door. Jim instinctively drew his weapon.

"Is there anyone in there?" he asked.

"In a manner of speaking," Gertrude said. She pulled open the door. The cold air rushed out. She hit a switch and the light came on. There were shelves filled with wrapped deli meats, ham and turkey and bologna. There were also bagged people hanging from the ceiling. Jim could see no faces, not even limbs, just the general outlines of human figures.

"From the stolen trailer?"

"Yes. We had plans to do more." She realized that she was confessing. "But then the other things started happening. Copycats?"

Jim shrugged. He pushed a bag with the muzzle of his pistol and watched it swing. "This isn't even creepy anymore."

"I'm scared," Gertrude said. "It's like we started something."

The big door banged shut. Jim and Gertrude turned to face and hear the sound of the locking pin sliding into place.

"That's not good," Jim said.

Gertrude ran to the door and gave the handle a try. She turned to face Jim. "I didn't know anyone was here," she said. "I swear."

Jim pulled out his phone. No signal.

"What are we going to do?"

"You got me. I can't shoot it."

"Maybe there're some tools in here," Gertrude said, scanning the shelves.

Jim studied the door. "A crowbar would be good."

"How about a big screwdriver?"

"Might work." He took the tool from her. "Okay, how do you suggest I go at this? I'm not the handiest guy around."

Gertrude took the screwdriver and tried to forced it between the jamb and lock housing. Jim helped her push. Nothing.

"I'm freezing," Jim said.

"It's a freezer."

101

Florence, South Carolina. Macon, Georgia. Hope Mills, North Carolina. Selma, Alabama. Shelbyville, Tennessee. Blue Ash, Ohio. Bedford, Indiana. Muscle Shoals, Alabama. Irmo, South Carolina. Orangeburg, South Carolina. Los Angeles, California. Jackson, Mississippi. Benton, Arkansas. Lexington, Nebraska. New York, New York. Rolla, Missouri. Perth Amboy, New Jersey. Elsmere, Delaware. Tarrytown, New York. Grafton, North Dakota. Oxford, Pennsylvania. Anne Arundel, Maryland. Otero, Colorado. Coos Bay, Oregon. Chester, South Carolina. Petersburg, Virginia. Laurel, Delaware. Madison, Maryland. Beckley, West Virginia. Soddy-Daisy, Tennessee. Fort Mill, South Carolina. Niceville, Florida. Slidell, Louisiana. Money, Mississippi. DeSoto, Mississippi. Quitman, Mississippi. Elmore, Alabama. Jefferson, Alabama. Montgomery, Alabama. Henry, Alabama. Colbert, Alabama. Russell, Alabama. Coffee, Alabama. Clarke, Alabama. Laurens, South Carolina. Greenwood, South Carolina. Oconee, South Carolina. Union, South Carolina. Aiken, South Carolina. York, South Carolina. Abbeville, South Carolina. Hampton, South Carolina. Franklin, Mississippi. Lowndes, Mississippi. Leflore, Mississippi. Simpson, Mississippi. Jefferson, Mississippi. Washington, Mississippi. George, Mississippi. Monroe,

Mississippi. Humphreys, Mississippi. Bolivar, Mississippi. Sunflower, Mississippi. Hinds, Mississippi. Newton, Mississippi. Copiah, Mississippi. Alcorn, Mississippi. Jefferson Davis, Mississippi. Panola, Mississippi. Clay, Mississippi. Lamar, Mississippi. Yazoo, Mississippi. Mississippi. Mississippi. Mississippi. Mississippi. Mississippi. Mississippi. Mississippi. Mississippi. Mississippi. Mississippi.

102

The President of the United States:

Five hundred years ago, my people tell me, and they're good people, they know a lot, and they like me because I know a lot, they tell me that back then, the folks from Europe rescued the Africans from each other. As I understand it, African kings were selling their own children to other kings, and we sent our navy, the best navy in the world, to save them. We have for the past two years been worried about the criminals and the drug dealers and the rapists sneaking across our southern border, and I have made great strides, more than any other president in history, in plugging gaps, and we built a fence, didn't we? A beautiful fence, and we have a great economy, the best in the history of the world. It's something, isn't it? But it turns out that the real threat, and I've been saying this, but did anyone listen to moi, that's French for *me*, did they listen? No they didn't listen. Isn't it terrible how they treat me? The president of the entire country after the greatest victory ever, and there was no collusion. No collusion. And no obstruction. But I said, have been saying it, it's the Blacks we have to worry about and apparently the Chinese and the Indians, but the point is they are not White like Americans are supposed to be. Make America great again. Something terrible is happening in our towns and on our streets. Good White Americans are being targeted for violence, killed like animals. I will put an end to it. Believe me. I am creating a new division in the Department of Justice, the People's Agency for Law Enforcement, to address these crimes. I am also calling on my base, fine, loyal people, they love me and I love them, I am calling on them take up arms against this rabble. I wish I could find the leader of the Negroes. I would punch him in the face. You know I would. Such a punch I would give him, and not a sucker punch because he would see it coming. Pow. I know how to handle these people. Thugs. Our good policemen are out there on the front lines, doing battle, and I've got their backs. I've given them the only raise they have gotten in twenty years, and so they love me and I love them. I do. You've never seen anything like it. But these niggers have gone off the rails and off the reservation, and they have got to be stopped. I will do it for you, but I want your support.

[cups hand to ear and listens]

I did not use the word *nigger*. I would never say the n-word. I'm the least racist person you will ever meet. Some fake news sources are going to tell you that I used the word *nigger*. I would never say the n-word. Some of these Dems and CNNers will tell you I said *nigger*, but I didn't. Ask anyone who is here. Did I say *nigger*? You, over there, did I say *nigger*? Did I use the word *nigger*? *Nigger. Nigger. Nigger.* I understand that it might have sounded like I did. What I said was, we have to put things in the *frigger*, as in cool. You know the expression they use, like *the frigger side of the pillow*. They are some colorful people, aren't they? And they love me, voted for me like they never voted for anybody. I did not say *nigger*, would not say *nigger*. My mouth can't even form the word. *Nigger*. *Nigger*. *Nigger*. Didn't say it. No collusion.

BREAKING BREAKING NEWS
Reports are just coming in that the Senate majority
leader has been murdered. He was found in a room at
the Ritz Carlton Georgetown by a massage therapist.
The young tattooed woman ran down the stairs and
into the lobby screaming that the senator was bloody
and apparently dead and with his Black lover. Again,
because of the woman's hysteria, we are not certain
what she meant. All that is clear right now is that the
Senate majority leader is dead.

What do you mean I was interrupted? I'm the fucking president of the United States. I don't care if he's dead. I was talking. When did they break in? I almost had those assholes out there believing I didn't say *nigger*. Ha ha ha. I am the best. I could sell ice to Eskimos. Hell, I could sell rope to a nigger. What? We're back. I didn't say what you think you just heard me say.

103

Jim regretted leaving his jacket in the car. He stood close to the door and tried his phone again, but there was still no signal. He looked at Gertrude shivering beside the outline of a dead fat man.

"If I had my jacket I would give it to you," he said. "That's a testament to today's chivalry. Whatever that means."

Gertrude tried to smile. "I'm so sorry."

"So, who would lock us in here?" Jim asked.

Gertrude shook her head. "I thought everybody was gone. Everybody was gone."

"There has got to be a way out of here."

"The only other tool is this crescent wrench."

Jim felt the weight of the wrench in his hand, stared at it. He went back to the door and thought about pounding the lock with it. The tool was about the weight of his pistol. "I need a small container. A plastic bag. Anything."

"What about the corner of this?" She pointed to the bottom of a cadaver bag. "Do you have a knife?"

Jim handed her his pocket knife.

As she cut into the bag, condensation or formaldehyde or something wet her fingers and she stopped, repulsed. She stood and looked around again. There was a can of oven cleaner on a top shelf. She grabbed it and removed the cap.

"That's good," Jim said. He popped the clip from his pistol and removed the bullets. He then used the crescent to pull the lead from the brass and collected the gunpowder in the plastic cup.

"I see," Gertrude said.

"I'm not sure I do," Jim said. "But we'll try it."

"I'm sorry," Gertrude said again.

Jim tried to pry the lock housing away from the door, but could manage only a quarter-inch crack. "This is a stupid idea," he said. "If this works, I'll buy you dinner. Probably end up blowing off my hand. But it won't matter because soon I'll freeze to death."

"Are you trying to be funny?"

"How am I doing?"

"You suck."

Jim tried to pack the powder into the casing as much as possible, then stopped. "Are you a smoker?"

"Never have. Why?"

"That's too bad. I'm not either. I have no matches."

"Oh."

"Well, I do have a bullet left. I could try to set it off by shooting it.

I was saving this one for whoever locked us in here."

"Okay."

"Get back there behind the dead guys."

Gertrude did.

"What?"

"I've got one bullet and I just barely certified on the pistol range last time. Ready? It's going to be really loud in here. Cover your ears." He took a used tissue from his pocket, split it, and plugged his own ears. "Here we go."

Jim squeezed off the round. He hit the lock and thought he heard the ricochets, but nothing happened. The lock was dented, but the gunpowder remained unimpressed. "So much for that. I'm sorry, Gertrude."

She said nothing.

"As much as it seems completely inappropriate and unethical, I think we need to share body heat."

"I think that's right."

"What?" Jim asked. "That it's inappropriate or that we share heat?"

"Both."

They sat on a crate against the wall and hugged each other.

104

There was a sound at the door. The handle moved slightly, jiggled, and stopped. Then it snapped down with the sound of a hard strike.

Jim held up his empty pistol.

"Jim?" It was Ed.

"Jesus, are you two okay?" Hind asked. She removed her jacket and moved toward Gertrude, put it over her shoulders.

Jim tried to stand straight. Ed helped him. As they exited the freezer behind Hind and Gertrude, Jim grabbed Ed's arm. "Did you did find anybody here?"

"No one."

"It's dark," Jim said, looking up out the window at the top of the stairs. "I stopped looking at the time a while ago."

"I couldn't get through to your phone, so we drove up here. We saw your car outside. If there was anyone here, they're gone now."

"Well, someone locked us in there."

"What's the deal with Gertrude?" Ed asked.

"I'll fill you in. What's been going on out there?"

"Oh, man."

105

Some called it a *throng*. A reporter on the scene used the word *horde*. A minister of an AME church in Jefferson County, Mississippi, called it a *congregation*. Whatever it was called, it was at least five hundred bodies strong and growing and had abandoned all stealth. The congregation could be seen cresting a ridge then coming down toward town like a tornado. And like a tornado it would destroy one life and leave the one beside it unscathed. It made a noise. A moan that filled the air. *Rise*, it said, *Rise*. It left towns torn apart. Families grieved. Families assessed their histories. It was weather. *Rise*. It was a cloud. It was a front, a front of dead air. Survivors reported that the air felt thick and heavy in its wake, sitting near the ground like the mist of dry ice. There were clouds in Alabama, Arkansas, Florida, everywhere it seemed. The clouds merged into bigger clouds, the sounds of their moans growing louder with every step, every death. *Rise*.

106

Mama Z's house was completely dark, except for a very small flicker behind the curtain of the records room. Jim and Ed approached the front door. Hind hung back with Gertrude near the cars. The front door was wide open. The men switched on their flashlights and stepped inside. There was clicking, like a very old typewriter coming from another room. They were across the room when Gertrude entered.

Hind was behind her. "She ran away from me."

"Just hang back," Jim said.

"Is that a typewriter?" Hind asked.

Jim and Ed moved forward to the records room, pushed it open. Mama Z was sitting on the other side of the table, a candle burning in front of her. Damon Thruff was sitting beside her, pecking away on a manual typewriter. His eyes would not leave the paper in the machine.

"Please sit," Mama Z said.

The four of them sat at the table.

"Mama Z?" Gertrude said.

"There's always more than you see," the old woman said.

"Damon?"

"He's busy," Mama Z said.

"What is he doing?" Hind asked.

Damon snatched a page from the typewriter laid it on a

thick stack to the right, rolled in a blank sheet from a pile on the left, and continued to type.

"He's typing names," Mama Z said. "One name at a time. One name at a time. Every name."

"Names," Ed said.

"Shall I stop him?" Mama Z asked.

Jim looked at Ed, then Hind. Gertrude was clearly confused. They were confused, yet not.

"Shall I stop him?" the old woman asked again.

Outside, in the distance, through the night air, the muffled cry came through, *Rise. Rise.*

"Shall I stop him?"

PERCIVAL EVERETT is Distinguished Professor of English at the University of Southern California and the author of over thirty books, including *I Am Not Sidney Poitier, Erasure,* and *Telephone.*

INFLUX
PRESS

Influx Press is an independent publisher based in London, committed to publishing innovative and challenging literature from across the UK and beyond.

Lifetime supporters: Bob West and Barbara Richards

www.influxpress.com
@Influxpress

Also by Percival Everett and Influx Press

'A scandalously
under-recognized
contemporary
master.'
– *The Wall Street Journal*

'One of the funniest,
most original stories
to be published in
years.'
– NPR

I AM NOT SIDNEY POITIER
Percival Everett

I Am Not Sidney Poitier is a hilarious and
irresistible take on race, class and identity.

The sudden death of Not Sidney
Poitier's mother orphans him at age
eleven. He is left with a name no one
understands, an uncanny resemblance
to an Oscar winning actor, and serious
amount of shares in the Turner
Corporation.

Percival Everett's novel follows Not
Sidney's tumultuous life, as the social
hierarchy scrambles to balance his skin
colour with his fabulous wealth. Maturing
under the less-than watchful eye of his
adopted foster father, Ted Turner, Not
Sidney learns to navigate a world that
doesn't know what to do with him.

Published for the first time in the UK,
this novel ranks as one of the greatest
achievements of Percival Everett,
an overlooked master of American
storytelling.

The novel is introduced by critically
acclaimed British author, Courttia
Newland

Also by Percival Everett and Influx Press

'Original and subtle,
canny and soulful –
full, too, of sublimely
sardonic humour.'
– *The Guardian*

'Everett displays an
intellectual dexterity
and formal versatility
that few contemporary
American writers can
match.'
– *Chicago Tribune*

DAMNED IF I DO
Percival Everett

An artist, a cop, a cowboy, several
fly fishermen and even a reluctant
romance novelist inhabit these
revealing and often hilarious stories.
An old man ends up in a high-speed
chase with the cops after stealing the
car that blocks the garbage bin at
his apartment building. A stranger
gets a job at a sandwich shop and
fixes everything in sight: a manual
mustard dispenser, a mouthful of
crooked teeth, thirty-two parking
tickets and a sexual identity problem.

Everett skewers race, class,
identity, surrealism and much more
in this exceptional work.

Published for the first time in the
UK, *Damned If I Do* is a masterful
short story collection from a genius
of American storytelling. The book
is introduced by critically acclaimed
British author, Irenosen Okojie.

Also by Percival Everett and Influx Press

PERCIVAL EVERETT BY VIRGIL RUSSELL
Percival Everett

A story inside a story inside a story.

A man visits his aging father in a nursing home, where his father writes the novel he imagines his son would write. Or is it the novel that the son imagines his father would imagine, if he were to imagine the kind of novel the son would write?

Not only is Percival Everett by Virgil Russell a powerful, compassionate meditation on old age and its humiliations, it is an ingenious culmination of Everett's recurring preoccupations.

Percival Everett has never been more cunning, more brilliant and subversive, than he is in this, his most important and elusive novel to date.

Published for the first time in the UK, Percival Everett by Virgil Russell is like nothing you've read before, or will ever read again.

"[A] stark, shattering novel. . . . This meta-fiction is deeply moving."
– *The Wall Street Journal*

"Every sentence, indeed every word, has come to seem like a valuable key, not just to this puzzle of a novel, but to the meaning of existence."
– *Publishers Weekly*